The Devil's Garden

EDWARD DOCX was born in 1972 and lives in London. His previous novels are *The Calligrapher* and *Self Help*, which won the Geoffrey Faber Memorial Prize and was longlisted for the Man Booker Prize in 2007.

Praise for SELF HELP

'Masterful. A gripping read that will engage, delight and engross'
Guardian

'Unforgettable. Not since *What A Carve Up!* has there been such an absorbing indictment of the family'
Independent on Sunday

'One of the brightest young novelists on the Man Booker Prize longlist'
Evening Standard

Also by Edward Docx

The Calligrapher
Self Help

THE

Devil's Garden

EDWARD DOCX

PICADOR

First published 2011 by Picador
an imprint of Pan Macmillan, a division of Macmillan Publishers Limited
Pan Macmillan, 20 New Wharf Road, London N1 9RR
Basingstoke and Oxford
Associated companies throughout the world
www.panmacmillan.com

ISBN 978-0-330-46350-8

1 3 5 7 9 8 6 4 2

A CIP catalogue record for this book is available from
the British Library.

Printed in the UK by CPI Mackays, Chatham ME5 8TD

For my father

The term kamatsiri, "dead spirit," is virtually synonymous with the word kamagarine, "evil spirit." Both are derived from the root -kama-, "to die." The word kamatsiri is a noun made from the intransitive form, "the one who has died," while kamagarine is derived from the transitive form, "the one who kills." The two are used almost interchangeably, and both connote sinister and dangerous beings.

(*Families of the Forest:*
The Matsigenka Indians of the Amazon
by Allen W. Johnson)

I came here as a scientist to conduct experiments on other living things. I believed that the most fundamental questions of our existence could be answered in the lab. I believed in rigorous method and the unemotional reporting of results. But I have come to see that life itself is the real experiment and that the answers to these questions are to be found only in what we do – as individuals, as a species. What results there are might better be called experience, and experience soon teaches us that they are not the results we would want. I will leave here under another name because of what I have done. All the same, I will leave here as a human being.

J. Forle

Part One

ONE

I

There is only one way in and there is only one way out: the river. And so they arrived on the supply boat in the late afternoon, just as the worst of the heat was over and the caiman began to stir. I heard their voices as they passed outside my hut. We had been expecting them – yesterday, today, tomorrow. Sooner or later.

I switched off my desk fan the better to listen. Sole was showing them the path down to the washhouse and explaining how our makeshift showers work. I could tell by her tone that she was trying her best to be soothing. The one cursed the cramp of the boat, the heat, the insects; the other the lack of airstrips.

Perhaps I should have greeted them there and then – welcoming, cordial and buoyed from my work. After all, it was not every day that we were visited by a Judge and a Colonel. But some part of me wanted to make an impression. And so I decided that I would let our visitors settle and wait until dinner to introduce myself. Instead, I would go down to the river and help with the unloading.

II

On the path, the heat of my own body hung heavily about me, suffocating, and the humidity was so thick that to breathe was almost to drink. The only place to see the sun was where the river broke the canopy and so it had become my habit to look up whenever I stood on the bank.

Red and yellow macaws were flying downstream. A graceful heron-like bird, whose name I could not recall, stood opposite me on one leg, studying the torpid flow, its long neck ivory in the softening light. The air was filled with a hundred different songs, chirps, squawks and screeches – back and forth, far and near, all around. But, beneath these calls, my ear was attuned to the real buzz and hum of the jungle: the great electric simmer of the insects.

Vinton, the boatman, was passing up our supplies to Jorge and Felipe. Felipe waved his greeting. I felt the wood shift a fraction as I walked out on to our jetty, the stilts beneath uneven, thin and crooked as crane fly legs on the mud. The water beyond was the colour of cinnamon and still so low that the boat could tie up only at the furthest reach.

'What's left?' I asked.

'All the important things, Dr Forle,' Felipe replied. 'All the important things.'

Felipe was our guide. His habitual demeanour was to please and his habitual expression was a wide and apprehensive smile.

'They've brought quite a few boxes of their own,' he said.

Jorge had turned away to urinate over the other side.

I looked at the stack of electrical goods beside the handcart.

'Satellite dishes,' Felipe said and shrugged.

'Maybe they like to watch a lot of TV,' I said. 'People do. I'll help pass up.'

The boat was still half full. I descended the rickety ladder to join Vinton, who was standing on his makeshift deck below.

'Vinton.'

'Chief.'

This was the boatman's joke – a double insult aimed at both Felipe and at me. Rebaque, the true head of the Station, had been away for more than three weeks. Nobody knew where. No word. But if anyone was chief, then strictly it should have been Felipe. Though I moved carefully, the boat rocked.

'If the water gets any lower, we'll be cut off completely,' I said.

'It won't.' Vinton stood purposefully still. He was proud of his white cracked-leather seats; his was the only luxury craft between here and Laberinto.

'The river is on the rise?' I asked the question as if I had been waiting for such a day.

'No.' Vinton spat carefully over the side. 'You would know if the rains had come.'

A few years previously, the entire basin had suffered the most severe drought in living memory – passenger boats stranded even on the larger rivers, half the forest burning, the whole vast system down to dribble and seep. If the rain did not quickly begin in earnest, I understood that even this record would soon be surpassed.

Jorge's mud-smeared sports shoes came into view on the jetty's edge. He stood heavily above the boat – a big, glabrous Buddha of a man with an odd coffee-coloured birthmark spilt across his smooth brown head.

'Everything is crushed,' he said as he zipped himself up. 'The biscuits. The bananas. Crumbs and mush.'

'They'll be OK.' Felipe appeared beside him. 'You'll find a way to use them.'

Jorge scowled. He was constantly suspicious of a

slight and was the sort of person who must continually apply acid to all that was said and done around them as the only certain prevention. He was our cook. Sometimes, when we ate, I could not separate the taste of the food from the man.

Vinton threw paper towels up to Jorge.

I offered up the first big box of cigarettes to Felipe.

'You'll stay tonight, Vinton?' Jorge smirked.

'No . . . not tonight.' Vinton shook his head as though the decision were narrowly made, though he had never eaten with us, nor spent a single night on the Station.

'Another woman?' Jorge grasped a big tin of cooking oil from the boatman.

'Your sisters.' Vinton grinned – broken teeth, a glint of gold. 'A special show – free of charge.'

Jorge's smirk fattened into a smile; he would take this off Vinton though nobody else.

We passed up bottles of water without speaking for a while. The heat seemed to shrink tighter about my skin. A beetle ran the gunwale, *Brasilucanus acomus* – dense, heavy-armoured, a brutal tank on tiny legs.

Then Felipe asked: 'Which one is the Judge?'

He could not endure silence and must always force conversation; it was a trait I disliked in myself.

'The smaller thin one with white hair,' Vinton said. 'The big one says he's the Colonel. Wouldn't wait for his own boats but he complained all the way here in this one.'

Jorge did his favourite mime of masturbation. 'What are they doing here anyway?' he asked. 'Nobody comes to this place because they *want* to – nobody except you people.'

I inclined my head.

'It's the registration,' Felipe said.

Jorge scoffed. 'What did they say was really going on, Vinton? What did you overhear?'

'They didn't speak. Or not to each other, they didn't.' Vinton spat a second time. 'Not one word in seven hours.'

As far as we understood, our two visitors had been travelling up the river for a month, registering people to vote. For the last three days they had been on our branch. Our Station would be their final stop. Only day-long boat trips from here; it was too dangerous further into the interior, even for government officials – especially for government officials.

The boat was almost empty save for its heaviest freight lying ballast at the bottom, which included four crates of beer and the case of spirits that I had paid for. The others knew it was my intention to donate vodka and whiskey to our bar, such as it was. And I was unduly pleased that my order had arrived; indeed, it occurred to me that I had come down solely to check on its safety.

We handed the bottles up, self-consciously careful. Then Felipe climbed down into the boat to help with the fuel drums for the generators. We counted three and heaved. There was a moment when I thought one of the damn things might fall back. But then we had it high enough and Jorge had rolled it over the edge to safety. We burnt oil.

The job was done. We were all slick with the work but only I felt the discomfort in my collared shirt. In six weeks, I still had not learned to sweat freely. Across the river, another bird I did not know chose this moment to display the fan of its plumage – bands of carmine, tips of jade. There was a splash in the water. The weeds strung out in the sluggish current around the legs of the jetty. I climbed the ladder. Jorge and Felipe would drag and push our cart. I would carry as much as I could. Vinton would wait with the remaining stacks.

There came the sound of another engine – full-throated and growing quickly louder.

I turned back to face the river. We knew straight away that it could not be any of our near neighbours; the Indians and the river-people, the *ribereños*, travelled with their motors at the lowest possible chug to save fuel. A moment later and we could make out six passengers – all men – sitting line astern in a rigid inflatable. They wore uniform.

It seemed undignified to continue staring as the boat veered from midstream to make its course for our jetty but this is what we did until they were almost upon us. Then, abruptly, I put down the box of cigarettes I had been holding and offered to receive their rope.

III

The dusk was rising from the forest floor. I stood at the porch window of my hut and watched the soldiers on their way to the washhouse. They bunched where the wall of the jungle reared and then disappeared down the dark narrow fissure of the path. I wondered would they meet Kim, my assistant, returning. There was an unspoken convention: that the women bathed around this time; the rest of us earlier or later. There would be more men arriving we had been told. I had been expecting only the Judge and the Colonel – but it now seemed obvious that that they would not be travelling alone. My whiskey made me wince. I had a six o'clock rule, to which I adhered rigidly.

Sole appeared on the balcony of her hut opposite. She was wearing her white dress. I had only seen it once before – and never for dinner. She hesitated and I did not understand what she was doing for a moment . . . Until, with surprise, I realized that she was locking the door. The key was stiff for her. She had to lift the handle so that the heavy bolt would find the unfamiliar barrel. She looked around and then hurried off. I was certain that she had been waiting for the men to pass. I was certain, too, that she had never locked her door before. We only ever laughed at our keys – huge, incongruous, medieval. Rebaque had liked to joke that one of his predecessors must have purchased them from the Franciscans in the 1500s; he said he had a skeleton key somewhere that opened all the locks and that it had an actual skeleton designed into the handle.

I returned to my desk. For the last five years, ever since my wife died, I had been trying to write a book that combined the best of my articles for the science journals with my research and findings – something that would open up my subject to the public and raise me from the confines of my discipline. I had been pleased to be making progress following my arrival on the Station. But now as I began to redraft my introduction, '*The One Special Difficulty*', I found that I could not re-engage my concentration and that even my title seemed clumsy.

Two skull monkeys swung from my roof and raced along the wooden rail of my balcony, fawn-flashed tails held high and dancing, then perfectly still, then dancing again. They stopped a moment and began to copulate. I was still not used to the sound of their landing on my roof. When I awoke, they were always at the window waiting; two, three, four faces. Intelligent.

IV

Ever since my wife died ... That is another lie – or rather, it is a story that I told people afterwards; a story I offered to give them a reason for the way I lived my life and to avoid conversations I did not wish to have. She was not my wife – though I came to believe that she was the better part of me and that this part had died with her. The last time I saw her she was angry with me. But as she turned away to cross the busy street, I did not call after her, I did not run to catch her up. I thought I would see her again. We always do.

I made a false floor to fireproof myself from what feelings burned below; and the greater the heat within me, the greater my effort to seal it off. Outwardly, I grew colder. Science, method – I turned into one of those men who seem to others reserved. But I held back only because I believed that to let go would have meant to detonate everything. My work became my reason for living. I escaped from life by intensifying my study of life's secrets – biology. I wanted to make a contribution to human knowledge, a breakthrough. Of course, there were more immediate and practical reasons for my finally coming here – my colleague, Dr Cameron Quinn, not least among them – but most of all I wanted to make one last effort to save my soul. When a man is wounded in the river, he must swim as best he can upstream from his own blood if he is to have any chance.

Thus bound up in my leaving, I was shamefully ignorant about my surrounds when I arrived. I knew nothing of the endless land disputes, the trades (legal and illegal), nor the provenance of the different peoples. But an accurate history of our Station would be near impossible to uncover in any case. During the height of the rubber boom, it was probably used as some sort of a collection point – though we were situated a long way up the river. There had been slavery. Missionaries. An Indian settlement before that, perhaps. It was hard to know anything for sure. There is no stone with which to build. Tribes vanish. Iniquity is forgotten. Everything is subsumed back into the forest.

In physical terms, the Station occupied a rectangle of cleared ground, roughly the area of two sports fields placed end to end. The path from the river led directly to our main building, the *comedor* – a big open-sided construction, the size of a large cricket pavilion, though fashioned, as all, in rough-hewn dark wood and raised some three feet off the ground. The *comedor* was the Station's dining room, lounge and bar. At one end, there were two separate rooms closed off: the kitchen and the store. And at the other, the same: a tiny infirmary and Rebaque's office.

In addition, there were the accommodation huts in which we lived and those kept ready for visitors. They were unevenly spaced, unevenly built, of uneven sizes and at uneven distances to the walls of the forest. But all shared the same basic box-on-legs structure, and all had the same small balcony facing inwards. Mine was the last hut downstream and thereafter this same path ran on through the forest some fifty yards to a small secondary clearing for the washing stalls and laundry.

There was one other building – the lab. This stood alone adjacent to Sole's hut and diagonally opposite my own. Roughly four times the area of our huts and a good deal taller, it had been built, customized and equipped by Quinn. I had taken it for granted in the background of the footage we played to students and associates. But when at last I saw it for myself, the fact of its existence struck me deeply – that it stood so square and so purposefully fitted to its creator's ends. The sheer will: to have the thing constructed and supplied from nothing.

With Rebaque away, we were now seven. Myself and my assistants, Lothar and Kim; along with Felipe, Jorge,

Sole and her mother, Estrela, who were all on the pay-roll of the state – albeit to no great extent. We spoke for the most part in Spanish. Ostensibly, we were a scientific station, maintained for the purposes of research projects. But the real motivation for keeping the place manned and inhabitable (while indirectly paid for by First World universities) was that it was the last Government outpost before the impassable interior. For this reason, Quinn had told me that all kinds of officials and scientists dropped in. But in the last six weeks, aside from Tord, a missionary, and Tupki, our nearest neighbour, we had received no visitors at all. Until now.

V

By the time I set off for dinner myself, the croaking hour had begun and the frogs were already basking in the silvery glow of our little solar-charged lamps. I trod carefully.

On the far side of our mighty kapok tree, which stood with its vast vaulted trunk across the path, the *comedor* cast its welcoming light. But as I crossed the coarse grass in front of the steps, I was surprised to see Estrela hurrying toward the kitchen – Jorge's domain. Relations between the two were more typically characterized by a steady and mutual detestation – seasoned only by an oblique regard that each held for the other's obstinacy. They never worked together and Estrela never rushed anywhere except to judgement.

Felipe greeted me from the other side of the dining area where he stood behind our makeshift little bar. He was sporting a battered burgundy-coloured dinner jacket and he had been serving one of our visitors.

I crossed the wooden floor conscious that I was wearing shoes rather than boots for the first time since I had arrived.

'Good evening, Dr Forle.' Felipe's smile was wide as a freshly strung hammock. 'This is . . . Colonel Cordero.' He poured so much deference into the introduction that I was afraid we would all drown.

The man turned slowly – deliberately so. He introduced himself as if Felipe had not spoken and then shook my hand with a narrow-eyed expression by which he intended, I think, to convey some quality of far-sightedness or leadership. He was tall and bulky and he appraised me as though assessing my physical capabilities in relation to his own. His features seemed to occupy only the lower half of his face – on account of his high, bronzed forehead and his baldness, which extended from brow to crown. I detected some care in the black arch of his eyebrows and – taken in all – there was something fastidious about him that asked for admiration before engagement. He wore a tailored white cotton shirt tucked into a heavy belt with which he held up a pair of well-pressed combat-style trousers. I was immediately uncomfortable in my linen jacket. Why were we all dressing up?

Felipe poured me vodka and soda from the bottles I had newly donated. Cordero was sipping some sort of juice. I took a seat on an adjacent stool. We talked politely of the river, the lack of rain, the anxieties of the local villagers – though we avoided any subjects of wider concern. His men had bought their own supplies, he said; they would eat after us. They cooked for themselves. Meats. They were used to it. They were often forced to improvise on this mission. Which was why, as far as possible, he preferred to keep the numbers down. Some of the places they had stayed I would not believe. Filthy. But there were objectives. There were things that had to be done. There was progress.

'You're helping the Judge?' I asked.

'We have to keep order. You're a scientist, they tell me?' Who told him?

'I am a naturalist – an entomologist. I study insects.' There was something about his slow nod that made me loquacious. 'Actually, I am a myrmecologist. I study ants – specifically ants.'

'And how does this research benefit us?'

'That's a big question.'

'Is it?'

'Yes.' I hesitated. I had bought the vodka for Kim. I had never liked soda. And I preferred not to drink in dry company.

'That depends on whether you mean benefit in an immediate way or more widely?'

'Either?'

His manner was somehow both rude and courteous at the same time but I was a fool to be riled.

'My work will – I hope – prove that in some areas of the forest the ants that I'm studying are killing every single species of plant except those in which they nest. We had thought that it was the inhibition of one plant's growth by another. But I hope to show for the first time that it is the ants themselves who are . . . who are poisoning their own environment.' It was my intention to rebuff him with so precise and forthright an answer. But he merely swilled his juice and I found that I must again go on. 'My ants are very successful – because they cooperate. In one way, I suppose you might say we're studying the biggest question of all: who – or what – wins in the end? What is the best strategy for survival? Competition or cooperation?'

He smiled. 'You misunderstand me, Doctor. I mean

how does your work benefit us, the country, how does it actually re—'

'Good evening.' A low, smoky voice surprised us both. 'And you must be our great scientist.'

I turned on my stool. The Judge was spry, slight and a good six inches shorter than the Colonel. He was well dressed – outlandishly dressed, I realized – in a cream suit and tie. But what really lent him his distinction were his pale blue eyes and his wild white hair.

The Colonel said nothing. I stood and introduced myself.

The Judge offered his hand. 'Raúl Ruíz Ramones,' he said, but did not bother to look at me as we shook, preferring instead to address Felipe: 'Can this man get me a drink?'

Nothing could have pleased Felipe more.

'Good.' Obscure amusement seemed to bedevil the Judge's thin lips. 'Something overwhelming and quick, please.' He turned back to me and at last released his grip. 'A shame,' he said. 'I was hoping you might turn out to be a woman worthy of the name, Doctor. Since I left the capital, my eyes have suffered greatly – a succession of slack-breasted monsters. But it matters less – it matters much less – now I have seen the face of our welcome.' He sucked his teeth. 'Where did you find her, Doctor? Yes, that will do.' Felipe was holding up one of my whiskeys.

'Don't worry, man. Pour. I'll imagine the ice. I am required to imagine everything else.' He looked around. 'It is fortunate – is it not? – that I have so beautiful an imagination.'

The Colonel had remained facing the bar. I felt the need to speak: 'Did you have a good journey?'

'No. I did not. How is it possible to have a good journey? Has anyone ever had a good journey to this place?'

I smiled. 'At least it didn't rain,' I said.

The Judge reached for the glass before Felipe could set it down. 'Rain is a thing of the past, Doctor. We are on our way to becoming a desert. We are looking forward to it. Sand. Not insects but *sand*.' He took the glass in one and then looked directly into my face as if he were only now registering my existence as a fellow human being. 'But why are you trying to talk to me about the weather? Are you English?'

'Yes.'

His expression said that he had thought as much. He motioned to Felipe for a second. 'It must be difficult,' he said.

Felipe obliged. The Colonel continued to face the bar.

'I don't follow you,' I replied.

'I mean it must be difficult flailing between greater powers where once you held sway – watching your great nation decline until it is little more than an elaborate theme park.' He took his glass from Felipe but this time held it before his lips while looking at me over the top. 'But also I mean being English for you – for you personally – appears to be difficult: the inability to stand easy.'

I was taken aback by his perception and his directness. But his own position seemed to be a source of private entertainment to him; and I warmed to this.

'My nation struggles on,' I said, 'as do I.'

He smiled and said: 'You think me judgemental, Doctor. But I am a judge.' He despatched half the whiskey and continued with his index finger pointing from where he held his glass. 'And neither am I alone by the way. We are a judgemental species. And it's been like that since the dawn of time: these people chosen, those not; this man a saviour, that man a thief. We judge and we judge and we judge. Every minute – another judgement. I sometimes think that's *all* we do.' He finished what was left. 'The relativist is an idiot telling himself lies while he stands in the corner with his hands over his eyes.'

'I'm not a relativist,' I said.

But he did not hear me for he was already looking over my shoulder.

Kim had appeared around the kapok and was coming across towards the *comedor*. Internally, I flinched. She was the best postgraduate we had so far found. Besides her intelligence, she had the emotional stamina for success in life and the proper fieldwork rigour for success in science. And yet the way she looked gave her the appearance of innocence and idealism and she seemed to attract cynicism and attack like nobody else I had ever worked with. She had shoulder-length loose-curled blonde and light-brown hair, even features and clear skin that told of good health and the more gentle sun of the northern hemisphere and she wore the student's uniform – half scruffy, half considered. Her upper teeth were a little pronounced and it was (as now) in her nervous smile that you glimpsed the tomboy's ghost.

'This is Kim Van der Kisten,' I said, smiling. 'This is Señor Ramones.' Against any likelihood, I hoped that they might like each other. 'He will be staying with us for . . . how long?'

The Judge bowed to Kim. 'Raúl, please – call me Raúl.'

'We've heard all about the registration,' she said. She offered him her hand to shake but instead he kissed it. Disconcerted, she turned to the Colonel, who had risen from his stool and now hooked his thumbs through his belt.

'We've heard all about the registration,' she repeated. 'We haven't had too many visitors. We've been looking forward to some new people!'

The Colonel nodded, peremptory. 'Let's eat,' he said.

VI

In normal circumstances, dinner was the principal ceremony of the day. Jorge carried out whatever he had burnt and served us with an aggressively fragile curmudgeon as if to dare complaint. I dispensed whatever we had to drink. Lothar managed the cigarettes and ashtrays. Felipe cleared the plates. Kim peeled the fruit and shuffled the cards for afterwards. Estrela disapproved. We sat at our round, uneven table. We talked of nothing and of everything. Every so often, the capybara would wander into the clearing and we would chase them off with our head torches. We inspected our cards hoping for the ace we might have missed. Above us, the fireflies glowed like tiny stars and the darkness around about seemed almost like an ocean; the *comedor* our little lighted ship. If it was not quite civilization, then we enjoyed at least . . . equilibrium.

Tonight, not so. Lothar was on a rare trip away to the capital. So we were only five at the table: Kim, the Judge, myself, Felipe and Colonel Cordero. Jorge remained in the kitchen throughout, playing the great chef, sending us all manner of side dishes that we had never seen before, nor much wished to see again. The entente with Estrela must have ended because she soon settled heavily and defiantly opposite me. Felipe, meanwhile, fussed and fidgeted and dabbed at his lips in mimicry of what he imagined fine dining in the capital to be.

Unusually, Sole did not sit with us. Despite her dress, she preferred to hover and carry though there was no need for her to do so. She was quiet – sullen almost and short with Estrela. (As so often, I noticed that mother and daughter had in common most of all the knowledge of how precisely to persecute one another.) But I was alone in detecting anxiety as the governing emotion behind this irritation.

Cordero spoke only to ask questions. I could not gauge his intelligence, nor the nature of his relationship with the Judge, but I was forming the opinion that he was the sort of a man who took a steady satisfaction in rooting down for the worst of things – perhaps to prove to himself that nobody else was free from the fears and the weaknesses he harboured in his own mind; perhaps because he found that he could not be sure of anything but the lowest motives. He listened – but only as though he was at some obscure extension of his business. And he had a way of desiccating personality so that everything we said about ourselves and our work felt immoderate and self-indulgent. When Sole appeared with coffee, I took the opportunity of the interruption to ask more about the Judge's work and turn the conversation back on them.

'Everyone. We are registering everyone.' He was annoyed to have been distracted from looking at Sole's legs. 'Outlaws, smugglers, gun-runners, rat-eaters, monkey-fiddlers. If it shows up alive . . . we register it.'

'Surely they need some kind of proof of identity?' I was not so naive as to believe this, but because of my continued irritation with Cordero, I was determined to be affable with the Judge. 'Otherwise anyone could turn up and there would be no record for next time and the whole electoral register would become—'

'A farce.' The Judge interrupted me. 'A protracted farce. Like so much.' He paused to upend his remaining wine directly into his throat before setting down the stem of the glass with exaggerated care. 'Look, most of the people we register are barely human. So how can they have an address? An address . . . An address requires a sense of time and place, a sense of the world beyond. These creatures crawl out of the forest and stand there smelling of sweat and faeces until the soldiers frighten them away. First they come for the knives, then for the free drink, then for the televisions.'

'I think what you are doing is worthwhile.' Kim spoke to him directly for the first time since we had sat down. 'Those that want to have a say are getting that chance. We should let them know about their rights and what those rights mean. It's all about giving them an understanding of their situation, their choices.'

I tightened. This earnestness was not her true nature and evinced itself when she felt shy.

She sat forward. 'We should be helping them understand the processes of land registration and the reservations and everything. We owe . . . we owe the indigenous peoples that much.'

'They, the *indigenous* peoples' – the Judge returned the word as though throwing back an undersized fish – 'are not the slightest bit interested in registration, or voting, or the sham of their so-called rights.' He fingered a cigarette from his case, his pale eyes unreadable and unwavering. 'This entire question is an embarrassment to all who concern themselves with it. The map claims the Indians live on a reservation and yet they have not the slightest idea that any such place is reserved for them. They don't know what reservation means. Who decided this? Not them. They were simply existing. Now their men beg for alcohol and pornography while the women sell themselves for mirrors and cosmetics. What does that tell us about *Homo sapiens*?'

Kim's brow needled. 'Well, I'm not an anthropologist or a campaigner but I believe that people have the right to choose their own . . . destiny.'

The Judge's match flared as he spoke. 'Miss Van der

Kisten, we hear a lot of this kind of talk in our country. And so we ask ourselves, why do you people come to the jungle?' He raised his jaw and exhaled towards the sky. His voice had an incantatory quality so that his words seemed to range out into the blackness of the night beyond and to echo on into the silence. 'Let me tell you. Always, always, it is for one of two reasons: either to find the green hell and to see some kind of a freak show; or to find a green heaven and so rediscover some ancient truth that you pretend to yourself humanity has lost but that in reality has everything to do with your own feelings of emptiness and worthlessness and nothing whatsoever to do with the Indians or their lives. And what happens the moment your own way of life is threatened? You retreat – you retreat the better to commune with your narcissistic little sense of entitlement, which simply will not go away however much you recycle your packaging.'

'I come for the ants,' I said, softly. 'And the food.'

'We're scientists,' Kim said.

'So you say,' he smiled. 'But I have met many of your tribe, Miss Van der Kisten, and they seem to believe because they wear certain clothes and affect an innocent demeanour that this changes everything. And yet to me – and to most of my countrymen – they remain exactly as they are: the children of a thousand unseen privileges flown in from their own continents, where their every whim has always been met at the direct and continual expense of the rest of the world, to lecture us . . . to lecture us about rights and restraint. Thank you but no. We much prefer businessmen – the honest pigs of profit and war.'

In part, he was toying with us and Kim knew it. But she would not be so treated and there was anger entering her voice. 'You are wrong,' she said. 'There are lots of examples of honest science. And there are loads of aid organizations that achieve real things for the people they're trying to help. We know for a fact that educated tribes make good decisions about their circumstances and what they—'

'What *you* consider good decisions.' The Judge drew a backhanded curtain of smoke. 'What *you* consider reasonable and fair and thoughtful. Everything by your standard, by your laws, by your decree. There is a covert we-know-best in the dark heart of everything you do and everything you say.'

'That's just not true.'

'Isn't it?'

'No. Not always.'

I intervened. 'The majority of the non-governmental organizations do have good intentions.'

The Judge smiled his scabrous smile again. 'Doctor, as

you will soon discover, this place is the death-mire of good intentions. Ah, yes, you *mean* well. You mean well . . . until you discover that you do not know what exactly it is that you mean.'

This time Kim was silent.

The Judge extinguished his cigarette. 'I myself am a keen anthropologist,' he said, suddenly genial. 'An amateur, no doubt, but I have read my Durkheim and what fascinates me . . . what fascinates me is that it is always the same with young women: the good-looking ones, they secretly want you to admire them for their minds; and the intelligent ones, they want you to admire them for their bodies. Now why would that be? But I see by your face you are offended.'

Felipe's eyes were watering.

'I am not offended.' Kim blew her hair from her forehead. 'We are all entitled to our opinions.'

'I'm afraid to have an opinion, you must know something of which you speak. But please . . .' Kim had risen and the Judge's face lit up in a disarming expression of conciliation. 'I am a contrary man and I make no claim for superiority. I, too, am looking for a big house on a pretty hill wherein I can indulge myself and pretend great spirituality while I forget about the rest of the world. Consider me an idiot.'

I stood noisily and began to collect plates. I had been

aware that the Colonel was watching us throughout. He had not spoken – almost so as tacitly to encourage us, I thought. Such conversations with strangers – officials – were at best uncertain and at worst dangerous. And everything bled into everything else: land rights into land reserves, the un-contacted tribes, the recent killings; the reserves into questions of agriculture, science, conservation, development, energy, resources; these, in turn, into narcotics, policing, the guerrillas, arms and the government, the president.

'Kim, it's our turn to wash up,' I said.

Cordero rose and addressed Felipe abruptly: 'Do you speak the language of the local tribe?'

'No.' Felipe nodded and then shook his head.

'They are called the Matsigenka,' Kim said. 'Or perhaps you mean the Yora or the Ashaninka or the Ese Eja or the Harkmbut?'

'Sole speaks Ashaninka and a little of some of the other languages,' I said. 'Or there is a neighbour of ours who is Matsigenka – his name is Tupki.'

Cordero nodded curtly. 'The men will make their own provisions. But we take breakfast at seven.'

'You had better tell Jorge,' I said. 'He prefers to take breakfast at noon.'

'Surely we're all going to dance now?' The Judge

started laughing to himself. 'We eat, we discuss, we dance. Please tell me that you have music.'

'I hope you will be able to help us in our efforts, Dr Forle.' Cordero spoke to me like I were another man's choice for promotion. 'I am sure there are things that you and your colleagues know about this area that might be useful. I'm assuming we will be able to rely on you. Now, if you will excuse me, I must see my men. We have work to do. There are problems.'

VII

'The One Special Difficulty'

The ants presented Darwin with 'the one special difficulty, which at first appeared fatal to my whole theory.' His problem was this: that the overwhelming majority of any colony consists of thousands on thousands of sterile females who have foregone their own reproductive potential for the service of a single queen. More than this, these sister ants often appear to make suicidal decisions for the good of the colony. (There is even a suicidal ant, Camponotus saundersi, *that will kill itself by exploding its own glands to spray attackers in poison.) This extreme cooperative behaviour runs counter to everything we have come to accept about natural selection and the prevalent idea that* the genes that get passed on most often over time are the ones whose consequences serve their own interests. The societies of the ants must therefore be reckoned with at the centre of all evolutionary questions. How can there be so many altruistic individuals and yet so many successful species?

And they are very successful. More than any other creature, the ants saturate and dominate the terrestrial environment. There are something like thirteen thousand species with roughly that number again yet to be discovered. Their total population is probably underestimated at ten thousand trillion individuals.

We call them 'eusocial' insects, meaning 'truly social'. Some ants farm, some use tools, some fight terrible wars, others enslave and still others are inquilines – disguised interlopers who rely on their hosts for food and shelter. There are ants of every adaptation and form one can imagine: from a strangely motionless species to those with mandibles that shut like trap doors in less than a millisecond, the fastest animal movement on Earth.

The combined dry weight of all the ants on the Earth is about the same as that of Homo sapiens.

VIII

I was awake. The air was stifling-close and the night full of sound. Yet distinctly, I heard the voices that must have woken me: unrestrained, then laughing.

I cast back the sheet and climbed carefully out from under my net. I put on my boots unlaced. I did not light my lamp, but crossed the floor and stood to one side of my porch window in the darkness.

There were two men sitting on Sole's steps. Behind them, Sole's light was burning. I shrank back. I could see shapes through the translucent calico of her curtains. The shadows came together in the window and I could not be sure if the one were laying hands on the other or the two merely crossing paths. I was afraid to make sense of what I saw. We did not force our way into one another's huts in the night. We hung around the *comedor*, we drank, we smoked, we went to bed. We tried to sleep in the merciless heat. We did not lock our doors. We woke early to catch the only moments of cool that the jungle allows. We went to work.

The shadows parted and closed again. Sweat seeped my sides. I resolved to turn on my light and march out but the door opposite was thrown open and Sole was framed a moment: she was bare-armed and bare-legged, her black hair untied; I recognized the long white cotton shirt that she liked to sleep in. A man appeared behind her. He was wearing a military cap and there was a gun in his belt. She moved aside and gestured him to get out. I stood deeper into my darkness.

She was remonstrating. Her hair fell in her eyes. The man finally stepped outside and she closed the door behind him. As the other two rose, I saw that one was wearing what I took to be a pilot's headset. In the semi-darkness, it made his head appear much larger, grotesquely square. There was low laughter. Cigarettes were lit. Sole's shadow moved behind the calico. Perhaps they were arresting her, I thought. But for what?

Abruptly, the man with the cap discarded his cigarette, took both the stairs in a stride, pushed open the door and went back inside. Sole's voice was raised. I had never heard her shout before. More exchanges – louder now. Then Sole was coming out, leading the way. She was wearing her jeans. She passed the other two, ignored their flashlight, and walked hurriedly up the path towards the *comedor*.

I cursed myself for not going immediately. I was sure that the man had snatched open the door deliberately to catch her as she dressed. I stumbled on my laces and lit my lamp. I tried to yank my trousers on over my boots.

But I had to sit, take the boots off, pull the trousers on, and then put on my boots again.

Outside, the night sounded like the teeth of a thousand combs thumbed over and over and the walls of the jungle loomed tall and black. I hurried towards the *comedor*. The other huts were dark. The solar lamps were running down. I should have gone back to fetch my torch. On our familiar path, I was suddenly an impostor. And it struck me then that these last weeks had been false and this . . . this was merely a righting. I passed around the kapok tree.

There was a shriek. Inhuman. High-pitched. Some night bird very close. Yet such a screeching cry that surely I must have heard it before? I told myself that the Station was known-of, long-established, an outpost of science.

Lights. Not at the *comedor*, but beyond. I stole forward silently. Around the back of the building, they had started a fire. The jungle beyond was no longer a dark wall but branches, leaves, vines, fronds, all balking and shrinking in the updraught. They were too close.

I stood at the corner of the *comedor* and looked on. The capped man and the other two had their backs to me. They were standing around a fourth who was tied to one of our dining chairs with a sack on his head. He was naked. Sole was leaning in towards the ragged hole in the bag where his mouth must have been. She had to shield herself from the heat. The bag turned from side to side. The fire whispered and muttered. She straightened.

The capped man hooked his thumbs through his gun belt as he spoke to one of his subordinates who now approached the fire, crouching and picked something up . . . a stick, a thin metal rod? I could not be sure.

Sole was bending in to the prisoner again.

The subordinate stayed down on his haunches. In the firelight, I saw his face as he turned. He was a boy, fourteen, fifteen perhaps – no more. And he was not wearing a pilot's headset but some kind of heavy-duty old-fashioned dental brace. Two thick wire tubes emerged from the corners of his mouth, looped back along his jawline and then fixed into heavy leather straps that were fastened tight around his head.

I saw now that the soldiers had taken out the seat so that the prisoner was tied only to the frame and his lower body sagged through the hole where the base of the chair should have been. The Boy brandished the pole. The end glowed a bluish white-hot in the darkness. He came in behind and underneath the prisoner. I understood his intention at the same moment as Sole.

She turned and screamed in fury at the capped man. And this time I heard her clearly – a boiling stream of curses. She pointed sharply at the Boy. He hesitated, staying low. She extended her hands high into the air, halting him and driving him back. Reluctant, he withdrew and placed his pole back into the heart of the fire. Sole leaned into the chair again. And at last I grasped what was happening . . . she was translating. She did not know these men. This was nothing to do with her.

I dropped away from my corner. My plan – ludicrous, infantile – was to fetch my torch and then to walk casually around the *comedor* and up to the fire as though I was out on some innocent night stroll.

Another shriek in the trees then a gruff grunt-growling sound. Not a bird, I realized, but a red-necked owl monkey – swollen-eyed and yellow-toothed, a claw on the fourth digit of both feet.

Inside my hut, where before I had seen order, I now saw only contingency. I found my torch. I extracted my key from the inside of the door and turned the lock behind me.

I ran. In the darkness, there were yet darker black fists that swooped and darted. Bats.

She was coming down the path.

'Sole.'

She did not stop.

'I woke up,' I said. 'I came over. You weren't there. What's happening?'

She did not speak.

'Sole, where have you been? What's happening?'

She shut her eyes as she pushed past me. I walked beside her, lighting her way as if she needed me to do so.

'Are you all right?'

She was silent.

'Sole?'

'I'm going to bed.'

I could not say what I had witnessed at the fire.

'Sole, stop. Talk to me.'

'This has nothing to do with you.'

I reached for her.

She turned but kept on. 'Why don't you go and ask the soldiers what's happening?'

'I will.' I stopped and softened my voice. 'I'll be back in a few minutes.'

'Be careful.' She spoke tersely over her shoulder: 'People are killed here all the time.'

The prisoner had gone. The Boy and the other remained. They had replaced the seat in the frame and fetched out a second dining chair from the *comedor*; they seemed incongruous – absurd – sat thus in the crimson light with the jungle wall, lit and shadowed, a thousand gaping throats behind them. I noticed the smell for the first time.

A metal grill lay in the ashes. They must have been cooking. Meats. Before the questioning began? After?

The second man was wiry and wore his hair short in the military style though with a long rat's tail hanging down at the back as though he could convince himself of neither his brawn nor his wits. He must have been ten years older than the Boy. He was still eating, leaning forward on the edge of his chair.

The Boy looked up.

'I heard a noise,' I said.

He licked at the metal where it emerged from the corner of his mouth so that it glistened.

'I don't sleep.' I added this as a fact, but perhaps I intended it as an obscure warning. 'What's going on?'

'Who are you?' the Boy said.

Somehow, though there was no wind, I was standing in the smoke.

'I'm a scientist. I work here. Why have you lit this fire?'

'We've been keeping warm,' the other said.

I saw that the order of things between the two was inverted: the older man looked to the Boy; and the Boy considered him in some way his associate.

'We've got a prisoner,' the Boy said, his voice still toneless.

'We've been keeping him warm, too.' The associate sniggered.

'The woman you took from the hut – she works with me. She told me what happened.'

The associate grinned. 'She is working with us now,' he said. 'And she likes it.'

'Where is the Colonel? Who told you to light this fire?'

'Captain Lugo gives us our orders,' the Boy said.

'Where is he?'

'He's right here.'

The Boy was looking around me. I glanced over my shoulder. The capped man was coming towards us from the *comedor*. I turned to face him.

Lugo was a short squat man – gaucho-legged and densely muscled from training. He stood with the attitude of someone for whom every encounter was a confrontation.

'You're the doctor?' he asked. 'Yes?'

'I'm a scientist.'

'But you're a doctor?'

'I'm not a medical doctor.'

I realized with a shock that he was younger than me. He said nothing. Either he did not understand or he was not interested in the distinction.

'What do you need?' I asked.

'I need disinfectant. Maybe a breathing tube. Do you have supplies?'

'What happened?'

'It doesn't matter what happened. Let's go.'

I held the ground a moment and then turned back to address the others. 'You should build your fire away from the edge of the forest . . . and away from the buildings. This is the end of the dry season. Everything is tinder.' My trepidation had disappeared and now I included the captain as I spoke: 'And if you want to cook, you can use our kitchen. We've already got the biggest rats in the world here. We don't want to encourage them.' I did not allow him to respond. 'The medical store is round the other side. I'll see what we've got. What happened?'

'We have a prisoner.'

'I know. What happened?'

'That does not concern you.'

'Everything concerns me.'

'Ask the Colonel.'

'I will.'

TWO

I

My dreams were murderous and full of lust. I woke hot
and dank in the close-wrapped darkness. But I did not
wish to disturb her so I eased myself beneath the net and
slipped on my boots.

Outside, the light had not yet cracked the sky, for
there are no horizons in the forest. Instead, the dawn
was being born in the trees a wan and smoky blue. The
clamour of the canopy had hushed and I stood a moment
on her steps. It seemed that all the beauty of the world
had come and lain down in the clearing. Thin fingers of
mist curled through the trunks in search of something
lost. If ever I were going to see a jaguar, then it would be
a moment such as this: the great cat stepping silent from
the half-dark wall of the jungle, head low, quartz-eyed and
lazy-tailed.

The water in the bathing hut was tepid and smelled of
cold tea and clay; but I was pleased to wash the night from

my skin. My intention was to confront them as soon as they appeared. My intention was fury. And yet, even as I stood towelling myself dry in our crude cubicle, I was aware that fury could not really be intended and that anger in primates is only ever fear by another name. I dressed in my boots and my field clothes – a uniform of sorts. As I passed the lab on the way back, I realized that I was taking conscious comfort in the satellite link of our computer. Civilization was my authority. Already, I could smell the heat gathering energy; rich and close and foetid.

I was confounded: the Judge was at the *comedor* ahead of me. He was sitting on one of the lounge chairs, wearing striped pyjamas, with his feet propped up in expensive shoes on our low table. He was peeling fruit with a knife too big for the task and he regarded me with neither geniality nor hostility.

'Good morning, Dr Forle. You seem in something of a hurry. Are the ants on the march? Have some fruit.' He indicated the pile of *tucumã*. 'I found them myself. They're delicious.'

'I want to speak to you.'

'And I want to speak to that disgracefully obese cook of yours. I was hoping for eggs. Various teas.'

'Last night, your men – your captain – broke into the hut of one of our staff and attacked her.'

A parrot squawked – ridiculous, ridiculing.

'I'm not at all surprised. That man is an embarrassment to evolution.'

'I'm being serious.'

'So am I.'

'They forced her to help them interrogate one of the tribesmen.'

The Judge looked up at me from his fruit. I found his eyes disconcerting. Glacier-blue, they did not belong here. *Terra del fuego*.

'Your staff?' he asked.

'Yes.' I was further annoyed at myself for using that word. 'Her name is Soledad.'

He continued to peel. 'I know her name.' He blinked slowly as if he were negotiating some narrow mental pass. 'I have always liked women who do not like me. I admire their good taste. Have you noticed how in the beginning we are aggressive and awkward with the people to whom we are attracted? But she's old for a childless Ashaninka. What is she – twenty-five, would you say? What do you think she is waiting for, I wonder, Dr Forle? A decent man?'

'Your captain went to her hut. He pushed his way in – threatened her – then dragged her out. If I hadn't got up to—'

'Threatened her or attacked her?'

'They were torturing him.' The word should have resonated but it drowned in the sticky air and I had to speak again almost immediately – against the insect hum and the chirping of the birds and the Judge's silence: 'I want the captain reported.'

'To whom?'

'If you won't do it, I will.'

'You may well have more effect than I would.'

It was impossible to sustain any kind of conversation with the man.

'I find that hard to believe. You are a judge. You are—'

'Everything is hard to believe, Dr Forle.' He looked up again with a disturbing fixity. 'I am from the Ministry of Justice. They are from the Ministry of the Interior. An entirely different thing. They are not *my* men any more than Sole is *your* staff.' He softened his expression – and I realized that he was smiling sympathetically as one might smile at a simple patient. 'But you are in luck.' He gestured with a flourish. 'For here comes the Colonel – to whom I suggest you make your concerns known.'

Cordero's step was dense on the wooden floor. The timber shifted, creaked, shifted back. He was dressed in fatigues. To my surprise, Jorge was following him – already wearing his apron. I would not be deflected.

'Good morning, Colonel. I need to talk to you.' I

glanced in the Judge's direction. 'We were deciding what to do about what took place last night.'

'What about last night?' He passed his tongue from one cheek to the other.

'Your captain attacked Sole – the woman who works here. She's an employee of the Ministry of Agriculture.'

A twitch or a fleeting smile. 'Captain Lugo?'

'Yes.' The fact of having dealt with Lugo as a captain seemed to elevate Cordero as Colonel and now I felt as though I was petitioning rather than requiring. 'The woman is frightened and upset. Your captain forced his way into her hut and then dragged her out against her will.'

'At what time did this occur?'

'I don't know – late.'

'And you were awake?'

'No, I woke up – because of the noise.'

'There was a lot of noise?'

'Yes.'

'Did anyone else hear – or come out?'

He was interrogating me.

'No. Yes. They must have done.'

'Did you see anyone else?'

'I don't know. Felipe, the guide, might have heard something.'

'Is this woman injured?'

'Her name is Soledad. No, thankfully not. I intervened.'

'You intervened?' The suggestion of disparagement became tangible. Behind him Jorge shifted. The wood moaned.

'Your men forced her to go with them to a fire they had lit – too close to the trees.' I raised my arm in the direction of the forest. 'They were holding a man there. They had him tied to a chair. He had shackles on his feet and a bag on his head.'

The Colonel was silent.

'They wanted Sole to translate what the man was saying. They threatened her.'

'Where is she now?'

'She is in her hut – I told her to wait there.'

'Can she speak for herself?'

'She is very upset.'

'Of course. But if she has a formal complaint to make, then she must make it to me herself.'

Now he was using the policeman's manner of exaggerated calm.

'Fine – but your captain cannot stay here – on the Station. Not after this.'

'If she wishes to come and see me, then I will talk with her.' He pulled out a chair and spoke over his shoulder at Jorge. 'Bring coffee and whatever else you have.'

'I intend to write a report of everything that I witnessed last night.' I said this to assert without subtlety my independence, but I had no idea to whom I might give such a thing or what, if any, its effect might be. I was beginning to sound ridiculous even to myself. The daylight made the night seem unreal. The parrot dipped its head repeatedly.

Cordero sat down with the affectation of weariness. 'Try to bear in mind, Dr Forle, that this Station is owned by my government, and that decisions as to who can and who cannot stay here are government decisions. But please feel free to mention my name in your report. If nothing else, I am sure the mayor, the governor and even the president will be pleased to hear of our progress this far up the river.'

All the while, the Judge had been following the exchange with an exaggerated back and forth of his head. Now his pale eyes came to rest on me.

'I'll be back this evening,' I said. 'I will ask Sole to come and speak with you.'

'Where are you going?' He looked up from the table.

'To work.'

It was his turn to detain me.

'I mean whereabouts is your work exactly?'

'We have twenty-four different sites,' I said. 'They're all around.'

'Where are you going today, Doctor? Which one?'

'It's about half an hour away. Why?'

'Because some of the river channels will have patrols on them by now.' He thinned his nose. 'And you will not be able to pass. But if you let me know where this site is, we can check that your way is clear before you go out.'

'It changes every day. We rotate the sites.'

Again the weariness. 'Then let us know every day where you are going – in the morning. And we will try to help you avoid wasting your time.'

'If that's necessary.'

'It is.'

I hesitated. 'What are your patrols doing, Colonel?'

'Picking people up.'

'For the registration?'

'Yes. For that.'

'I'm sorry but I don't understand – surely we can just carry on – your men will know it's us, won't they? We won't be interfering with your work.'

I looked towards the Judge, who smiled.

'There are also security issues,' Cordero said. 'Which are my responsibility.'

Jorge had brought out the coffee.

Cordero turned back to the table.

'Please let me know what you have done about Captain Lugo when I get back,' I said.

I walked away full of intention and, in this, like so many whose lives pass busily and who in the end do nothing.

II

Our boat chugged the sullen backwater. We were travelling upstream but this no longer felt like a journey back to the earliest beginnings of the world, rather to its end. There was no visible sun and the matted tangle was strangely motionless – monochrome, petrified. Everywhere the roots were exposed and the brown flats suppurated. Where once there had been tributaries, now there were pools, cut off. A slow asphyxiation: more and more seeking less and less. The season of low water had gone on too late and too long.

I was thirsty. I needed to break the spell. Tord, the missionary who sometimes visited us (and who liked in our company to be considered a linguist), said that most of the Indian languages had a special word that described the power of the jungle to mesmerize. I could well believe him. I turned around. Felipe's smile flew across his face to greet me.

'Do we have anything to drink?'

'Yes, of course, Dr Forle.' He prised open the Styrofoam cool box with one hand and made to stand and lean toward me. I was afraid that we would swerve and that he would ground the boat. We had been snagging the propeller a lot recently. I am skilled with a knife – anatomy, dissection – but, still, it was blind, wet, dangerous work to cut free the heavy tendrils. And though they say the piranha only attack those with open wounds, the caiman and the anaconda are less particular.

'Throw it,' I said.

He did so with exaggerated care.

I sat back and cracked open the can. After the anger of the morning had come a burning urgency to work. I had left the *comedor* and gone straight to the lab to collect my pack and my equipment. I did not know what else to do. Perhaps I had already begun to feel that my work – as a naturalist, as a scientist – was somehow against them. I had then walked back up to Felipe's hut, where I had found him already neatly dressed, sitting at his table, cutting pages from the lifestyle magazines he collected and drinking a glass of milk. He had been surprised to see me at the door of his hut. We needed to make faster progress, I had explained, even if that meant working alone in the field from now on. I wanted him to take me out immediately.

Now, I sipped my drink and watched the river. We were passing an unusually reedy stretch of bank. Heavy, raven-coloured birds sat high-shouldered on a fallen trunk as if at some last council. I swung both my legs over the bench and sat facing backwards so that I could talk with Felipe directly.

'Did you hear anything last night?'

'Yes.' He rubbed at his cheeks; there was a line above which he did not shave but the bristles grew up further, towards his eyes.

'Did you get up?'

'I was very concerned, Dr Forle,' he said uneasily. 'I was very concerned.'

'Did you come out? Did you go to the *comedor*?'

'No.'

'Did you see anything? Did you see Captain Lugo going into Sole's room? Before?'

'I saw him going back towards the *comedor* with her. Then I saw you following them and I thought to myself – oh, that's good, the Doctor is awake – since I knew that you would come and knock if there was a serious problem.' He tilted his head to one side. 'And you know, Doctor, nobody bosses Sole about. Not even captains.'

Felipe was pretending to a certain delicacy – as though the night had been about something else and he was chary of intrusion. But his hut was next along to Sole's and he must have been woken by her shouting, just as I was.

'You didn't hear Sole – when the captain went into her hut?'

'No.'

'You didn't see the captain go in?'

'No.'

'You didn't hear anything from the direction of the *comedor*?'

'No – nothing.'

Now he was lying. I felt for him. In his own way, Felipe was ambitious. He liked to talk about the trip he had once made to the capital and though he was unsure as to what prospect the visitors might present, he was eager not to let any such opportunity pass. It occurred to me that he had not left his hut because he was employed by the government – like Jorge, Estrela . . . and like Sole. Inwardly, I cursed the Colonel and the Judge and the studious calm that their arrival had so quickly poisoned. More than ever, I wanted to work.

'If I were going to report the captain – I mean report his actions – who would I contact, Felipe?'

'The captain is not police. It would be impossible . . . even if he were police.'

'What about an ambitious lawyer?'

The question dismayed him – his innocence was his armour not his nature.

'This is politics now, Dr Forle. The mayor, the governor, even the president most likely – everybody is involved. These are matters for the government. Who knows how anything is decided? I would say that the best thing is to wait and see, Doctor, wait and see.' He brightened. 'This is all part of the bigger picture – the registration. It is better not to be involved. We stay focused on the bigger picture by staying focused on the little picture.'

It was one of the idiotic phrases that I brought with me.

'After the registration process, they will be gone,' he continued. 'And then things will be back to normal. You will see. Mr Rebaque will be back and we can get on with the science.'

He was doing his best. He had worked on enough expeditions to understand scientific vanity, too; he knew that I feared a full-scale disruption of the work.

'All the same,' I said. 'I'd like there to be a note on the Colonel's file or something. And it might be important that you corroborate my story.'

I realized that I sounded naive, and that this offended his sense of my status, my international authority. But my thoughts would not leave the white-hot pole. And it was true: I would have liked to place a similar rod in the fire for the enemies of Cordero – something easy to hand if ever they wished to torture him.

'What do you think Dr Quinn would do?' I asked after a while.

'I don't know what Dr Quinn would do in this situation.' Felipe crossed himself. 'Nobody can know that.'

'He would do something. You told me that Dr Quinn was involved in lots of things.'

'Not like this . . . Nothing like this. He would visit the villages. That's what I meant.'

'Which villages?' I was persecuting Felipe now, I knew, but I could not stop. 'The *ribereños* or the Indians? The Matsigenka? The Yora?'

'Dr Quinn was friends with Tupki and lots of the others. He would go and camp. Sometimes after his work. Or for a few days. With Lothar. He was interested in looking at their medicines and how they lived. But he was not . . . He was not involved with the government or the police . . . or soldiers. Not at all.'

Something swam just beneath the surface of the water.

'Did they find the wreckage of the plane? I hear different stories.'

'I don't know. But, Dr Forle, there were more than a hundred people on the plane. Not just Dr Quinn.'

'Not just Dr Quinn.'

'Dr Quinn is with God and all the saints and the angels,' he said and crossed himself again.

'And we are finishing his work.'

'Yes.' He nodded. 'Yes.'

'With your help, Felipe,' I said.

He smiled but he did not speak. We had come to a bend in the channel where the shoals narrowed our passage and he looked past me, partly to verify his way, partly to pretend an absorption not permitting of conversation. He too was seeking refuge in his work.

III

The jungle has been compared to an ocean: the canopy is like the coral where the fruit grows and flowers bloom and the forest floor is like the seabed where all dead things must eventually fall and rot. Man is a monster of the deep, therefore, a creature of casual atrocity and low cunning lumbering through the perpetual gloom.

We progressed steadily. After a while, we found a rhythm to our going and in this rhythm a kind of ease. We carried our machetes; we swigged from our water; we clambered fallen trunks and bent beneath the hanging vine. The ground rose and fell. Amidst the green and brown of the trees, I began to see flashes of white and gold, red and blue – birds, flowers, epic butterflies in the quavering grace of their flight.

I had grown fond of following Felipe – specifically I had grown accustomed to watching his white gloves dancing ahead of me. I had thought them ridiculous when I arrived, but I quickly came to see their purpose. Only a fool would throw out a hand to steady himself in the primary forest: thorns and spines were on every side – great barbed trunk-teeth, lethal hooks, scimitars and spikes. And all five kingdoms have their formidable defenders – their bites and stings and scratches, their toxins and poisons and venoms, their bacteria and their viruses.

In order to ensure our study was thorough and robust, Quinn had chosen twenty-four separate field sites. Roughly half were less than fifteen minutes' boat ride from the station. But it was difficult to try and remember the subsequent foot journey even to most of these. As for the more distant, it was impossible; and though I must have passed along the way that we were now walking a dozen times, I recognized little and the path we followed seemed barely that – appearing to fork and fork again, merging, circling, disappearing altogether, trickery and chimera, all directions identical, no direction at all.

It was our usual arrangement that Felipe and I went out together while Lothar worked alongside Kim. But with Lothar away, we three had been working all together at the closer sites. Up to now, I had been strict: neither Kim nor I had gone into the jungle alone – for obvious reasons to do with the risk of accidents, but most of all because we would both have been utterly lost within ten minutes. Anyone not thoroughly familiar with the forest is desperate within an hour of finding themselves alone. Most die after a surprisingly short amount of time; usually because they make themselves fatally ill as they start to believe – consumed by hunger and maddened by thirst – that every berry, nut, root and leaf is edible. Even a compass bearing is useless since it is impossible to walk in a straight line for more than two paces at a time. You cannot proceed except in the direction the forest allows. And though Kim and I both carried satellite navigation systems in our packs, they were little better for the same reason – and, in any case, the reception beneath the understorey was notoriously unreliable.

Felipe stopped and I looked up, startled afresh each time to see the canopy broken. We had arrived without warning and the sun was poking through and the light flaring from leaf to leaf, bright and shocking. Dead ahead, the customary riot and profusion of the forest had vanished and there were no plants in view save one species – a thin, bare and bleached-looking tree with crooked branches that reached towards the sky like claws: *Duroia hirsuta*.

IV

The Devil's Garden

The Indian tribes call the glades in which we conducted our research Devil's Gardens because they believe them to be gardens cultivated by an evil forest spirit, Chuy-achaqui. For the most part, the local tribes are animist. But of course the anthropologists remind us that all forms of spiritual belief are about the same things underneath: through our magic and our cosmology we project ourselves onto the universe and the universe back onto ourselves. We place ourselves in the centre of our own drama. Our religions become the means by which we worship ourselves and our societies; a way to get the business of living done. And thus, like all human beings, the Indians conjure up their devils to make sense of that which is otherwise psychologically intolerable to them; to accommodate their anxieties, their disasters, the terrifying arbitrariness of the world. As once with our own witches, the worst of these malevolent spirits are always located away from the villages – deeper in the forests – because established power seeks to maintain itself and devils threaten the status quo. All this the scientist knows well. And yet it was not difficult to understand why the Indians ascribed magic to the forest and malevolence to these anaemic glades. Besides which, most of our time in the Devil's Gardens was spent on our knees measuring necrosis.

V

Stage One

There are three stages to our fieldwork – each important in its own right.

The first is the task we are engaged in every day: an experiment to demonstrate that the Devil's Gardens are created not by the inhibition of one plant by another, but by our ants, Myrmelachista schumanni. *In effect, we hope to prove that the* Myrmelachista *are engineering their own environment.*

*With this in mind, we plant some common forest saplings (*Cedrela odorata*) in the midst of the Devil's Gardens. Then we either allow our ants onto these saplings or we exclude them with tape. We watch and record what happens.*

As predicted, we are finding that the ants immediately attack the Cedrela odorata *saplings from which they are not barred; but that the ant-excluded saplings grow as normal whether they are in the Devil's Gardens or not. In other words, it is the ants that are doing the poisoning.*

Of course, this is a classic mutualism: the D. hirsuta

trees of the Devil's Gardens flourish thanks to the ants; and the ants live with staggering success in the hollow stems of their beloved hosts. It is also one of the single most impressive evolutionary successes to be found in this, the most ferociously competitive environment on Earth. By our calculations, some of the Devil's Gardens are over eight hundred years old.

VI

Felipe returned to the Station to pick up Kim and take her out to one of the other sites. I forced myself to be meticulous in my work. We were recording as much as we could; we had over thirty thousand photographs on the spare hard drive back at the lab – all coded for site and time. I wanted my foundations to be firm again and my dealings with the world authentic. Ninety per cent of the labour in our field was in organizing the appended material – the documenting and the display of the evidence to support our findings.

Every so often, I looked up and breathed in the forest – the trees beyond, the layers of sound, the smell, the thrum of life all around, the great non-human flourishing of it all. I wasn't anxious of being alone until I heard a crashing sound.

Something large was moving through the under-growth. I stopped dead still, listening.

Nothing.

Peccary, soldiers, tapir, a jaguar, tribesmen; it was possible to be less than three metres from any of these and a First World man would never know. The sound came again – ahead, louder.

I called out: 'Hello?'

I stood motionless, my field camera hanging from my wrist, the sweat pouring off my body, an entire continent of jungle in all directions.

'Who's there?'

My breathing stopped and my body tensed ready for I did not know what.

'*Guten Morgen, mein Freund.*' Hat, machete and grin – Lothar emerged from the thicket. He was holding up his palm in a childish gesture of greeting. 'You know what I want to know? I want to know why the little bastards don't take over the whole forest. It seems to work so well – this beautiful system? Why don't they poison the entire planet? If I was them, I would not stop until the world was one big Devil's Garden.'

I heard birdsong again.

Lothar made a rueful face; he was a little surprised by the nervousness of my reaction. 'You look as though you've been bitten in both nuts by a *naca-naca*,' he said.

'You're back.' I raised my forearm to my brow and removed my hat. 'Thank Christ it's you.'

'Who were you expecting?'

'I thought you were one of those marauding pigs.'

'You'd know all about it if I were three dozen peccary, my friend. They like to travel noisy and all together.' There was amusement in his eyes. 'But you're right to worry: it is not such a great way to die – to be mounted by a herd of angry pigs.' His face softened into his rare, soft, ugly smile. 'You are not having so much of a party here today?'

'I've been to better.'

He looked about as if weighing up our chosen field of operations for the first time. 'Maybe if we had some disco lights.'

My brim was sodden and I did not want to return it to my head. 'What are you *doing* here, Lothar?'

His expression became businesslike and with unusual deliberation, he took out a cigarette from the packet he kept in one of his breast pockets.

'On the way back, I stayed at one of the villages. They told me the Judge and the Colonel arrived.' He paused. 'I heard about this Captain Lugo, too. There are rumours. I came straight to find you. I think it might be better to talk away from the Station. They took one of the Matsi-genka prisoner – correct?'

'Yes. And that's only the start of it. I've been going insane wondering what the hell to do.' More often than not I found Lothar's boyish pride in knowing things ahead of time slightly irritating; but today I could hardly restrain my feelings of relief. 'Can I have a cigarette?' I asked.

'Let's sit,' he said.

He was a rangy man with steady grey eyes that seemed a little sad and a face that forty-five years of experience had scored deep so that it creased and wrinkled as he cycled through his various expressions: cynicism, disparagement, black humour, lugubriousness. He smoked as other men breathed – fifty, sixty cigarettes a day. He had short, fair hair, almost no eyebrows, and a small wart on one ear. He wore a leather hat at all times and a wedding ring in which a tiny diamond was embedded.

He was one of those men whom nobody liked on the first few meetings – certainly not women – but whom, in time, all came to love and with such a surety and vehemence that they could not explain or understand their initial aversion. He had lived and worked in this region of the river for fifteen years or more: a translator, fixer, guide, the veteran of a dozen or so expeditions. Quinn persuaded him to join us and he had been living on the

Station for the last three years. I would have thought the place too remote – even for a man of his daunting self-reliance; but we paid him well enough, his hut was free and he had the use of the computer – this last a near-priceless boon. I did not know whether his entomological knowledge had been collected as a result of working on other research or whether there was some part of his early life that had been passed in such study. Either way, he was a far more natural naturalist than I. He knew the names of tens of thousands of species of flora and fauna and his love of the forest and his curiosity for all that lived there were as affecting as those of a child. Of his wife, we knew nothing.

We walked together – back into the forest a short way from the glare in the glade. There was a fallen tree on whose branches I had sat before. Self-conscious of having summoned one up, we checked carefully for *naca-naca*. (*Micrurus spixii*, probably the most venomous of the snakes – neurotoxic, a grown man lasts no more than fifteen minutes, whether he is lucky or not.) Then we sat side by side and smoked and I told him everything. When it came to the fire, the white-hot pole, I found myself covertly watching his reaction. He was surprised; but he was not appalled and I realized with discomfort that my intentions had begun to dissolve. Neither the requirement to act nor the guilt of inaction felt quite so insistent any more. The thought rose up that I had not felt any outrage at all but was merely behaving in this way out of a conviction that I should.

'How normal is this kind of thing, Lothar?'

'Not.' He looked across. 'It is not normal. Not in the last few years. Not in this area.' I had never seen him in this engaged mood before – more sober and without the mock gloom. 'But whatever is happening is happening for another reason. Nothing about the registration. Probably, they are trying to flood the place with votes – yes. There will be bribes for one thing or another. You can be sure of that. They want the vote for something else – something specific.'

'For what?'

'I don't know.' He shrugged. 'All the usual possibilities are with us . . . mining, logging, drugs, cattle, agriculture. You know the list.'

'Aren't we too far in for agriculture?'

'You would think so now. But maybe there's another road coming. There's still a lot of very valuable hardwood here because it has been too difficult for them to get to.' He crushed out his cigarette and placed it carefully in the empty packet that he always carried in his other breast pocket. 'There will be a deal somewhere. It might be land rights. Or it might be some kind of concession. Who knows? But I have not seen it like this before. Not here.

Everybody is tense. And one thing is for certain, my friend, this Colonel sends no more than two of his men out with the Judge. He goes out separately most of the time. The Yora have been watching them.'

'Are they registering the Yora as well?'

'They don't know which tribe is which.'

'I thought it was all about the Indians?'

'Indians, *mestizos*, *ribereños* – they don't seem to care. They register whoever they want. Who is going to check?' Lothar shrugged. 'Two weeks ago, when they were downriver, lots of Ashaninka turned up – but they are organized and their leaders were making the people go. Some of the Matsigenka who already live on the rivers are coming out for the bribes. The Ese Eja are staying out of the way and the Yora will wait for what they think they can get ahead of the other tribes. And as to Mashco Piro – well, what does any of this *Scheiße* mean to them?' He exhaled. 'They tell us that we must develop to relieve poverty. But the un-contacted do not consider themselves poor or undeveloped – they say, "We have the forest to live in. What are these things called rights? What is poverty?" '

'That's more or less what the Judge said.'

He shrugged. 'The facts are the same the world over. It's what we do with them that is the difference between people.'

'Now you sound more like the Colonel.' I winced against my smoke. 'By the way, he wants us to tell him where we are going every day. He says that we can't go where his patrols are.'

'That's not good.'

'I don't see what is so dangerous about rounding up people to register them to vote.'

'Exactly.'

'So where are we in all of this, Lothar?'

'That depends on what you decide to do and what is really going on.'

'We are doing science. It's a research station.'

'No, it is a government facility that your university rents off a poorer country that will do whatever it can do to make itself richer – just like your own. That's what countries do. That's what we *want* countries to do – no? And it's only been used as a scientific station for the last five years – which is no time at all.' He exhaled. 'Welcome to the mess.'

I looked at the tree opposite. I remembered that the last time we had been at this site, Felipe had cut me some of the fruit.

'We are only just beginning,' I said. 'We are booked in for four months. We have brought all our gear. I'm not abandoning everything and going home. I can't do that.' I coughed. 'This work is all I have. We're going to prove something about the way life works. Something that is nothing to do with human beings. Something real.'

'Well . . .' He folded his second cigarette and offered me the carton so that I could discard mine. 'It looks like it will be a real pain in *der Hintern* to have these guys hanging around and telling us where we can and cannot go – but they may not stay so long.'

'So you agree: we carry on as if nothing has happened?'

He looked at me with his grey eyes. 'I am not telling you what to do, my friend. We must all decide that for ourselves.'

THREE

I

A week passed. And the truth is that we worked harder with the soldiers around – reporting in with our site destinations at dawn, leaving for the forest earlier, staying in the lab until later. But this was because the Station was no longer a place of gathering and conversation. We had lost our sense of companionship, the pleasure of society. We kept to our huts.

Every morning and every evening, Cordero was at the *comedor*, waiting. When he was alone, he studied maps and read yellow documents that he took ostentatious care to turn over as soon as we entered. When he was with one of his men, he would immediately and self-consciously break off their discussion. He would nod his curt greetings but he seldom spoke save to ask questions – and when he did there was always that same mixture of indifference and contempt in his voice though nothing that could be specifically defined. I had been right about his concern for his appearance – his clothes were incongruously clean and he used various sweet-smelling lotions on his skin. He ate slowly and methodically and never fewer than three courses. And though our table was round, he seemed always to be sitting centrally so that we found ourselves divided on either side of him.

Jorge became Cordero's personal chef and took an obvious delight in his new-found sponsor. He came and went from the kitchen with his little round jaw thrust forward above his chins, daring us to comment and refusing to work much before the Colonel's sitting or much after his rising. We were served the dishes the Colonel liked at the times the Colonel liked them.

Felipe hovered and fussed, meanwhile, half envious of Jorge and half embarrassed by his disloyalty to Kim and me. Plainly, the Colonel had no use for him. And this realization only served to drive him to greater anxieties and the protracted performance of all manner of needless minor tasks. When he came out into the field with us, he was distracted. When he stayed at the Station, he was dejected.

Sole, conversely, did nothing. And though we carried on as before, it was not the same. She refused to talk about what had happened. And in the evenings, she preferred not to leave her hut at all. Instead, she performed her washing and cleaning tasks in the dead time of the mid-morning or mid-afternoon.

Estrela was the only one of us seemingly unaffected: surly, silent, she continued to sit in the tiny store room day and night in near darkness before her candlelit shrine devoted to La Virgen Madre de Dios, praying for God knows what.

Though there were half a dozen other uniformed men around, I saw nothing of either Captain Lugo or the Boy. And, after a couple of days, I began to convince myself that Cordero had acted on my insistence, that they had been disgraced and sent away to be disciplined, but that – for reasons of pride – he had decided not to tell me.

I said nothing to Kim of that first night. And she gave no indication of having heard anything. She had been thrown off balance by the Judge, I realized, but her unease and her upset had manifest themselves in a renewed application to our field studies and a more businesslike tone to our conversations in the lab.

The Judge himself seemed to work as he pleased, coming and going at hours that did not coincide with our own or the Colonel's. I did not see him at breakfast but he arrived most evenings for dinner, always in his suits, always drinking from our bar, which he promised loudly to replenish. Like Kim and Lothar, I sought to avoid him and exchange only civilities, not least because I found something disturbing about his ability to force me back on my core – so that I felt I must always be defending myself against the acuity and implication of everything he said. One evening he surprised me, though, and I could not but talk with him.

Seeking some relief from the endless green, I had gone down to the river. The sun's blast was fading and the perfumes of the plants were uncoiling so that the air was filled with subtle fragrances. I had sat down at the furthest reach of the jetty with my legs dangling over the water like a boy and I was listening to the burbling song of the oropendola birds and watching their bright tails flash across a sky streaked in peach and pale vermilion. My senses had become so subsumed in the forest itself that there was no longer a border between my body and the world. And so I heard his voice as one might hear a deep low splash – a large caiman entering the water.

'Another beautiful sunset, Doctor. I can't help but think they are wasted on humanity. I would like my wife to see this.'

Startled, I turned.

He was walking towards me: 'I have never been able to process much above pleasure, of course, but my wife is remarkable – she really enjoys beauty where she finds it, breathes it in, lives it. There are too many people who wait for death to enlighten them about life, don't you think? Please, don't get up.'

He laid down the light rug that he was carrying rolled beneath his arm and sat down beside me. A pair of blue-headed macaws flew past.

'They're famous for their monogamy as well as their colour – is that true?'

'I think so.'

'Do you have a wife, Dr Forle?'

'No.'

'But there are strands of silver in that scruffy golden hair of yours and it is obvious you are a man who knows love.' He looked across at me. 'There have been women? Or is it one woman in particular?'

I said nothing.

'Don't persecute yourself, Doctor. It will be no more than half your fault. And women understand men more than it suits them to pretend.'

He took out his cigarette case and I had the sudden thought that his capacity for such quick intimacy must have been honed through the long years of questioning people under oath.

'And you – have you been married a long time?' I asked.

'Yes.' He smoked with a flourish that suggested a peculiar strain of happiness. 'We're lucky. When we are together we are very happy.'

'And when you are not?'

'I mope with my mistresses.'

'It must be difficult for you.'

'Touché.' He smiled. 'I like you, Doctor, you remind me of myself before I knew who I was. But there's something else there . . . something visceral. Sorry, forgive me – would you like one?'

'I'm giving up.'

'So I've noticed.' The smile became a laugh.

A green kingfisher dived into the water.

'What are you really doing here?' I asked.

Another flourish. 'Bringing democracy and enlightenment.'

'You said yourself, though: most of the Indians don't wish to vote.'

'But we have told ourselves a great story about our world, Doctor, and the progress of mankind. And democracy is what happens next. Surely you must know that mankind is forever *becoming*?'

It was impossible not to respond to his odd mixture of charm and challenge. 'You don't need to be a scientist – or an amateur anthropologist – to know that life does not lead up to something else, something better. Life leads up to life.'

He exhaled. 'And yet each man – in his own mind – tells himself a story, Doctor: about who he is, and what he is, and how he should be reckoned. And each man follows this story that he tells himself: what happened before, which is why he is where he is now; what happens next, which is why – pretty soon – he won't be where he is now. So it goes. No wonder he cannot then resist the idea that there must be another story – that of mankind itself – of mankind's progress. And no wonder he gets the feeling that his little story must be part of this . . . this much bigger story.'

'*Homo fabulans*,' I said, 'man the storyteller.'

He looked at me candidly again, his pale eyes shining. 'I have not heard that phrase before.'

'I may have just made it up.'

'Well, it is true, Doctor: we are the only animal that is compelled to fashion narrative.'

'It's still a fallacy,' I said. 'A scientific impossibility. The individual organism cannot participate unconsciously in some great narrative of the species toward a collective destiny.'

'Well, then, it's a fallacy that the evolutionary scientists share with their religious enemies – the notion of narrative, the notion of becoming.'

'Again, no. You can have the first without the second.'

'I'm not so sure.' We could hear the unmistakeable sound of a powerful outboard. He began to get up. 'And in any case the need for both springs from the same place inside the human psyche. Although it's true: I myself much prefer *being* to becoming. This must be them.'

I stood and asked: 'Do you know how long your work here will go on?'

'Why?'

'Because you're getting in the way.'

Dusk had stolen upon us.

'What's the Colonel really doing here?' I pressed. 'Why are there so many patrols?'

'Doing – that's the word.' The Judge rolled his rug under his arm. 'The Colonel is keeping order and fashioning the future. And what could be more admirable than that? Ah, here she is.'

A military boat came into view. We watched it gliding in.

'His men are his responsibility,' I continued. 'And they were behaving like animals the other night.'

'You should meet Rafaela,' he said.

I hesitated. A woman in a red floral dress was sat between two khaki soldiers. One of the men stood to reach for the jetty below.

'You will like her, Doctor. There are those women who understand men and there are those who do not; and there is no way of accounting for this, nor explaining one to the other. A drink later on?'

'Not this evening. I want to work.'

'Ah, yes: your work.'

Again, I hesitated. 'But will your wife be staying with us a while?'

Amusement danced in his eyes. 'Rafaela is not my wife.'

Dark-haired, she appeared at the top of the ladder and stepped towards him with all the assurance of a milonga queen. She smiled but said nothing.

'Rafaela, this is Dr Forle. He tells everyone that he is a scientist.'

II

The following day, Felipe and I arrived back from the field earlier than had become usual. We emerged from the river path and approached the *comedor* with by now routine circumspection, braced for the Colonel or the Judge, uncertain as to whether we would wish to stay for dinner. We were both surprised to see everyone gathered: Kim behind the bar, Lothar in one of the lounge chairs, smoke curling from beneath his hat, Sole fixing the wire mesh in the little doors of the kitchen hatch that kept the squirrel monkeys out. Though the mood was subdued and had nothing of its old ease, I was pleased to feel some sense of our communality at least. Estrela and Jorge were working together at the dining table again, soaking two mighty birds in steaming hot water, a blue tarpaulin spread out to protect the wood from the feathers and innards.

I stood on the steps. 'Where are our new friends?' I asked, addressing nobody in particular.

To my surprise, Tord appeared from where he must have been lurking at the back beyond the bar with Kim. 'Actually,' he said, 'the Judge is at Tupki's place. He has set up for the afternoon, I think.'

'Hello, Tord.' I had no previous love of the missionary but our new circumstances had polarized my view of people and, as our only visitor prior to the arrivals, I saw him now as one of us. 'You mean he is registering people there?'

'Apparently, yes.' Tord had a way of loosely binding his fingers before him, even when he was walking, as if on the cusp of prayer. 'Not that many people are going, though.'

'And the Colonel?'

'Now that, I am afraid, I do not know. Good to see you, Dr Forle,' he said.

Tord's smile was brief and wan and never the consequence of humour – though his eyes were quick and green and intelligent. His hair, which was the colour of pale straw, was always exactly the same length all over –

serviceable, sensible – with his fringe a feathery and irritating half-centimetre above his brow. He suffered from mild eczema and his skin was pitted and reddened here and there with the vestiges of acne. There was something disconcerting in his overall bearing, I always thought, a disjunction between the resilience that his life required and the wispiness of his appearance. I had never seen him undo more than a single button of his shirt.

'We've been missing you and the Lord, Tord,' I said. 'There's been a lot of excitement and sin around here these last couple of weeks.'

'So I understand.' He placed a second pastoral palm over his handshake.

I addressed Lothar by way of antidote. 'When do we expect them back?'

Lothar shrugged. 'I have not heard anything. I came straight back here. There was nobody in the bathing huts when I went to scourge myself half an hour ago.'

'Jorge?'

Jorge did not look up to answer me but worked his hand at the smoothness of his bald head as though trying to rub out his birthmark: 'They went out this morning about an hour after you. First the Judge – with a couple of them. And then the Colonel with the rest.'

I wanted to force Jorge to engage with me. 'But they didn't mention where they were going?'

'No.' He wiped at his sweating neck. 'I made breakfast for them.'

There was a whisper of a challenge in this. We were provided with food and a cook. But I paid personally for extra provisions to make our diet less monotonous. Kim and Lothar contributed, too. There was now a question, therefore, as to what food Jorge could cook for whom.

'Did they say if they were coming back?'

'No.' Jorge continued to pluck at his bird.

'Well, did anyone think to look at the guest huts to see if they have left anything?'

Kim came out from behind the bar, carrying the board of fruit she had been preparing. 'Their personal things are still there. If you can call porn magazines personal. So I'm guessing they will be back at some point. Who wants *cherimoya*?'

'Yes, please.' Felipe's voice was determinedly cheerful.

'Actually . . .' Tord enjoyed this word as no other for it signalled that he was in the business of correction. 'Actually, the villages all think that the Judge will be staying here for a while longer.'

Lothar leant forward to fold out his cigarette. 'If the tribes think he can overrule their own laws, then pretty soon the entire state will be bringing him their lives to deal with. Land disputes. Boat crashes. Divorces. Children. It is going to get very Italian down there. The Judge will be bribing them to vote. They will be bribing him to judge.'

'Justice.' Kim twisted her free hand in front of her face the better to lick between her fingers.

I smiled. Then, because my hands were still in the straps of my pack, she held out a piece of her favourite fruit on the end of a fork. The gesture was obscurely intimate. The fruit tasted of strawberries and custard.

I caught Estrela's eye. She was pulling the intestine from the bird, wielding her favourite carcass knife – a blade so ferociously sharp that when she took their heads, her poultry could have known nothing about it until they looked up from the earth and saw their own bodies still gripped in her thick fist above them.

'When do we get to eat those?' I asked.

'They're for the soldiers,' Jorge said. 'When they come back.'

III

A hundred shades of khaki were darkening along the walls of the forest by the time Felipe and I reached the lab. At the door, I put down my pack carefully, conscious of the test-tubes I was carrying. I took out my flashlight. I was annoyed to be bothering with our flimsy padlock.

Unlike the huts, the lab, which was built years later, had no key. Quinn was nothing if not an idealist.

I left Felipe to unpack and walked through the plastic screen into the 'dry room', the area that Lothar and Quinn had painstakingly dry-sealed to hold its twice-daily air conditioning and the place where we stored our meagre computer equipment, our papers, our vials, our refrigerator unit and our microscopes – anything that the inexhaustible mould would thrive upon.

I turned on the monitor. Felipe pushed his head through the plastic to say that he was leaving. I thanked him for all his help and turned back to the screen. But he lingered a moment.

'Shall I fill up the water bucket?' he asked.

'Yes, if it's empty.'

It was a strange question. We kept a wooden pail of water for moisturizing our formicarium and squirting drops into the bottom of the test-tubes which contained various specimens we had collected in the field. Keeping this pail full was about the least important task in the entire laboratory. I turned but did not help him out of his discomfort.

'While the Judge is here . . .' He hesitated. 'Could you ask Mr Rebaque – if he replies – to confirm that I'm still supposed to work alongside you, Dr Forle? Or should I be guiding our other guests as well?'

'He hasn't replied to any of the emails I have sent, Felipe. Anyway, you should ask him yourself.'

I worked quickly and efficiently. I connected my camera and transferred the latest batch of pictures. I entered my data and my notes.

Our usual routine was to return to the Station in good time to do the lab work, write everything up and prepare for the next day long before nightfall. We had power for two hours every evening, but we preferred not to consume the oil for the generators with unnecessary lighting. Each evening, we recharged the computer's battery. Then, when the power went off, we ran it down halfway again. This way we could use it for four hours rather than two.

We took turns in staying late to send email or do any personal work or correspondence and that night was mine. So I set about trying to read and then rewrite a draft of one of the early sections of my book, struggling to make simple the complexity and implications of the ant's reproductive system. But even my notes would not hold to their purpose. Pages wandered and my tone and observations became tangled. The advances I had been making prior to the arrival seemed to have halted; it was as if the jungle had started colonizing the clearing of my own mind, confusing me, distracting me, planting a hundred rogue seeds in what should have been the clean-kempt prose of scientific method.

Did I feel myself slipping into the old lassitude? Certainly, this lack of progress frustrated me. After all, this was supposed to be my side of the partnership with Quinn. He did most of the practical work. I wrote up our findings and kept our studies in the front pages of the influential science journals. And the harsh truth was that I had never relished the field. I was a talented collator – collegiate, collaborative – the communicator. But I was not really a scientist of any originality save on paper – and even then, it was seven years since I had written anything of depth or value. Anything new.

Quinn, though . . . Quinn was forever fearless and unbound – in his imagination, in his work and in his relations with his fellow human beings. He carried with him some great affirmation towards life. Ideas just poured out of him as though from a never-empty bottle; you pulled the cork and there they came – dancing and chattering and laughing and frothing; silly, mad, serious, insightful, profound, primitive, emotional, glorious, fool-ish, generous ideas; about man and God, science and myths, creation and extinction, and always – always – his own ideas.

I know that I'm painting a flattering picture of my friend. And I do myself down the more to do him up. (It

is true: Quinn could not write or structure his thinking.)
And yet the larger part of the portrait is accurate. I have
come to believe that the greatest divide in humanity is
neither age nor race nor gender but between those few
who possess self-belief and the rest who must thrash
about in uncertainty or communal delusion.

Most of all, I was conscious that Quinn would have
dealt with the Judge and the Colonel differently and
that he would not suddenly be finding our work . . .
inconsequential, minor. Perhaps I was annoyed with
Felipe, too. I disliked the way he sought to hide behind
me – or, rather, to confer jurisdiction on me when I
had none. Nonetheless, having given up on my book,
I wrote another email to Rebaque – my third without a
reply – and another to the head of administration in my
department. Our satellite connection was slow, fragile
and intermittent – we had long ago abandoned trying to
send our photographs and heavy data files – and, after the
third attempt, I rose and went through the plastic rather
than sit waiting for the confirmation that they had gone
through.

I stooped to look into one of the thin sealed glass
tanks in which we kept a colony of my favourite ants:
Daceton armigerum, a strange-looking species – voracious, omnivorous, powerful – and yet with these sad
and oddly beautiful heart-shaped heads.

'Hello, Dr Forle. I am sorry to disturb you.'

Tord appeared unctuously around the door.

'I've finished for the day,' I said.

He had the trick of watching me closely and yet when I sought his eye he was looking away.

'How is the project going?' he asked.

'Well. We are on the right path – but, of course, proof takes time.'

He nodded slowly. He affected to take an interest. But he addressed us like we were all well-meaning children – vague and deluded and a long way from what was important, but good-hearted all the same and not necessarily exiled from hope for all eternity. Perhaps he was merely reflecting our opinion of him back at us.

'Who told you the Judge was at Tupki's?' I asked.

'I gave one of the villagers a lift on my boat. Everyone is talking about it.' He said this to emphasize that he alone could speak the Indian languages well enough to know what they were discussing among themselves.

'What do you think is going on, Tord?'

'I don't know, sir. Nor can I be sure whether it is for good or for evil.'

'That must be awkward for you.'

'I'm not saying that I cannot be guided by the Light once I have learned the true nature of events. Just that I have yet to learn that nature.' He closed his eyes a moment as if to make inward enquiry of whichever Evangelist might recently have begun to whisper within his breast. 'Kim says that the Judge is rude, that the Colonel barely talks and that the soldiers are disgusting.'

'Judge not, lest ye be judged, Tord.'

'Do you not know that we will judge angels? How much more then the things of this life?'

I admired his quickness. 'Maybe you should ask one of them to deliver the homily at the next get-together of your mission, Tord, how about the Sermon on the Mount? Blessed are the pure in heart.'

He joined his hands. 'You seem even more subversive than usual tonight, if I might say so, Dr Forle.'

'I'm sorry. Maybe it's just that I never really understood the Sermon on the Mount.'

'If I thought that there was anything other than your usual mischief behind that statement I would offer to sit down and have a right and proper conversation with you about it.'

'Sorry, Tord. Not tonight. I have to check my emails have gone through.' I crossed back to the dry room. I was, I realized, obscurely pleased by Tord's visit. The screen told me they had been sent. I sat down and logged out.

Tord had followed me. 'It must be very disruptive,' he said, gentle almost.

I looked up. 'Kim is right – about the Judge and the

Colonel. And yes – I'm anxious about the work and I don't like the idea of the Station turning into some sort of cod-military base while we are here. But there's nothing we can do and there's no reason why it should affect us.' I was suddenly desperate for soap and our lukewarm water. I sat waiting a moment but still his eyes were fixed above my head. 'What can I do for you, Tord? I'm guessing you didn't come here to hear all about my progress on the questions of multi-level evolutionary selection?'

'Oh, I wondered if you would mind if I borrowed the computer again. Just for fifteen minutes or so.'

'Be my guest.' I stood and gestured toward the chair. 'Shut it down when you have finished.'

'Thank you kindly.'

I stepped through the plastic but could not resist adding over my shoulder: 'Keep it clean, though, Tord, keep it clean.'

I realized that I had covertly been looking forward to my single malt all day. I did not stint. I collected fresh clothes. I regretted not putting a password on the new sections of my book since they included some more diary-like side observations about the Station and how the others were getting on – nothing that I needed to hide but still Tord was inquisitive to the point of deviousness and he intuited things astonishingly well. Many of the missionaries did. Their work required a great deal of non-verbal perception. They spread their lethal cult-lore (and their lethal viruses) among the tribes with patience and great perspicacity. Our region, because of its remoteness, was host to the best of them. And Tord's sect was among the most steadfast and sophisticated. They operated under the burnished fig leaves of health, education and an improvement in living standards. They founded schools and hospitals. Most of all, they studied the languages. They affected that the linguistic emphasis was coincidental or academic, but the simple truth was that they sought keenly to translate the Bible. Indeed, this was why Tord was great amongst them – he was already at work on rendering the Gospels into the hitherto unbreached language of the Yora. In the tribe of the missionaries, these were the feathers of highest distinction

I stepped out of my hut into the trill of the forest night. Why was I so pleased to see him? The answer further dismayed me: it was because I was hoping for moral support in the event of any further brutality. I was hoping that Tord's indignation – partaking, as it must, in the wider indignation of the Son of God – would be righteous and forceful and that I would be able to ally myself with him and splint up my own conviction. For one thing I was sure of: if Tord was here, he would not let evil pass. And though I knew that his convictions were based on enduring falsehoods, I was – it seemed – profoundly grateful for the cover those same falsehoods provided for me.

IV

I was awoken by the violence of her kick. I said her name but she was deaf to me. Her anger had dissipated but we had not been the same together since the night of the fire.

There were unfamiliar noises coming from the direction of the *comedor* – the intermittent sound of men and alcohol, cries, raucousness, the repetitive grunt of music just audible beneath. The soldiers must have returned. Where had they been so late? I had slept for no more than two hours – less. With all my being, I longed for the Station to be returned to us.

Something was rustling in the dry leaves below the hut. We were drowning in the lack of rain and it was impossible to breathe. Sole shuddered; dreams were passing through her, whispering their solicitudes one to the next. I sat up. The darkness was close in the room, but here and there a faint pearl light pooled. The moon must have risen above the forest. She stirred. I was still. I waited. Her murmuring became words I neither understood nor recognized. A frown passed across her brow. Then she curled deeper into her sleep. I thumbed her hair from her face; it was unwaveringly straight and so black that in the sunlight it seemed almost blue. Aside from a year in the capital, she had lived mostly in the physical world of the river and the trees and her body was dense with such a life; sure, strong and well-proportioned. Sometimes, when everyone else was asleep, we went to the bathing huts to wash one another by the dim light of a hanging lamp and I found that my fingers rose and fell across the muscled contour of her shoulders and that her calves were full to my palm. She slept without a pillow.

She stirred again. I soothed. She settled. I lay still. Whenever we slept together, these wordless duets of ours played on through the night; though we were barely conscious, it was as if our bodies were about some quiet communion that they wished to protect from the searchlight of the mind.

Now, without warning, she turned herself onto her front, raised herself on her elbows and hung her head. I reached for the kerosene lamp behind me. The room flared into view; the shadows stretched and shrank back. The animal moved again beneath the hut. Her cheekbones were fiercely broad and high, so that she seemed both defiant and shy whenever she looked up.

'I hate this,' she murmured. 'What's happening?'

'They got back about half an hour ago. They're having some kind of a party. Here – have some water.'

She remained on her front and swigged awkwardly from the bottle. The white sheet fell from her shoulders.

'My husband came here,' she said.

I made myself hold her eyes.

'I saw him,' she said.

'It was a dream, Sole. You woke in the middle of a dream.'

'Why does he come back?'

'I don't know.'

'He wants to speak to me.'

She passed the water and lay down on her side, facing me. As a younger man, I would have recoiled. Now I was drawn further in – I wanted to show solidarity with her experience. I wanted to tell her that I knew some of what the human heart is required to endure.

Her body tensed: people were coming up the path. It was too late to extinguish the lamp.

'I'm going to buy a gun,' she whispered.

Her husband had been a miner but he was poisoned by the mercury and then shot for his gold.

'No,' I said softly.

'If you were me, you would have already got one.'

There were two voices. And an eerie rhythmic

squeaking sound that I both did and did not recognize. They stopped directly outside. We breathed the wet air. Our door was locked but I was afraid that they were about to demand Sole out again. They were arguing. I could not make out what they were saying. Where had they been? I did not believe that they would bother with the bathing hut to urinate. They had not done so thus far. The squeaking began again.

Sole rose and soundlessly crossed to the window. She motioned me to douse the light.

'Who was it?' I asked. 'Lugo?'

'No. The youngest one with the metal mouth and his rat friend.'

'What are they doing?'

'I can't see. They're using our cart.'

The cart, of course: the wheels squeaked.

'What for? What are they moving?'

'I can't see. It looks empty.'

'I'm going to go out.'

She turned from the window. 'Stay there.'

'They won't do anything to me, Sole.' I threw back the sheet. 'It would cause them too much trouble.'

But I hesitated. The cart was moving away. I twisted again to light the lamp at its lowest burn. She stood looking towards me in the flickering light, fingering the hem of her T-shirt. My heart was filled with feeling for her.

'They're going,' I said. 'Come back to bed.'

'Everything is changed.' She shook her head. 'They are changing everything.'

'What, Sole, what are they changing?'

'Ministry of Agriculture to Ministry of Interior.' She said these formal, masculine words with a terrible finality.

'How do you know?'

'Everybody knows.'

'Do they?'

'Yes. That's why Rebaque went away. That's why he won't be back. Right now, I bet he's in the capital getting a new job somewhere else. Maybe he already has one. This place isn't about research any more. It never was. It's about money. Like everything.'

The noise from the *comedor* was dying down. I spoke softly: 'You don't know that. It's just rumours. Nobody official has said anything.'

'There *is* no official.' She raised a single shoulder in her habitual shrug and scoffed. 'Maybe they will send one letter in a few months and maybe – if it makes it as far as Laberinto – someone will open it before they wipe their ass. But even then they won't be able to tell us the good news because they won't be able to read.' She leant back against the wall and raised her eyes to the ceiling. Quiet again, she said: 'Our jobs will go.'

'If that happens . . . if that happens, I can increase the

money I pay you. We need more help, we're going too slowly.'

'I do not want you to give me your money.'

Inwardly, I cursed my clumsiness.

From somewhere in the night came the sound of a small plane.

'Cocaine,' she said.

'Sole, come.' I reached out. 'I will massage your head.'

She moved from the wall but only as far as the end of the bed, where she sat down sideways with her legs curled beneath her.

'Perhaps you are the reason for my dream,' she said. 'My husband wants to talk to me about you.'

I wished only to crawl across to her.

'Tell me about your dream,' I said.

'You tell me about yours.'

'I don't dream.'

'But sometimes . . . sometimes when you are here you are not with me.'

'Everything before – it's gone, Sole. With you, there is quiet. That's the truth.'

'I don't believe you.'

'I am not dishonest.'

'But you keep yourself hidden to me – to everyone.'

'Ask me anything.'

'Even when you answer, you do not answer.' She looked at me, her eyes unmoving and so dark they seemed completely black. 'You're like the men who come out of the forest – you sign your name to the register with a cross. Except that I know that you can write.'

FOUR

I

I found Felipe bustling about at the *comedor* as if but half an hour from opening the family restaurant.

'The Colonel has gone,' he said, stepping towards me and unable to contain his delight.

'What – with the soldiers?'

'Yes – all of them – the Colonel, the Judge and the soldiers – and this time they really have gone.'

'How do you know?'

'Their huts are completely empty. No equipment. Nothing. All that they've left us is some beer.' He smiled his widest smile. 'Twenty-four bottles. We are saving them for when we go to Machaguar – for the party.'

'Twelve bottles,' Jorge murmured – he was standing by our dining table wearing his black and white oven gloves, holding a hot metal tray on which he was keeping half a dozen fried eggs warm.

With finger and eager thumb, Felipe began tugging

first one shirt cuff then the other. 'Two of the men were carrying the Judge's red boxes,' he said. 'The registration documents are in those boxes . . . I think they have finished here, Doctor, I really do.'

I could not hide my excitement any more than Felipe. 'All right, we should do something about the mess – especially where they had their fire.'

Jorge slid the eggs ever so slightly one way then the other on his tray. 'Where is Sole?' he asked.

'I don't know. She'll be here in a minute.' I tempered my tone. 'We'll clean up together – it won't take long. We'll have a meeting here in half an hour – everyone. Then we'll get to work.'

I had forgotten about Machaguar until Felipe and Jorge reminded me. Every party on the river believed itself the best but Machaguar, a remote and little-visited village, had a particular reputation as 'the enchanted carnival'. In the main, so Lothar had explained, its fame was to do with an accident of nature: there was a giant beach there – a rare, relatively flat expanse of mud and sand on the inside of a great slow bend that allowed them to erect a stage and a huge sound-and-light system. This beach then became the biggest dance floor in the jungle. They dressed up the surrounding trees and the village behind with thousands and thousands of torches – and it was these lights that were supposed to cast 'enchantment' over the two nights. People travelled hundreds of miles to come – down from the mountains, up the river, in from the jungle, out from the cities.

We would need two full days to get there. We would first have to go down our tributary and back up the main river as far as Laberinto; from there, we would take one of the passenger boats. Clearly, Jorge still intended to go with his stolen beer; Felipe, too, judging by his tone. The others would take their cue from me. I would have to decide.

Eggs were one of the few things Jorge cooked well. I was considering a second when I was startled by a high-pitched squeal . . . A tiny boy was running full tilt down the path from the river towards the *comedor*: it was Mubb, Tupki's youngest son. He seemed to be in the grip of a maddened exuberance at his own mobility. His excitement doubled as he realized that I had seen him and he appeared to lose all control of his toddler self, holding both his hands out in front of him and waving as though to stop a taxiing air force. I stepped down from the *comedor* and gathered him in before he could stumble.

'Hello, Mubb. Hello hello hello.'

'Dig dig dig,' he shrieked. Digging had obsessed him

ever since we had passed twenty minutes together digging a hole for a *D. hirsuta* I had planted near the lab.

'Dig dig dig.' His shiny black hair had been trimmed again so that there could be no better example on Earth of a bowl cut; and his cheeks bulged so far up his face with his grinning and his squealing that they squeezed his eyes half closed, giving him the appearance of a deranged boy-emperor – life, death and all the kingdoms of the sun at his whim.

José, his older brother, sloped up. He was a sombre four to Mubb's two and yet already he had the bearing of one resigned to an existence of fraternal glossing and oblique compensations. He stopped short, placed both his hands behind his head and looked up at me with an expression that said: I know he's mad; I have talked to him about it; but there's nothing further we can do; we just have to persevere.

'Hello, José.'

'You come eat *tambaqui*?' he asked.

How could I refuse such an invitation?

'Yes,' I replied.

Mubb shrieked.

José nodded and winced and nodded.

'Dig, dig, dig,' Mubb began again.

Tupki himself emerged from the trees, holding up his hand in salutation.

Rebaque used to make a point of maintaining good relations with our neighbours – the river folk, the missionaries, the farmers, the various workers and the Indians alike. And now that the Colonel and the Judge had left, I wanted very much to continue in that spirit. I placed Mubb back on his feet and offered him and his brother some of the juice on the table, which they drank at terrifying speed.

Tupki climbed the stairs and murmured his thanks and then said something to José that I did not understand. The two brothers set off down the path towards my hut and Tupki and I sat down together at the low table.

'Brothers who are friends need fear nothing in the world,' I said.

Tupki had no true smile but his pained eyes softened momentarily and the furrow of his brow shallowed a fraction.

'All my children are different,' he said. 'Same mother, same father, same food. I don't know how it happens.'

He was a short man with a thick black-and-grey moustache and though brawny-armed he had a tight little belly as if he had just swallowed his sons' football. His face told of hard work and harder liquor and he had the odd double manner – solicitous and yet scornful – of a ticket tout. He always wore the same things: a nondescript T-shirt, football shorts, sandals and a tattered straw hat in the last possible stage of disintegration. He was a fisherman. And he was a father – nine times over.

He had come, he said, to see if I and 'my ant people' (here he did manage a grin of sorts) would like to eat with him and his family. He would have asked us earlier but he had not been finding the fish.

'Thanks,' I replied. 'Of course, we would love to . . . José tells me that it is *tambaqui*. I've never eaten it. They say it's the best.'

He nodded and began to explain that certain fish had vanished, returned, disappeared, required libation, become plentiful. I neither understood nor quite believed him.

'I will bring something to drink,' I said.

He made no effort to hide his satisfaction at that.

'Come tomorrow,' he began. There was the faintest note of distraction in his voice and I had the sense that there was something he wished further to say.

'The day after is better for us,' I said. I wanted us to have some free time together again – to eat in the evening as before and play cards. 'I'll bring my assistant, Kim.'

There were squeals from beyond; Mubb had escaped his brother's attempts at distraction. They were coming back at maximum speed across the clearing.

'They can help with our work today,' I said, 'if you want to stay for lunch. We're cleaning the whole place.'

Tupki could not prevent his eyes going to the bar.

'Thank you. I will wait.'

I understood his need. And I wanted only to indulge it. A flood of good intentions was rising inside me. I knew that the spring was guilt over my inaction regarding the prisoner and that the source lay deeper still in my previous life. But I wanted now to encourage this flood in the hope that it would drown the weeds that had flourished since the arrivals and bear me back to the hope I had previously begun to feel in the steady business of our work. And in the company of Sole.

II

Stage Two

The second phase of our research will be a concerted effort to address the constraint question: what limits the Devil's Gardens?

During the course of our work, we have become ever more astonished at how effectively the Myrmelachista *go about the destruction of the environment to suit their purpose – how they poison it, then populate it, then police it. We are growing certain, too, of what can only be described* as a 'language' employed in these feats. For the most part, our ants use chemical secretions to communicate, but these in combination with a vast array of touches and even sound; they tap, they stroke and they squeak. Indeed, we have come to believe that they are very close to what we might call 'syntax'; each chemical 'word' is used in a sequence to convey a 'phrase' and this communication is modified and further directed by contact and auditory signals. Demonstrably, they teach and they learn; running in tandem, meeting, 'embracing', 'pointing', passing instructions back and forth.

The question has arisen, therefore, and will not go away: if the Myrmelachista build, and then maintain, their great monocultures, their cities, their empires, then what constrains them? Why do they not take over the whole forest? Given the right conditions, might they do so? Is there some advantage to the species as a whole in limiting the expansion of one group and, if so, what kind of intelligence is this? Such a thing would be an anathema to evolutionary biology, of course; for how could the individual (or the colony for that matter) 'know' what was good for the future of the species and act upon this – at its own genetic expense – on a day-to-day basis?

Our working hypothesis provides a simpler and less heretical explanation: because a larger number of plant eaters are attracted to the altered environment in Devil's

Gardens, there must come a point where the Myrmelachista *cannot keep them all at bay. In other words,
through the very act of engineering the world around them
for what appears to be their own benefit, the ants eventually bring about their own demise.*

The difficulty, as ever, is how to prove this.

III

I passed the morning of the departure in two tasks.

First, I took José and Mubb and I cleaned the washhouses. José was helpful; but Mubb wanted only to climb
into our wooden buckets and put José's sponge on his
head. Every five minutes he got soap in his eyes and
started to wail as if he had been shot. He was, however, a
dedicated sweeper of the floor; though in this, too, less
than helpful since he could not control the big broom
and yet insisted on monopolizing it while José attempted
miracles with the dustpan.

Second, I entered Rebaque's office, which doubled as
our infirmary store. I had been intending to form a mental
inventory of our medical supplies since Rebaque left; but
I had always anticipated his imminent return and such an
undertaking had felt as though it were an invasion of his
domain.

I went through the shelves. As a student, I had studied anatomy but not medicine. I often wished I had been a doctor – a purpose so clear, so daily, so undeniable. We were short in most things though long in aspirin and, unaccountably, laxatives. We had splints and bandages and surgical tubes for sprains. There was nothing for venom. I put everything on the desk. I wiped down cupboards and then replaced the various pills and packets to a new and more ordered system of my own.

An unwholesome curiosity made me open the drawers. The three down the right were empty. Those down the left the same. Only the central one had any weight. Inside was the grotesque master key with its death's head at the bow end. I sat back and looked around the office with fresh eyes. The place was bare of personality. The pictures on the walls were generic – an aerial shot of the river, a child in feathered headdress, a chart of poisonous frogs. Perhaps Sole was right: perhaps Rebaque was not intending to return.

IV

The trip to Tupki's was twenty minutes downstream and there were no other major channels in which we might lose ourselves. So I was piloting and Kim was sitting in her T-shirt facing me. The fierceness of the sun had given place to a kinder glow that flattered our complexions and lightened her curls. Like myself, she had grown leaner and fitter since we arrived; it was impossible not to do so – we were covering a minimum of four difficult foot-miles a day and in sauna conditions.

On a bend in the river, amidst the exposed roots of some giant overhanging tree, we sighted an unusually large family of capybara on the bank. I cut the engine and lifted the propeller so that we were gliding. Kim swung round, eager with her camera. They were red-brown and the size of pigs or sheep though with larger hind legs than fore – the largest living rodents. As ever, this family seemed to know little fear but simply paused to watch us as we passed by. There was, I thought, a certain dignity in their indifference.

'They get sunburn.' Kim spoke from behind her viewfinder.

'They remind me a bit of hippos,' I said.

'Isn't there a pygmy hippo?' she asked.

'*Liberiensis*,' I replied.

'Very impressive.' She lowered her camera and smiled her tomboy's smile in my direction. 'Especially for an entomologist.'

'I live with the ants.' I shrugged. 'But my heart is full of even-toed ungulates.'

She grinned and swung back round. 'Ever wish that you'd done something other than insects?'

'No. I'd miss the money and the respect and the VIP tables wherever I go.'

'I guess the danger is you start to take it for granted.' She pointed the lens at me.

'Plus you can't do sinister experiments on the mammals – or take them home and watch them mating in your bedroom.'

'Which we would all feel as a loss.'

'We would,' I said. 'Nor do they hold the key to a counter-theory of evolution.'

We tied up the boat. Over the rise of the riverbank, we could see his house standing alone – oblong, wooden, built on stilts and set back a hundred metres or so from the river in a natural glade. Lashed lianas covered the roof and there were four unglazed holes cut into the walls. The forest's edge was thinner here and round about there were fruit trees, some cultivated, others wild.

Lothar had once explained to me that it was best to think of the indigenous peoples and their lands as circles in a Venn diagram. Each circle interacted with the others around its boundaries – sometimes deeply, sometimes hardly at all. In the heart of the forest there remained the few un-contacted peoples. Then there were a good number of tribes (or parts of tribes) who had been contacted but who had very circumscribed dealings with the outside world – they lived (or tried to live) as they had always lived. Then there were the tribes – like the Ashaninkas, Sole's people, and some of the Matsigenka – who stayed on their own homelands (or sought to do so), but who were politically organized and had regular, overt and more or less modernized relations with the incomers. And then there were those that had dissipated and now pursued lives in the towns and the cities of the river much like the *ribereños* and the *mestizos*. 'Like everything about everything,' Lothar had said, 'it is an unhelpful simplification but you can start with this idea and maybe you will understand more in a few weeks.'

Tupki was Matsigenka. They had always been a notoriously difficult tribe for the missionaries and the anthropologists to understand. They were non-hierarchical and disinclined even to the customary rituals and cooperations of village life. They disliked school, they disliked leaders and they disliked war. Through most of the conflicts that had swept through their territories – with the old civilizations, the conquistadors, and more recently, the communist guerrillas, the military fascists and the narcotic barons – they had always preferred to vanish into the forest unlike their neighbours, the more warlike Yora. Often, the Matsigenka solved their disputes simply by leaving the conflicted village and starting a new one. And perhaps this had once been Tupki's intention. If so, nobody had followed him.

He greeted us by the great fixed black iron skillet, which sat in an open-sided construction adjacent to his house. His wife stood with two of his daughters – her eyes shy, her hair still black, her arms muscled from carrying children. She was throwing in the manioc to roast. A flame flickered beneath. Beyond, in a little clearing, there was a wide grill on which was cooking the giant fish.

Something I could neither place nor articulate hung in the atmosphere. At first, we sat together with Tupki and various sons in a slightly awkward line on the only seating – a long bench. This made it difficult to talk together so we swigged the beers that I had bought and watched the women work. Their refusals of help were so adamant and severe that even Kim gave up after a while.

Mubb and José saved us. Sometimes they whispered under the table, sometimes they skulked behind a tree, sometimes they peeped up from behind the nearby cart, until, after about ten minutes of this, we heard a sudden series of piercing squeals and they broke cover. José sprinted past first in his red shorts, twisting and turning, clearly desperate with trying not to laugh. Mubb was ten paces behind him, wearing nothing save a patch of sand on his bare behind, bowing down his head in an effort not to burst apart as he went pounding by . . . with a tiny startled kitten jolting in his arms.

Tupki stood up, shaking his head. His wife was smiling, while behind her back another of her daughters made a just-playful slapping motion with her hand as if to suggest that her youngest brother might benefit from some gentle corrective.

We ate in appreciative silence – stared at by the younger children while those in the middle sought to avoid eye contact altogether and the older ones continually offered us more. The *tambaqui* meat was plump and white and firm and succulent and tasted more like veal or pork than anything else. I had noticed a couple of plates being carried off in the first serving but it was only towards the end of our feast, when I rose to rinse my hands with the cup from the water bucket, that I heard the banging and looked up to see two of the elder boys spread carefully across the roof of the main house fixing up a satellite dish.

When Kim enquired, Tupki's eyes went a moment towards his wife before he said: 'From the Colonel.'

'What for?'

Tupki pinched a bone from the end of his tongue. 'We helped him.'

'With what?' she asked.

'They used here.' Tupki indicated the area in which we were sat by holding the neck of his bottle out in front of him and describing a lazy circle. 'For the registration.'

Kim nodded. 'So they gave you a satellite dish?'

'Yes.' Tupki gave his wincing narrow-eyed version of a grin. 'Nobody came.'

He obviously thought this amusing, or at least a deal well struck; and yet, without doing anything beyond collecting our bowls, his wife emanated a powerful sense of . . . what? Anger, hurt, something I could not read.

Tupki seemed to assimilate this censure. 'It was my son – the oldest – Kanari,' he said uneasily, raising a thumb in the direction of the banging. 'He was the one who suggested this. He liked the idea.'

'Did *you* like the idea?' Kim pressed.

Tupki finished his beer. 'It's the same with the soldiers as it is with the *narcóticas*. Once one person is in, then everybody is in – the whole family. They come for sons, they come for daughters. You must choose.' Again the sweep of the bottle to indicate the area, the buildings, his homestead. 'Perhaps I would not have said anything myself. But Kanari . . . he's at the age where I cannot tell him what to do. Or, if I do, he does the opposite.' He sighed. 'So now we are a military family and we have a satellite dish. The problem is we need a new television to work with it. And that is a lot of fishing.' He spat.

I do not know if we would have ever been asked to look at Yolanda had it not been for Kim inveigling her way into the washing-up circle with two of Tupki's daughters. Their mother had just set down the fruit when one of these girls came over, holding both her arms in front of her and trying to shake the soapy water from her hands. She must have been eleven or twelve and she stood before us with that same mixture of defiance and solicitation that I had noted in her father.

'The lady says the Mister will look at Yolanda,' she said, simply, in her broken Spanish, addressing her parents. 'The lady says he medicine.'

Beneath the brim of his hat, Tupki's eyes registered anger but they were caught and held by those of his wife with such a silent intensity that within a second he was swigging from his bottle and looking away. I exchanged glances with Kim who had quietly followed the girl over after eliciting the information.

'Yolanda is your sister?' I asked.

'Yes.'

'And Yolanda is sick?'

'Yes.'

This, then, was the real reason for our invitation.

And now, at last, there was an expression of relief and alertness on the face of the girl's mother. I looked across at Tupki again. But he was picking at the label of his bottle. Neither spoke. Perhaps there was too much anger, too long tended between them; perhaps they had arrived at a place where their children were not merely their unique physical enterprise but also their sole remaining conversation. It struck me that the girl was articulating exactly what they would have wished to say – if only they could have communed again and somehow spoken with one voice.

'What's your name?' I asked.

'Virima,' she said. 'Yolanda is bad sick. Mister is a doctor?'

'I am not a medical doctor.' Now it was my turn to feel uneasy and embarrassed. Her face began to fall. 'But . . . but let's go and look. Maybe it's something we've got medicine for.'

Closely attended by wife, daughters, sons, a chastened José and a sister-restrained Mubb, we followed Tupki up the stairs inside the main house.

The rooms were interconnected by open door frames that ran the length of the building. The first was a kitchen of sorts, no more than six paces long by three wide – dark, crowded and cramped with cracked crockery and a makeshift freestanding cupboard. Unknowable pots and jars and vessels were arranged side by side with cheap branded tins of cooking oil or salt or beans. I had the sense that Kim was trying to shrink herself out of politeness. Diptera skittered every surface.

We passed through into what I assumed was the room Tupki shared with his wife – a giant bed and little else save for two crooked shelves resting on a row of huge nails hammered into the wall and a series of wicker baskets containing clothes.

The third room seemed at first to be similarly a huge bed, though as we edged along the wall in the semi-darkness, I saw that it was in fact broken up into little areas – each presumably given to a different child. Brightly coloured rugs and tattered blankets lay in faded piles and twists as if the night's inhabitants had been required to kick their way free. There was no wind and some mighty tree outside shadowed the window. The room smelled of must and sickness. We crowded in and the heat seemed to close about our shoulders and press forward with us. In the corner, turned away, a motionless figure was lying.

Tupki knelt. I did the same but hung back. Kim dropped beside me. The light was dim but I could see that Tupki's expression was too hard – as though he wished his daughter would make more of an effort. I shuffled forward quickly and motioned with my hand to still him.

I realized with surprise that the girl was not asleep. Rather, as I was about to lay my hand on her arm, her head moved a slow quarter-turn and two deep green eyes gradually came round to hold my own. I clasped her hand. The room behind me seemed to retreat and her shallow breathing became the only count of time. Her lips parted but she made no effort to talk. Instead, with neither anger nor sorrow, something I can only call her spirit began to well up in her eyes and speak to me of one thing and one thing only: the terrifying certainty of its own death.

In the very corner of the hut above her head, I saw threads of light, cracks in the wooden slats where ants were moving – appearing, disappearing. I turned to face her family.

'I don't know what is wrong. But we must take Yolanda to a doctor.'

Their eyes were all on me. Mubb's face was buried against his sister and now he shifted his head deeper into her chest. José was holding his mother's hand and was on a level with me where I knelt; his expression contained enough intensity for the entire family over again. Tupki stood leaning against the wall, holding his empty bottle of beer.

I stood. 'It's serious. We need to get help.'

'Before she said where it hurts,' the older sister who

was holding Mubb spoke. 'Now, she does not know. Everything hurts and she does not speak.'

'I am not a medical doctor,' I repeated. 'But I may have something. It will not make her well but it will ease her pain.' I could feel the tension in Kim's stance. 'Then we must take her to the capital.'

Tupki cleared his throat like he was about to spit. 'This is a white man's sickness,' he said.

Kanari came noisily in through the door and pushed forward past his brothers and sisters. He was strong and taller than the rest and still in the first rage of his masculinity.

'Do you work for the Colonel?' he asked, his shoulders thrown back and his Spanish more fluent than his siblings.

The older sister turned on him sharply and said something I could not understand.

'Then he's with the Colonel and Lugo,' Kanari said to her in Spanish. He put his fist to his chest. 'Any friend of the Colonel is a friend of mine.'

Tupki's wife shifted.

'I am a scientist,' I said, caught out, my eyes moving between them. 'I don't work for anyone. We need to help your sister.'

Virima moved next to her older sister to block Kanari, then glared up at me: 'When you come here again?'

'I'll come straight back now.' I addressed Tupki, then his wife. 'I'll bring medicine. We'll work out what to do.'

Tupki grimaced. 'Yolanda cannot go to the capital.'

Kim's voice was soft but not yielding. 'Why not?'

'Don't worry about the money,' I said.

Tupki showed no sign of having heard but he stood upright and said something in Matsigenka. One by one, the family began to back away whispering among themselves.

Kanari, however, waited by the door. 'Don't worry about the money,' he said, grinning and rolling one shoulder then the other. 'Don't worry about the money.' He waited for Kim to pass, jejune and aggressive as he watched her body. 'Soon we have plenty of money. Nice woman. Party every day.'

V

Once, late one night, when we had taken our lamps down to the bathing hut and we were washing together, Sole told me the story of how the Matsigenka believed the virakochas, the white people, came into the world. Some people were digging for shiny metals, she said, when the virakochas suddenly poked their heads up out of the mud. The astonished diggers desperately shovelled the earth back on the emerging creatures but it was futile: the virakochas came pouring out too fast for their efforts. Hastily summoned, Tasorintsi, the blowing spirit, rose up and rained down many arrows on the heads of the virakochas – killing a great number. It seemed the flow had been staunched and Tasorintsi left, warning the Matsigenka never to dig any more holes. Thereafter, things looked like they might be OK . . . But then, one day when Tasorintsi was far away in the forest, the virakochas unexpectedly started to pour out of that hole again. And this time, they came so quickly that there was nothing that could be done – even when Tasorintsi returned. The virakochas, it turned out, had been created underground by Tasorintsi's great rival: the evil trickster, Kentivakori.

FIVE

I

We were surprised to enjoy a sweet pancake breakfast prepared not by Jorge but by Estrela, who was staying behind with Lothar and was delighted to see us go. There was then half an hour of dispersal before we assembled on the jetty and climbed into the canoes. We were excited – glad to be leaving the Station, glad to be together again, and glad, too, for a purpose besides our own pleasure. We would be travelling all together as far as Laberinto. And from there, Sole would accompany Yolanda with Virima down to the river city while the rest of us would travel upstream on one of the specially chartered overnight boats to Machaguar.

Sole had spent the morning constructing Yolanda a bed in the bottom of Tord's canoe – pulling out seating planks, securing a simple frame so that it would not slide, and then laying down bedding, sheets, pillows. Tucked away somewhere, she had a thick cylinder of my banknotes and she had slipped one of my cards into her tatty old hiking boots. I was paying for their passage and whatever hotels and medical treatment were necessary. There was some additional business that Sole had in the river city – though she would not tell me what exactly and behaved instead as though she were buying me some big secret of a birthday present. Her mood had improved with each day following the soldiers' departure. And for my part, I had not realized how dependent on her happiness my own had become until it now returned.

We would lose working hours, of course: all of that Friday, the Saturday morning lab-time and much of the Monday for the return. But since one trip was absolutely necessary and the other was likely to do us good, my decisions had been easily made. As we set off, I heard a Paradise tanager calling somewhere close by – a high-pitched whistling sound – earnest, childlike. An augury, I thought, though of course I did not believe in auguries.

They were waiting on the shallow muddy headland above the reeds. Kanari and his brothers carried Yolanda down to the boats on an improvised stretcher. Nothing was said but hope now hovered in the air and there was a certain operational fortitude in the faces of the boys as they lifted their sister gently into the boat.

Jorge left Tord's canoe for ours to make room, bringing his precious case of beer with him. Tord, meanwhile, stood upright by his tiller, doing nothing, and yet performing this ministry with such a sedulous and determined attitude of pastoral care that he would have us all believe that the afflicted of the world had ever been his personal charge and that their best chance on Earth, as in Heaven, lay solely with him. (Who can blame the Achuar for shrinking the missionaries' heads?) There was no point in my offering yet more hands to get in the way – so I remained in our boat and watched Virima and Sole ease a near motionless Yolanda off the stretcher and into the bed that Sole had made. Somewhere, Sole had also found a great umbrella to protect Yolanda's face.

Mubb and José were waving. Tupki's wife appeared beside them on the bank, looking on as we pulled away. I never knew her name.

It was a beautiful day: a clear sky and – midstream at least – drier air and the breeze of motion. I was deeply cheered to be in our company. Sole and Tord were up ahead in the missionary's boat with Yolanda and Virima; Felipe, Kim, Jorge and I were now in the second. We dropped the engines to their downriver chug. We rearranged whatever padding we had bought to make the plank seats more comfortable. We settled back – Tord and Felipe piloting, Jorge sipping his beer, Kim taking pictures, me with my notebook and the jungle sounding like a pair of maracas shaking out its rhythm on either bank.

Time on the river is like time at sea. It is not measured in minutes but in the way the light changes the colour of the water. And I felt a deep and unusual contentment that day as I watched the current and the passing frieze of the banks. I had imagined something like this before – I had seen myself drifting along with mankind's Latinate checklist of creation to hand, ticking the boxes as I went, all five kingdoms intimately described. One of the thoughts that I have always liked in Tord's Bible is the idea of humanity as steward – caretakers of a paradise entrusted. Of course this leads on to questions as to who has done the entrusting . . . But is there not some secret back channel – muddy and shallow – that links even the most avid atheist's urge to classify with the preacher's teaching of stewardship?

Children stopped their play to watch us go by. We waved and they waved back. Many of the riverside houses were little more than raised platforms, haphazardly roofed. The number of other canoes and skiffs increased as we went. Men were fishing here and there – with nets and spears and trailed hooks. I watched women laughing as they washed clothes at the water's edge.

On the near bank, we passed the oyster-backed heron birds whose name I still did not know, standing in the cracked mud of the holms. The way they swapped from one foot to the other was mystifying: the free leg gradually offered to the earth in one long slow-motion bend until – abruptly – the decision was made and both feet were firmly planted for a glorious second before – just as quickly – the other leg was snatched up an inch or two and then retracted the rest of the way with that same measured movement. What possible reason could there be for this? Must there always *be* reasons?

I watched a pair of turquoise butterflies dance about a heliconia flower; *Lasaia agesilas*, the rarest of the rare. And as I fell asleep, the forward sky was full of swallows. Through half-closed eyes, I saw them wheel and swoop. Fast and keen. So many beating hearts in those chasing breasts; alive alive alive.

II

Speculations on the Nature of the Devil

Sometimes, when I cast aside the tools of taxonomy and the great tapestries of language that we have spun about ourselves, I recognize afresh that there is no sense in evaluating creation merely by the measure of its most exotic creature – Homo sapiens. *Instead, I see clearly that the ants that walk in tandem are teaching one another* the way, however we may define teaching. I see that the ants that raid and forage have memories, regardless of what we might call memory. I see intelligence whatever our definitions of intelligence might be. I see super-organisms.

I see, too, that my own ants and these hollow trees in which they nest need not even be two species but one. When the world was young there were one-celled organisms that did not have chlorophyll, that could not turn light into energy, and there were others that did. These combined to make single species of plants. Why not, then, another word for this amalgam creature in the Devil's Garden – part ant, part plant?

Indeed, my ants are very like trees already. The colony releases thousands of seed queens. These queens must scatter and fall to the ground. Almost all will die. Those too close to the parent colony, like saplings too close to the parent tree, cannot thrive. But the few colonies that make it are stable and unmoving; and they set about the exploitation of local resources, guarding them jealously.

In this cast of mind, I come to consider Homo sapiens. And in the self-delight of two hundred thousand years – almost nothing – I see that he has lost all humility and blinded his own eyes to the true nature of his circumstances. That, despite his intelligence, he alone of all creation looks to the gods to save him. But I see, too, the ants who track him, settle where he settles, thrive where *he fouls; I see them swarm across the world, destroying, colonizing, voracious* – Solenopsis invicta, *the red fire ant, that he can neither control nor repel.*

III

We arrived in the late afternoon and even from a distance we could see that Laberinto was in chaos. Mindful of Yolanda, we cut the engines and hung back while we assessed our best course. Everything centred on the crowded pier, which teetered over the mud and vegetation, reaching out desperately for the water. Two big riverboats had drawn up perpendicular to the end but no care was being taken to load the outer vessel first and so commotion massed on both decks while more goods and boxes and carts and cages continued to arrive from the town. There were smaller boats all around. I called across to Sole: 'Is there somewhere else we can tie up?'

'No,' she yelled back. 'We'll have to pull up on to the mud and walk.' She indicated where the riverbed was dry beneath the pier. Filth and refuse choked even the weeds. A cadre of vultures kept desultory station on an upturned canoe.

'Is there a path?'

Tord raised his voice from behind his tiller as if he had not heard us. 'We cannot climb up with Yolanda.'

Sole ignored him. 'Yes, there's a way to the main track. They use it as a dump.'

Two hundred yards downstream, we stepped into the mire. A fouler-smelling place could not have been imagined and yet there was no choice but to cross it. Jorge volunteered to stay behind with his beer until Tord and Felipe could get back and secure the boats somewhere. Sole went ahead to requisition a room at the town's only hotel, the San Mateo. The rest of us set off after her, carrying the stretcher as best we could – Tord, Felipe, Kim and myself with Virima beside us – sometimes tiptoeing, sometimes slipping calf-deep, sweating through the slime, parting the tangle and weeds where they rose up, passing by the rusting fridges, the bed frames, the stain-soaked mattresses, the oil drums, the cans, the bottles and endless plastic bags. The worst was a rotting dog – the bristled yellow skin of its bloated stomach suppurating beneath a fume-brown cloud of flesh flies; this horror doubled by the vultures; and then tripled by the realization that, if ever it began properly to rain, this tip would soon be the river *bed* again and was deliberately sited in order that all of this detritus would be washed into the system. In every blessing – a curse.

We were filthy, thirsty and slick-faced when we

emerged onto the pot-holed track. I had never known such heat. Water left my body across the entire surface of my skin – even my knees were sweating, my wrists, my knuckles. We rested and swung our aching arms about. I had given Yolanda some more paracetamol. She was still conscious. We swapped sides to alleviate the strain and hoisted the stretcher and walked on, Virima beside us leaning in to her sister whenever we jolted or paused.

Inland a little, the track joined a second – muddier and wide. Dead ahead and away to our right lay the Laberinto favelas. The trees had been cut back and the ground bared, creating these terrible fields of mud. Great holes had been dug without pattern or obvious purpose – some filled with standing water, others with refuse. There were no cross-streets, but instead ill-defined footpaths wound and narrowed between the hundred corrugated-iron huts, the lean-tos, the plastic sheeting and the tents.

A motorbike bounced past. Boys ran alongside. Matted heads emerged from beneath tarpaulin. A woman with a bucket of water was washing a child that would not stand still. Capuchin monkeys followed along behind us, too close.

We struggled on in the direction of the centre. The stretcher drew eyes from all sides. Perhaps it saved us from the worst of the leers and drunken shouts that I knew from my last visit attended the arrival of the unfamiliar. I had not been down this far before but I had come through Laberinto on my way in – eager, clean – and was pleased to leave as fast as Felipe and Sole could find Vinton the following morning. Felipe had then explained to me that there were no serious prospectors left in the town – that the thousands encamped here were the mad and the desperate: men who slept guard at the entrance to their tunnels day and night; women who claimed to have discovered a new gold-yielding stream so secret that they walked three days in circles to throw imagined thieves off their trail. For everybody else, Laberinto had become merely another frontier town, a last stopping-off place before the various river tributaries went deeper into the interior. Apart from the supply stores and the depots, the only people who stayed here worked for the only people who could provide employment – those in charge of the trades that paid; drugs, guns, timber and sex.

We had walked no more than three-quarters of a mile but it felt many times that distance. We stopped at a liquor shop guarded by a man with a gun on his lap and a military cap. Felipe went and found a truck and driver to take us through the centre – a narrow grid of dirt roads parallel to the river roughly three miles end to end. We climbed in and shook and thumped and juddered into town, Yolanda murmuring and Virima grimacing all the way.

My time at the Station had altered my perception. I remembered thinking before how dangerous the bare wires seemed – strung up roof to roof between the shacks and sagging as if to garrotte the unwary. I remembered how the dim bulbs threw an incongruous fairground light on the mud and the dogs at dark. But now this felt like a high street and Laberinto all but a metropolis with its bars and ready supplies and motorbikes and the possibility of strangers and a life beyond nightfall.

I remembered the San Mateo, too, the town's only boarding house. I had stayed a single noisy night – full of an anticipation that was half fear and half elation. And it was the same stout manageress who now stood to greet us as we came in through the swinging doors, her biscuit-fed features as attentive as I had remembered them indifferent before. Sole must have worked her magic.

'Hello, Doctor. Your room is number three.'

'Thanks. Do you have the other keys as well?'

'Yes, Doctor.'

'Please bring them up with us? We all want to wash.'

She hesitated by her desk.

'I'll come and settle all the bills straight away – as soon as we have this girl in a bed. Is there a doctor?'

Confusion slackened her jowls still further.

I asked again: 'Is there another doctor?'

'The señora has gone to look on the boats.'

I turned as best I could with the stretcher. The short lift in from the truck had nearly killed us.

'Everyone OK? Or do we need to put her down?'

'I'm OK,' Felipe replied.

Across from me, Kim tried to blow her hair from her forehead but it was stuck with the heat. 'Never felt better,' she said.

'Tord?' I asked, over my shoulder.

'Ready.'

'OK. Let's go straight,' I said. 'Can you bring us twelve big bottles of water?'

The manageress nodded and forced herself to smile. 'Please, this way.'

We were lucky: the stretcher went through the door frame. But if the room was really the San Mateo's largest, then it was by a matter of no more than two or three square inches. There was a bed, a clothes rail, a chest on which a television squatted and two tattered chairs – exactly the same as I remembered mine on the way through. Mercifully, Sole had found three separate fans from somewhere and at least the air was moving. We crowded in. I lifted Yolanda in my arms and the others pulled the stretcher out from beneath her.

The door opened, pressing Felipe against the wall. It was the manager. I remembered him from before, too:

porcupine hair and a face that always seemed to be calling in a favour. He eyed the fans: 'How long will you be staying?' he asked.

'We're not all staying.' I turned so that he could not approach the bed. 'We've just spoken with your wife. I'm going to check us in – and settle the bills in advance. Is there a problem?'

'I'm the boss,' he said.

Felipe's thumb knuckle went to his eye. Tord appeared to be praying over Yolanda's feet. Kim was busy in the tiny bathroom wetting a towel.

'This woman will be here with her sister until the boat leaves for the river city tomorrow,' I continued. 'My friend will also be staying. She's the one who spoke with your wife. The other rooms you can have back this evening at six – that's what has been agreed.'

He leered. 'We don't do day rooms. You pay for the night. We're busy.'

'But you do rooms by the hour – right?' I took a step towards him, widening my arms to sweep everyone out of the door before me. 'Let's go and sort this out. Tord – come on – Jesus hasn't helped anyone here yet. I don't think he's going to start now.'

The manager backed out but stood waiting in the corridor, picking his teeth. At the door I paused. Kim looked up and I acknowledged her expression of exasperation.

Sitting on the other side of the bed, Virima was stroking her sister's forehead. Quietly, she began to sing.

IV

The ceiling fan was broken. I lay down, clean if not cool, and I listened to the voices, the fizz of the electricity and the motorbikes in the street below. Two men were discussing the price of petrol and the price of women, the one rising as the other fell. They must have been sat on the porch directly beneath my window. Our other rooms were all upstairs – something of a novelty since this was one of only half a dozen buildings in Laberinto to have a second storey.

Everybody passed through the San Mateo. Downstairs, at the bar, young working girls smoked and joked together, fussing with their counterfeit handbags in various simulations of sorority. Middle-ranking cocaine and logging bosses sat down at the tables for fried river fish with scientists and missionaries and the occasional anthropologist from Paris. The prospectors were the first joke in common – mad from the mercury, everyone said, crazed on hope. The environmentalists were the second. Lothar had told me of a zealous faction of undercover activists who blithely talked football and bought drinks

all night for two gun-runners, who had convinced them
that they were elders from a local village come in to cam-
paign for clean water. I had some sympathy with the poor
fools; I, too, had found it impossible to know the real
provenance of any man or woman beyond their claims
– the various Indian tribes, the *mestizos*, the *ribereños*,
some moved down from the mountains, others left behind
after previous booms, others again terrorized into stasis
by the recent guerrillas; farmers, miners, adventurers,
pioneers, narcotics, counter-narcotics, soldiers, rebels.
Quinn's words: 'Whatever people say, in the end, the
only sure measure of a man is what he does – everything else is commentary. You'll understand when you
get here.'

There was a knock on the door. I rose and slid the
buckled chain. She slipped inside. I trapped her against
the wall and we kissed.

'The doctor was like you,' she said, looking up at me.

'What do you mean?'

'Not a doctor.'

She had a way of only just touching me with her
fingertips.

'Does the water work?'

'Yes.'

She ducked beneath my arms.

'It's a rubber pipe but the floor is clean.' I passed the

towel that I had stolen for her from another room then lay back down on the bed watching her. 'How is Yolanda?'

'I don't know.' She undid her shirt. 'Alive. Drinking water. Some juice. No worse.'

'I've arranged a truck and four men to carry her to your boat tomorrow morning.'

'Good.' She stepped from her jeans.

'I will leave you the money to pay them.'

'You have given me enough money. Just leave me the men.'

She stood naked a moment at the end of the bed but before I could reach her she had stepped back and edged round into the washroom laughing. She turned on the tap and held the pipe away to test the temperature. Then she raised it to her head and let the water run down. I lay on my side so that I could see her through the door frame; there was something to do with the casualness of her beauty about other business that touched me deeply, something that summoned feeling again from my blistered heart. Sometimes, when she slept, I would press myself against her and she would murmur and seem hardly to wake, hardly to acknowledge me, save to shift by slow degrees until I was inside her and she was pushing her body against mine – and afterwards, without once speaking, she would sleep again and I would imagine that

I had made love to some night creature now vanished, leaving sleeping Sole behind.

I rose from the bed. She started to laugh and sprayed me. I cornered her, twisted the hose from her hands and carried her back. We twined together and soon we were alone in the world. When she was close, she opened her eyes and looked up at me, reaching for my hand and spreading it wide across her stomach.

V

We walked the late afternoon across the broken kerbs. At the Bar Gotica – painted in startlingly clean bands of yellow and blue – we stopped and chose two plastic chairs and sat down. We were protected a little from the worst of the fumes and the mud by a moped propped against a weathered wooden pillar and a row of sacks that might have contained nuts or beans or anything.

'We have an hour,' Sole said. 'Time for three or four drinks – if we go at your speed.'

'I wish you were coming.'

She raised a single shoulder in her favourite shrug. 'When I was a girl, we went every year. My father took me.'

The barefooted waiter must have been no more than seven. The simplest thing for everyone was beer.

'Two bottles of Cusqueña,' I said.

He nodded – oddly formal – and set off for the ramshackle stack of crates at the back.

'Did your father take you everywhere?'

The shoulder again. 'He had no sons.'

'It must have been fun.'

'Not always. He had no money either. And most of the time we were fighting for something or other with crooked lawyers and bent politicians and then there was our own people and, well, you know the mess of everything . . .'

I nodded.

'And there are some things a daughter shouldn't see,' she added.

The boy came back and flipped the lids with his prize opener. I lit a cigarette and watched Sole watching the street. Her eyes were so dark that it was impossible to distinguish her pupils. The boy hovered, still holding the necks of the bottles. I dug out some money and paid him; clearly, lines of credit in Laberinto did not extend even as far as two beers. He nodded and then pushed the bills into the front of his underwear.

'How long will you be away?' I asked.

'I don't know. As long as we need to be. Will you survive without me?'

I smiled but beneath I was startled. Not once had Sole

acknowledged our relationship in such a way, let alone joke about it. Neither had I.

'Yes,' I said. 'But that's different from . . .'

'From what?'

'From being alive.'

I was sure that a reciprocal smile quivered at the corner of her mouth but just then the boy arrived with the change.

'And you?' I asked.

'And me what?'

'Will you survive?'

'I don't need you. I can take care of myself.' She sipped her beer but looked at me over the top of the bottle. 'But if you are serious, then I am serious. I like your company. You make me laugh. Not so many men do that.'

I felt something I could not articulate so I said, simply: 'I am serious.'

Immediately she danced backwards into mockery. 'How do you know I am not just after your money?'

'I don't think you are. But just in case: you should know that I don't have all that much.'

'And you should know that we don't trust anyone from outside.'

'I can understand that.'

'Why are you really here?'

'I'm a scientist.'

She curled her lip. 'Oh, please – don't – you say the same thing to everybody. You're worse than Tord.'

'I'm here because . . . I was trying to get away from myself. The man I was before – I didn't like him.'

She shook her head slowly – half in ridicule, half in earnest. 'The Judge is right. Everyone thinks that the lost tribes have been looking after their souls for them here – while they have been busy filling their lives with poison and crap.'

The dogs rose. Above the noise of music from the other bars came the sound of a larger engine labouring in first gear. Opposite, a group of women sitting outside the grilled-chicken shack stopped shelling nuts and looked up. An American off-road vehicle with tinted windows lurched into view, leaning precariously into a pot hole while the wheels spun axle-deep in mud.

'Who's that?' I asked.

'Cocaine,' she said.

'Did he have to boat that car all the way in here just so he could drive it up and down this street?'

The shoulder again. 'Yes.'

This time I shook my head.

'I know him,' she said. 'Everybody does. He is a nice man. He doesn't shoot anybody if he doesn't have to.'

I put out my cigarette.

'And everybody knows?' I asked.

'Yes.' The car drew level and Sole must not have liked my expression because now she narrowed her eyes. 'Why shouldn't he have his men drive him around in whatever car he likes? The people in your country who buy and sell his cocaine – they do.'

'Cocaine is illegal in my country. They still—'

'Listen,' she scoffed, 'sometimes the Americans come and they give us money so that they can take it away and stuff it up their noses. Sometimes they give us money so that they can burn it. But then what happens? All the farmers who are not already growing coca start to do so – as fast as they can – because the money they make if they give over their crops for this burning – guaranteed – is way more than they could make from anything else. They – you – you're the same – you have no idea what you want. Cocaine is not our problem. It's your problem. Your presidents and your leaders – most of them take it – or they have done – before. Their sons and their daughters – for sure. But what do they say? What do *you* say? That it's illegal.' She laughed. 'So why should we care about your hypocrisy? Why not buy a stupid car and boat it here all the way? At least this guy is a good criminal – he keeps the peace.' She sneered. 'I told you. Nobody cares. Not when it comes down to it.'

'That's not true.'

'It *is* true.' She put down her empty bottle and leaned in. 'On the TV, when I was working in the capital, just for that one year, there were maybe fifty things on the news or on the documentary channels about cocaine or the trees or beef or soya or something. Maybe a new thing every week. And I bet there is ten times that in your country. Do you think that there can be anybody left – really – who does not know all the bad stuff about what happens? No. Everybody knows everything. Or they know *enough*. Lothar says that in Europe it's even taught in the schools – everything – about the drugs and the guns and how many acres we lose a day. And, Jesus Christ, everybody has computers. So who doesn't know? Which people? Where are they?' She looked around as if to find them. 'So what is the answer? The only answer is that they don't care. How many times do I have to tell you? People are killed here – casually – all the time. It's the same with diamonds and heroin and weapons and oil and everything like that. Everybody knows. Nobody cares. Simple. This is the world we live in.'

'Sole, I want to go back to the hotel.'

'Good. I hate talking. We still have half an hour. We can be quick. Let's go.'

VI

Two hours later, I stood alone at the prow, bound for Machaguar. This was no minor tributary but the mighty river itself, greater in volume than the next eight of its rivals combined. The far bank was little more than a painter's smudge of indigo and violet and the early stars were spread across a sky so wide it seemed to vault a sea. As the current began to whisper around the bow, I breathed in air that was truly fresh and forgot the long weeks so tightly hedged about, inching up those foetid back channels, sweating through the nether gloom of the forest floor. I stretched out my arms and let the wind ripple through my sleeves.

There had only been a few cabins left, so we had split up. Felipe was with me. Kim, Jorge and Tord were on the second boat, which now began to draw up alongside, a twin to our own: two decks tall and top-heavy with the crowds so that every conceivable space on the railing above and below was taken by people leaning out and struggling past, by dangled legs and waving arms. In between, cluttering, strapped and loose, were innumerable bags and crates and boxes. A llama. Two vast black speakers. A moped. Pigs. More boxes – cardboard, plastic, wooden, mesh. Packs and sacks. Drums of oil.

Smokers. Gamblers. An old woman crouched on a stool, seemingly cooking on a tiny gas stove – a ghostly blue flame – elbowing off her crowding patrons. And above it all, nearer the back, a crown of children sat in a line so high on a mound of bags that they must surely have slid clean over the guardrails and into the water with the slightest swell. In the trees of the near bank, the twilight skull-monkeys screamed and raced – maddened outriders to these tottering human arks.

There were shouts from the deck above. A spotlight was switched on; it rolled and wandered across the water like a cataractous eye. People above and behind me were moving and the extra weight was making the boat lurch. For a moment I thought that someone must have fallen in, but the chug of the engine had not changed. I stared out into the water, following the spotlight. Pink dolphins.

The night darkened and the moon came and went behind clouds. I found a seat and drank awhile and watched my fellow passengers settle themselves to sleep: children on the floor, mothers propped up, fathers sprawled out. The other boat had dropped behind us and all that lay ahead now was the blackness of the water, the blackness of the nearside bank, mile after mile, and beyond even that, the pristine jungle, rising above the waterfalls and on into the upland mists. The last place on

Earth where people lived who did not know what the world had become.

VII

We heard it long before we saw it. Low and deep; a deadened thudding. Sleepers twisted in their hammocks. Children fell silent. The jungle absorbed the sound, so that it throbbed in from all sides, spread and seeped between the trees and, strangest of all, drifted up from behind us where the river disappeared into the darkness. The boat began to turn and the bend ahead to open up, the music swelling with each degree until, at last, we rounded the corner and there it was: the great beach, curving away as far as we could see, glimmering dark in the light of a thousand torches. Machaguar.

The scale surpassed all that I had imagined. At the near end there were twin towers of burning lights that cast gold and platinum streaks across the water, black and shiny as oil. Fireworks arced the river and flared across the thousands of dancing arms raised as if in worship. More lights were draped through the trees of the opposite bank; necklaces, pearls; the branches super-illuminated and ghost-white where these bulbs were set. The entrance was a banner between two giant poles and under-lit by crimson spotlights so that it reached out into the water ahead of us like a red tongue lapping us in to some fantastical city born only of the night.

There was no pier. Somehow, our pilot manoeuvred us so that we were able to tie up alongside our twin, several boats out from the shore. Below, we could see hundreds of smaller craft but the congestion was such that it was impossible to tell which were floating on the river and which had been hauled up onto the mud.

Felipe, who was wearing what appeared to be a luminescent pink waistcoat, had gone to find the others. Now he was waving to me as though there was a chance I might not be able to see him. I found the break in the rail, crossed to the other boat and made my way towards where they were standing to one side of the main crush. He was not alone in wearing his party clothes: Kim was dressed in her shorts and some kind of silver-sparkling vest top that I did not know she possessed; and Tord was wearing a T-shirt with a big white arrow pointing heavenwards on which the words 'I'm with Him' were inscribed in a Gothic typeface.

'Where's Jorge?' I asked.

'He says he is meeting some friends,' Felipe replied.

'He has friends?' Kim widened her eyes in mock reconsideration.

'Let's go,' I said.

We crossed one deck after another with the throng, the music insistent and the excitement impossible to resist. Beyond, the wide beach rose gradually up towards the tree line of the forest in which were hung more lamps, Halloween orange and ladybird red. We reached the long wooden ramp and walked down, one at a time, the drop twenty feet either side. There were several thousand here already. They pressed in on all sides and we stayed close as we moved towards the entrance. The music heaved and pulsed so that, when we stopped, we had to speak directly into one another's ears or not at all. We passed beneath the banner and paid for our stamps and our ultraviolet marks. Then we linked hands and snaked our way up the beach through the dark mass of dancers.

Crocodiles of boys pushed through in haphazard directions, brash and careless, jumping to the rhythm. I fought a rising wave of claustrophobia and felt Kim's fingers tighten behind me. Underfoot, there was glass and plastic and cans and I was glad of my boots.

We stopped at a blue tent that despatched only spirits and mixers – the former served in little paper thimbles that everybody tipped carefully into their cans. Over to our left below was the giant stage. A woman with a beautiful voice had started singing.

'Worth coming all this way for,' Kim said. 'We should

have been here last night as well.' She poured her rum into her can. 'I'm blaming you for not organizing things better.'

I smiled. 'I'm blaming me, too.'

She looked up from behind her straw. Few people were wearing much more than she, but her lighter skin and the sparkle of her vest attracted attention. Most thought that she was with me. Passing men glanced up for that male-to-male fraction of a second – acknowledgement, envy, challenge, then blank.

She held out her free arm and offered the cool of the can to her wrist. 'Where did you disappear to in Laberinto?'

'I went for a drink – with Sole.'

'Did you?'

'Yes.'

'That's probably a good thing.' She looked away and waved at Tord and Felipe, who were buying chicken. Then she handed me her can.

'Will you look after this?' she asked. 'I've just got to go dance.'

I watched her as she walked down the incline to the top edge of the beach. There had been no animosity but there was a constriction in her voice that she could not hide – either her feelings of sisterhood with Sole or something at odds with those feelings.

Tord came over. Without speaking, he ate his food and stood watching Kim dance. Then he drew a deep breath and eyeballed me before turning about and setting off for the sand, moving to the music with one arm in front and the other behind in the manner of an Egyptian hieroglyphic. I felt for him and his strange and patient pursuit of Kim. Almost uniquely on the continent, he could be trusted to face down temptation; and I admired him for that, too.

I caught Felipe's attention. He turned, eager, and began to move his shoulders up and down alternately. I nodded to him to join the others but he kept on with his jigging and it occurred to me that I had never seen him drink spirits before. He came and stood by me and I leant over and cupped my hand to his ear: 'Stay with them,' I said. 'And rescue her if she looks like she wants to be rescued.'

Then, before he could protest or start his shoulder dipping again, I walked away, conscious of the flask in my trouser pocket.

From the top of the beach, I looked to the shoreline where flickering fires burned between the hundred hauled-up boats. I could see the river again, just beyond, black as a scarab's thorax save for the liquid shard and glitter of reflected lights. Smoke was drifting between the larger riverboats and out across the water. Spotlights crisscrossed the crowd, revealing countless black heads rising, falling, nodding, dense and tight together.

I walked on, sipping as I went. Beneath the roar of the music, I could hear the heavy drone of the generators away to my left. I stepped across the snaking cables, moving closer to the trees. Already the mixer was thinning down and the whiskey's edge was a strengthening wall against which I would soon be able to lean. There were fewer bulbs but I could smell paraffin and kerosene from the lamps. I stood awhile and smoked. Groups of people were passing me on their way back down to the beach. Eyes shone and every face – beautiful, ugly, young and old – was caught a moment in the glow of the torch-light. For the first time since I had arrived I saw tribesmen painted in earnest: red semicircles on their cheekbones, darker streaks beneath, white lines, beaded skin, gleaming white-bone jewellery bolted through noses and tiered in hoops around ears, the flash of gold.

Further on and further in, the ground flattened out and the way narrowed. The trees began to muffle and distort the music from the river and I could hear the sound of the jungle night rising once more. I found I was walking on a raised wooden walkway and ahead there was a clearing – the village of Machaguar itself. The path split right and left and then split again, each branch haphazardly lit.

Between and besides and beyond were scattered huts. They were tall with steeply raked liana roofs and larger than any I had yet seen; some were illuminated from within, others were dark. The crowds had gone but everywhere there were groups gathered and people going in and out of doorways. I was walking in the trees and I could not tell any longer how far below me the forest floor was. A man came towards me carrying a burning torch, his skin shining, black paint rising in a v from his nose, white discs hanging from his ears, a thin peccary tusk curved through his nose. I stood aside in the entrance to a hut. The music was distant now, the air stultifying. I could not see within but I could hear breathing. One, two, three ... I did not know how many people. I realized with a shock that I was outlined in the lighted doorway and that they were waiting. As I turned away, a woman let out the unmistakeable moan of pleasure. I hesitated, sipping from my can and looking back at the river of torches along the walkway. And only then did my breathing deepen and my limbs ease; I had passed beyond the jurisdiction of my better self.

'What do you want?'

The voice came from behind me and was followed by a low murmur of laughter. Startled, I spun about. A man was standing – too close. I stepped back. But he continued to look at me with the quick and searching frankness of a far greater intimacy – as though my entire being and history would be instantly plain to his perception. My mind had not yet left the hut's darkness, the woman's sigh, and before I could speak came the low laughter again.

'What do you want?' he repeated.

'I was just—'

'Tell me what you are looking for.' He inclined his head slowly and then held it still. 'I might be able to help you.'

'I was just wandering.' I was not sure how apologetic to be. 'I came up from the river.'

'Wandering about. We see a lot of it in the world, Mr . . .'

I told him my name.

He considered it without reciprocation as he took out a cigarette. He was my own age, my own height, my own medium build; but he was dark featured and his hair was luxuriant and tall above his head – a black that seemed almost to shine, though with the strange greenish tinge of a carrion crow. *Corvus corone*. He was unlike anyone I had seen on the river; but his manner was so self-assured that I was certain he must be locally powerful – perhaps the man behind the entire carnival.

'You should know, Mr Forle,' he said, 'that you do not have to be bashful. Not with me. If there was something you . . . something you might *want*.'

'I'm OK.'

'Are you? Good. Well . . .' He described a circle in the air and then pressed a long finger to his own chest. 'Merely ask,' he said.

I took him to mean the carnival itself and assumed he hoped in some way to make money out of me. Self-consciously, I sipped from the straw.

He fired the cigarette with a match that he sparked on his thumbnail.

'Might as well smoke,' he said.

To my embarrassed surprise, he now offered this same cigarette to my lips. I was too unnerved to do anything but accept.

'Don't concern yourself. Tobacco only. Might as well.'

He lit his own in the same manner and then flicked the match over the balcony.

'Don't concern yourself. There's a stream down there – more of a river when it rains – which it no longer seems to do.' He indicated the clearing beneath, leant forward on the railings and looked down.

I was relieved not to be the subject of his strange intensity. Below, there were human shapes squatting in circles around a fire, which cast a dull gleam in the water.

'It's polluted, of course,' he said. He smoked like he could hardly stand to do so. 'And in the wet season it floods the entire field. It's from the cocaine preparations.

Kerosene and sulphuric acid – among other things.' A short murmur this time, not quite laughter. 'The *refinement* process.'

'I didn't get your name.' I looked over. I could not help but be pleased to be talking to someone new after the long weeks on the Station.

'Oh, they call me lots of things, Mr Forle. But Wilson. Wilson, I like.'

It was not clear whether this was his Christian name or otherwise. 'What brings you here – Wilson?'

'Work. I am always working. Or rather, I am never working and I am always working.'

'You're something to do with the carnival?'

'Wilson supplies the generators and all these torches you see. Your eyes doubt me. But I am the bringer of light. Yes, I do all the festivals and the parties – among other things – on the river.' He looked across to see how I liked this information. 'Among other things that I do and that I *can* do. Don't concern yourself. And you? You are?'

'I am a scientist.'

'Climate, animals or pharmacology?'

He was quick.

'Insects,' I said. 'Ants.'

'Which shall inherit the Earth.'

'Yes, though they will not see it that way.'

'On account of?'

'There's no before and after in the world of the ants. As far they are concerned, the Earth is already theirs.'

'Do they not have souls, Mr Forle?'

'Consciousness is notoriously difficult to test for.' I sipped the last of my can. 'Even among humans.'

'It begins in dreams – does it not?'

'What? What begins in dreams?'

'The soul. Everything thereafter.' He threw his cigarette so that the glow arced before it fell below us. 'Let us say that there was nothing.'

'Nothing?'

'No civilization, no religion, no science.' He inclined his head sideways again and held it there as if his eyes were indeed in the side of his face and he need not turn to look at me. 'Nothing but a man. A man sheltering in a cave long ago as he waits for the winter to pass.'

'A man.'

'When he falls asleep, he dreams. And in his dreams, he leaves his body behind, he sits down with distant friends, he meets his ancestors. In his dreams, the dead live. He discovers that neither time nor space binds him, that he is a wandering spirit, that he is more than the flesh and blood of his daily struggle. In other words, Mr Forle . . . in his dreams, his soul is born.'

I pressed out my cigarette on the rail.

'In time,' he continued, 'is our man not certain to conceive of another world beyond that which he can see, touch, taste, smell and hear? Inaccessible by day, perhaps, but there – always there – just around the corner of his mind?'

From the fires below, I could smell oil burning and the thick heady scent of green leaves smoking. I dropped the dead cigarette.

'And when the interpreters of dreams, those who claim they can speak with the dead and the gods and monsters that he has met in his sleep . . . When these interpreters make themselves known to him, is he not certain to follow them? Is our man not on his knees with desperation for an explanation? If only someone would tell him *why*, Mr Forle.' The low laugh returned – sardonic or genial, I still couldn't be sure. 'You see how it is . . . Man needs no more than a single dream to fashion for himself two thousand years of delusion.'

'I'm not an evangelical,' I said. 'I'm a scientist. I try to proceed by reason and proof.'

The laugh again. 'Here. Might as well.' He lit another cigarette and passed it across. 'So . . . ants ants ants: in a way, it's interesting, isn't it? The inner workings. Perhaps you knew Dr Quinn?'

'Cameron Quinn? Yes. Yes, I do. I do.' Now I straightened and turned and regarded him with a cordiality that I could not even pretend to suppress. 'Cameron Quinn was my colleague. We work on the same thing! You knew him?'

'I did and I did not.' He continued to lean, waving his cigarette. 'He came here last year. He was very nearly shot. I became involved. He appeared to have made a number of enemies.'

'He could be difficult but he—'

'Not difficult – I would say instead that he believed himself immune . . . from death. Which is not something that will make you popular in this part of the world. Death is such a common currency here, Mr Forle – *tender*.' He was watching me again. 'In my opinion, he was insane. He was on that plane that came down – yes?'

My expression must have betrayed my incredulity because he added: 'It's my work – to know. My business. The river.'

'It was terrible,' I said. 'So sudden. Just gone. He was my closest friend. I can't . . . . do you know, were there any survivors?'

'Come.' He peered at me. 'There is a place where you can get a proper drink. We can talk as we go.'

I was eager now. I flicked away my second cigarette

and followed him. He walked quickly. The few people we encountered stepped aside.

'What do you mean – he was insane?' I asked, struggling to keep up.

'The recklessness. The rashness. He did not care about himself.' Wilson spoke over his shoulder. 'And yet he cared for many things a great deal. He liked to take matters into his own hands.'

'Did you speak to him? About what?'

'We spoke about the same things as we have been speaking about, Mr Forle. I can see why you are – why you *were* – colleagues.'

Though they were the words of a stranger, I felt pride stir. I attempted to walk beside him. He seemed unaffected by the heat. A noise I had never heard came up from below – a bird that sounded like a frightened calf lowing.

'What do you mean?' I asked again. 'You talked about dreams?'

'We talked of explanations.'

'Did he say about his work? Was he in good spirits?'

'Oh, he was well. Very well.' He half turned. 'He told me a story about how one of the Matsigenka huts fell down and killed a child just before he visited. The mother and father called the death witchcraft but he

pointed out that the beams had been eaten away by termites. They said that they knew this but asked him why
did their son have to be sleeping beneath the beam at just
the moment when it collapsed? *That*, they said, was the
witchcraft. I remember the story well because Dr Quinn
said that previously he would have ascribed the disaster
to "coincidence" or "chance", which, now that he had
thought about it, was no explanation at all. He thought
this *very* interesting. Explanations, you see, Mr Forle.
Here we are. After you.'

He indicated a small path off the walkway to the left.
There was music again. We were far from the water now.
The hut was the largest I had seen and the noise from
within rose as we came to the door.

'This is where I first met Dr Quinn. He was with a
woman. Had brought his own. Which is *unusual*.'

'What was she like?'

'Ashaninka. Please go ahead. It's all in here.'

It was a bar of sorts – some kind of meeting hut,
I guessed, when the village was functioning norm-
ally. There were rough wooden chairs and tables with
hurricane lamps on each – though somewhere there must
have been a generator because strings of amber bulbs
ran like fat fairy lights all around the walls. In the
middle was a dance area where nobody was dancing

save for two semi-naked girls. The music was softer than elsewhere. Men sat in clusters while the women moved among them. On one side, a dozen or so were gathered around a bigger table where money was changing hands. These were *mestizos* – wiry loggers, rheumy miners, coca-pool gangs; red-eyed and raw-skinned men, unshaven and with the affected bravura of cowboys. But there were wealthier people here, too, proud of their boots, their machismo protocols and the spirits that they sipped.

Wilson stopped at one end of the bar, close by the wall. I must have been watching the dancers because next he said: 'If you want a girl, then ask for a girl. The young ones are better . . . but worse . . . if you know what I mean. It's an old problem.' The murmured laugh. 'If you want two girls – might as well – it's best to ask the first to recommend the second so that they'll be good together. Usually, they will do everything but not each other. This is a difficult area, I'm afraid. Nobody knows what is expected – not the house, not the girls, not even God. Perhaps, with three girls, these issues begin to diminish. Please, allow me to buy you a proper drink. This can you are carrying is rather . . . childish.'

'Thank you,' I said.

He nodded. 'I like to maintain good relations with

whoever is on the Station – with the ant people. You never know. Whiskey, I presume. He has something you will like. Vincenzo?'

The bar man left off the group he was serving and came straight over with a nod. Wilson must have given some sort of a signal for now Vincenzo pulled up a bottle emblazoned in blue and gold. He held up an ice-tong. I nodded. He pushed the drink across and I turned to thank my guide but he had moved away and I had to look around until I found him. He was sat at a nearby table, talking quietly. Long-fingered, he beckoned me over. I turned back to the bar wondering if I should offer to pay – or leave a tip at least. But Vincenzo was already about his work elsewhere.

The man with Wilson rose and I saw that he was a giant – six and a half foot at least and broad with that. He had a buzz cut and he wore a white vest in the manner of an off-duty combatant. His face was sombre – but sombre in the way of a young boy who is aware that sombreness is expected of him.

'This is Abideus,' Wilson motioned his introduction from where he sat. 'He was sent. By various parties. Most of which came through me. He is ex-army. It doesn't matter which one. I think it would be helpful for you to talk to him.'

I extended my hand. He must have been thirty-five though his manner suggested no more than fourteen.

'Please sit down.' Wilson winced at his own cigarette then offered me another. 'Abideus, kindly tell Mr Forle what you saw.'

'I saw bits of the plane. The seats. Somethings like suitcases maybe. A lot of metal. Everything burned.'

'The bodies,' Wilson breathed.

'I saw everything burned. Some whole bodies. Some just heads.' He made the shape of a skull with two huge hands. 'Most was nothing but black bits – twisted like rubber after fire.' He looked upwards as though he were still seeing what he spoke of. 'There were more bodies up there – in the trees. One thing big and white – from the wings. And the tail of the plane was up there, too. There were rags and shoes in the branches. Then everything else everywhere – all around – pieces of plastic and clothes – I don't know – cans of spray and toothpaste tubes. After the planes collided, I think this pilot came down slow – and he try to land on the top of the trees. Maybe one or two survive the crash but then the fire kill them.'

'Could you identify anyone?' My question sounded hoarse even to my own ears. 'Would someone be able to recognize a face?'

'No. Not everything burned completely – but – but the bodies – they were all filled with maggots.' His giant fists uncurled. 'This is what happens here. The flies lay eggs and the maggots eat the bodies from the inside and everything is rotting in three days.'

I did not speak.

'When I got there, the brains were already gone.' He raised two index fingers and pointed out from beneath his brow. 'The flies were being born from inside the eyes.'

Wilson spoke softly and leaned forward. 'Nobody survived, Mr Forle. I am certain. Nobody is alive in the jungle somewhere. There is nothing lost here. There is nobody to find.'

My cheeks were wet though I did not know I had been weeping. 'Quinn would have liked to have died in the forest,' I said.

The cocaine was astringent but there was no cheap detergent sharpness, no sear; instead, a purity, smoother, sweeter, a single line, and then – powerful, muscular and shocking in its speed and potency – it reared up inside me, swelling out to seize and fill my shape, taut against the borders of my skin. And suddenly my heart was screaming, and my blood was beating in my temples, my teeth tight atop of one another. I felt the shudder and then the certainty, and the rise become a soar, and then, just as fast, I felt the world shrinking to nothing more than the narrow circle of my skull, and everything beyond that fortification seen anew by two lidless eyes that looked out from deep inside my own hollow sockets.

Part Two

SIX

I

We should never have come back from Machaguar. We
rounded the last bend and I saw in a single moment
that everything had changed at the Station. There were
fifty or more canoes – some tethered, others beached, a
few idling in the river, more arriving. Indistinguishable
figures clambered our frail ladder. Our jetty was visibly
lurching under the weight of people. There were bare-
chested tribeswomen gathered in groups and naked
children playing in the mud on the bank. Men formed a
queue that disappeared up our path towards the clearing.
Above, a bird of prey turned in slow circles watching
something I could not see.

'Beach us,' I ordered.

Something was happening with the weather: the air
was like warmed glue. I jumped, Kim followed. Together,
we hauled the boat up. I threw in the rope and did not
wait to gather my pack. Ignoring the alarmed glances of

the women and the children racing beside me, I ran along the bank. Mud reached up my legs. I climbed the steep rise – slipping, cursing – until I was standing where the jetty's stem met the forest.

'You've got to get off,' I shouted. 'Everybody – the jetty is collapsing.'

There was laughter as well as alarm in the eyes of the men around me.

'Please. Get off.'

Nobody moved. I reached for the shoulders of the man closest and clasped him forcibly towards me – past me. I did the same to the second but he stiffened. He was younger and wore paint. I met his eye and held it for a moment before I felt the resistance leave his body and he too was shuffling up, pressing those on the path back into the jungle behind. I edged out onto the jetty, signing collapse and shouting.

'Climb down. Climb down.'

The structure sagged further to the right. I looked to the left – eight feet down – I'd have to land like a parachutist. The others had felt it, too, and now two or three ahead turned and began shouting with me. Some were laughing, others pushing. One jumped into the water at the end of the peer. Then another and another. People began scrambling down the ladder. Boats attempted to manoeuvre away, swimmers held up their hands and called. The water became dark with the disturbance. I felt the sway again beneath my boots. I had made things worse. The wood could not take all this rapid movement. I turned. There was a great splintering and tearing behind me and I was running at an angle, each step more of a leap.

I made the bank with three or four others. We pressed together, penned as though by an electric fence. The far end of the jetty had completely disappeared into the water; the rest had risen up in a broken twist.

Kim had climbed up and stood wiping her hands on the backs of her trousers. She looked at me. I saw fear tighten her features for a second.

'Whatever they're doing, they should have organized this,' I said. 'Stay close.'

We pushed our way along the path, past groups of men. Felipe caught up with us and I took my pack from him. There was a rumbling in the sky and the canopy was filled with unfamiliar sounds, as if every bird in the forest were in a rising panic. The insects were screaming.

We were almost at the clearing when it broke. Water fell in great vertical streams – solid ropes that battered us even as we struggled on. Mud was being born from mud – oozing in all directions, a measureless and filthy creature rising up from the forest floor. Men ran past us, cowering, though to no purpose. Some dissolved into the trees, many others we now saw were huddled and crammed and jostling several deep in the shelter of the *comedor*. We stopped short, too waterlogged and disbelieving for haste to matter. I wiped my eyes. There, at the top of the steps, sat the Judge.

He was alone behind our heavy dining table, which he had repositioned to the fore. And from this vantage he looked down to where we stood in the mire like some great prelate presiding over an uneasy rabble. The curtain of water that marked the boundary of the *comedor*'s shelter fell between us. Thickened papers slopped and slid from the table into the mud, congealing, destroyed.

'It's not enough,' he shouted, pointing both index fingers to the sky. 'A flash squall – over as quickly as it has begun – it's not enough. You'll know when the real storms come.'

The normal sounds of the forest had been deluged and there was only the racing wet swish of the rain. Barely twenty paces apart and we had to bellow at one another to be heard.

'What are you doing here?'

'It's good news, Doctor. Good news.' The pointed fingers became two open palms. 'They're pouring in from everywhere. They're coming out of the forest to register. I give them knives. I give them televisions – those that bring more than a dozen. And now we are no longer looking for them. They are looking for us.'

'The jetty has collapsed.' I took a few steps closer to the bottom of his stairs. 'There's chaos down there. People could have been killed. Children. Where's the Colonel?'

'If they are already registered, Dr Forle, then we will be able to attest to their deaths.' His voice seemed to resonate up from inside the sound of the rain. 'If not, then the question arises: have they truly died? Indeed, have they truly lived?'

There was a bottle on the table. Felipe started forward, then stopped, stranded between us.

Again, I shouted: 'Where's the Colonel?'

'He's gone out – ethnic cleansing. I would have gone with him but for my work. I didn't realize he was such a great friend of yours.' The Judge leant forward, reaching lazily at the papers – some floating away on a mini-stream, some draped forlornly on the stairs. 'Why are you so angry, Dr Forle? I thought you were a great democrat – a democrat-*izer*. And look at the face of our beautiful Miss Van der Kisten. Oh, the confusion. Did you ever see such confusion? But surely we are all in agreement – even science must make way for our wonderful democracy.

This is what is *supposed* to happen all over the world – no? Isn't democracy the great hope of all mankind? Or have I misunderstood everything? Have a drink.'

Already the rain was easing.

'Tell these people to go.'

'Go where? Go where? We are here. Where they go – is here. We are here – where they go. This is it. This *is* where they go.' He sat back and stretched out his arms. 'We must register. We need more opinion. More voices. More votes. We are all going to decide everything together for the good of everyone. All nine billion of us.'

His laughter sounded like a bird.

The Judge raised his voice again, a little louder for each step we took away from him. 'This love affair with the individual is a disaster, Doctor. Yes. Yes. Look at us. We're all obsessed with ourselves. We can't think about anything else for more than a minute. And your tribe is the worst. You have created this – the age of hypocrisy. This will be your legacy: hypocrisy in everything.'

Kim and I held on to one another's arms. It was difficult to pull our boots up from the mud. Behind us, I heard Felipe fall. I turned back to help him up. And I saw that the Judge had risen and was standing behind the table.

II

The forest was the loudest I had ever known it, thronged and teeming with newly emergent life after the rain; and even inside my hut, the air smelt of the wet earth.

'We're not stopping,' Kim said. 'And we are not going home.'

'We're not,' I nodded.

She cursed violently. 'We shouldn't have gone to the party. We've wasted five days. Every day here is a day we should be working.'

I lit my desk lamp.

'We've been behaving like tourists,' she continued. 'Like students on some rancid gap year.'

For different reasons, anger had consumed us both. We had washed together: Kim first while I kept station outside. Then Felipe. Then me. But time had not so far tempered the mood. Now, we were avoiding the *comedor*.

I sat at the desk and reached for my cigarettes. She was right. But I could not concentrate or deal with anything. The residual cocaine rushes were still coming and going; and with them a paranoia that I knew and discounted, knew again, and again discounted. My own emotions were intolerable to me again. And I had begun to suspect something in Kim's attitude to Quinn. Apart from her ill-masked fury at being 'abandoned' at the party, her reaction to my conversation with Wilson had surprised me with its vehemence. I should have found her, she said. I should have come back and got her straight away. What had this man seen? Who was he? The last leg of the journey back from Laberinto in our little boat with her and Felipe had been hell.

I offered her a cigarette. 'Did you see the Colonel or any of the soldiers?' I asked.

'No. Why?'

'Me neither. I think that's good.'

'Is it? I wish the Colonel would come back and clear up this mess.'

'On his own, I can deal with the Judge.'

She looked up. 'Can you?'

'Yes.'

The matches were damp. I threw her my lighter.

'Good,' she said. 'Because we *will* finish the work whatever it takes. We've been messing about—'

'Kim, I know. I know I know I know.' My voice rose and I forced myself to calmness. 'Believe me, I feel as bad as you do. Worse. I knew Cameron for fifteen years. Longer. We spent most of our working lives together. He more or less kept me alive. So don't think—'

I was interrupted by a knock on the door. I stood. There was the unfamiliar chink of crockery. Then Felipe came in backwards carrying a heavy tray, his smile like a ceremonial mask.

'I thought you would want to eat here tonight,' he began. 'Don't worry. Don't worry. Almost everybody seems to have gone. But there are still a few people about. And, my goodness, the *comedor* is covered in mud. Tomorrow is going to be one big clean-up.'

'Thanks, Felipe,' I said. 'We were going to come over.'

'No need.' He busied himself unnecessarily with plates. 'In any case, Estrela has locked herself in the store room so there's nothing to eat except this, which I had to beg off her. Would you believe it? She has made a bed on the floor. I had to speak to her through a crack in the door!'

I felt a surge of affection for Felipe. He was behaving like a head waiter following an atrocious accident with the soup – and it was contrived and ridiculous and silly. But it was working.

'She wanted me to say which person slept in which hut to prove that it was me!'

I glanced at Kim. The ire was softening.

Felipe opened the beers with a flourish. 'Even then she would not unlock the door. She would only pass all of this through the window.' He handed me a bottle. 'Please, I have already eaten.'

'Thanks, Felipe,' I said, again. 'You're a good man.'

I ate at my desk in silence. Kim balanced her plate on her knees. Bats were squeaking. My appetite was returning. I was glad to be clean at least.

Felipe sat on the bed, sipped at his water and talked while we sawed the meat into edible strips. The Station would be empty by morning, he reckoned. All the families had vanished with the rain. A few men were still sitting on the steps of the *comedor*. He believed they were Matsigenka. Everyone was friendly. They were talking among themselves. He wished Sole or Lothar or Tord were here so that he could have spoken with them. There was no sign of Cordero, Lugo or any of the soldiers – just the Judge. He had not been down to the river since the storm. What a mess. The Judge seemed not to care in the slightest. He was playing chess with a woman.

'What's left of the bar?' I asked, swigging deeply at my beer.

'I checked that, Doctor.' He smiled. 'It seemed OK, it seemed OK.' He nodded vigorously. 'I think the Judge may have taken a bottle or two but we will still have a few good ones left.'

I realized that Felipe's attitude was merely a different expression of what Kim and I were both starting to think: that the Judge's return was a colossal inconvenience, but that alone. Chaos, not disaster; the real apprehension had always been the soldiers.

'Will you let me know when the Judge goes to bed?'
I addressed Felipe. 'I don't think there is much point
speaking to him tonight. He was drunk four hours ago.'

'Or pretending to be,' Kim murmured.

'I will come and have a look and talk with Estrela. We
can see what needs to be done.'

Felipe stood, seemingly glad of his charge. 'Yes,' he
said. 'I will start now with the *comedor*. And tomorrow –
tomorrow hopefully Sole and Jorge will be back to help
us and we can make everything spick and span.'

'Thank you, Felipe.'

He left and I sipped from my bottle.

Kim put down her knife and fork with mock solem-
nity. 'Do you know what kind of meat this was?' she
asked.

'Monkey,' I said. 'Or some kind of rodent, maybe.'

She made the face of the delighted gourmet then rose
and placed her plate on top of mine and sat back down
with the tinned pears Felipe had bought.

After a while, she said: 'Dr Quinn would love all this.'

'What do you mean?'

'I mean he would have wanted to know which of these
people was from which tribe. For all we know, there could
be Mashco Piro making first contact. Smoke. I don't
mind.'

I lit a cigarette and said: 'Cameron used to tell me that

of all the amazing things in nature, the thing that amazed him the most was how such a staggeringly intelligent species could make such a mess of running the world which gave rise to its existence. One time he went on a television panel just to expose how little the other guests – politicians, senior journalists, the usual crowd – how little they knew about the human story. He said that not teaching anthropology in schools was like locking people in the basement of their own lives and making them think the abuse was normal.' I watched a moth fret the netting where the window was ajar. The light asked it in, the smoke warded it away. 'Is there anything you want to say to me, Kim?'

She looked up from her pear-spooning hunch. 'Such as?'

'Anything.'

She returned my look with a level gaze. 'Nothing. Except . . . can I use the computer tonight? I could do with an hour or two. I feel the need to connect.' She blew her hair.

'Sure. Do you want me to come with you?'

'No. I'm fine.' She put down her bowl by the chair and indicated that she wanted a second cigarette of her own.

'Can you hear the bats?'

She smiled. 'I was just thinking – thank God we're

not studying them: all of this again – but at night and airborne.'

'There are plenty of nocturnal ants,' I said.

She stood and lit her cigarette, her tomboy's grin returning.

'Do you want Felipe to sleep on your floor?' I asked.

'No thanks. Do you?'

I smiled. 'OK. Here, take another.'

'Thank you, Doctor. You seem to have imported all the vices.'

'It's my pleasure.'

She picked up her bottle. Perhaps it was just that I was beginning to see her as she truly was, or perhaps she was becoming even stronger and more self-reliant before my eyes – a woman with purpose and the surety that purpose brings. But our relationship was changing and I saw clearly that she would surpass me in science – and that this work would be hers to push into other disciplines and on as far as she wanted to go. A woman once told me that she believed confidence to be the greatest aphrodisiac, and she was not far wrong, but confidence comes and confidence goes, and in the end it is purpose that surpasses all; purpose in a purposeless world.

She hesitated at the door. 'What are you going to do tomorrow?'

'Tomorrow,' I said, 'I am going to sort things out.'

III

However brief and insufficient the rain, when I rose the dawn felt cooler. I dressed and stepped out into the clearing. Clouds had slept in the forest. The rivers would be wreathed in mist.

The lab padlock was undone and for a moment I was ready to blame Kim. But I had forgotten that Lothar had his own keys; and there he was – sat in the dry room, his weathered face bathed in the pale blue light of the screen.

He half turned in the chair. 'Good morning, Herr Doktor,' he said. His smoker's cough rattled him a moment. 'How was the party?'

I hesitated.

'But you're still alive anyway – and this is a good thing. After Machaguar.'

'I am. I'm still alive.' For a moment I thought I might tell him everything. Some part of me called out for his shriving.

'You have to see these things.' His lips curled but for the first time the rubbery grin was not wholly natural.

'Where have you been?' I asked. 'What time did you come in last night?'

'I came in this morning. I have been in the gardens.'

'What? All weekend?'

'Yes.' He glanced at the screen and clicked with the mouse. 'Friday and Saturday – they were good days. And then yesterday – after the rain – I worked with torches until late. I have been sleeping in the storage hut to save time coming backwards and forwards.'

He meant no reproof but I felt guilt leaking into my bloodstream like quicklime into the river.

'The good news is that I have been round half of the sites.' He pulled at both ear lobes simultaneously. 'I think so – we should keep going, yes?'

'Yes.'

'Everything is entered on the computer. And I have labelled the pictures, of course. *Ruhig fließt der Rhein.*' He clicked again then wheeled the chair all the way around childishly with his heels so that he could face me properly. 'So. What happened here? It looks like the circus came? Or was it the famous swine?'

'The Judge is back. He is using the Station as a registration post.'

He drew heavy breath. 'Why must it be that whenever I think the worst I think the truth?'

'You should have been here yesterday: anarchy.'

'I saw the jetty, my friend.'

'He is mad,' I said.

'No, he's not mad. You do not survive in the way he survives if you are mad. He survives in the capital. He survives here. He works by himself. He considers himself separate from everything that happens in the world. And yet people of every kind do his bidding. Not mad – much worse than that.' Lothar scooted himself forward and backwards a little. 'What's the plan?'

'I am going to talk to him now. He has to get a grip of it. Even if he is treating the whole registration as a joke – he can't let it be dangerous.' I stood upright. 'Have you heard anything more?'

He coughed again. 'No. Nothing since you left. I have been in the forest.'

I hesitated. 'Thanks, Lothar.'

'For what?'

'Thanks for your work.'

I had never seen him blushing. And I took it then as embarrassment – embarrassment at me thanking him.

'I love this place,' he said.

IV

Only twenty yards beyond the *comedor* and the Station felt different. The walls of the jungle were closer on the upriver side – a slight tapering of the clearing. I realized with a start that I had not come this way since the Judge and Cordero had arrived. Somehow, this side had become . . . theirs. Before, when Rebaque was here, I would walk up blithely and often and sip bourbon on his porch.

The heat was growing heavier. Soon, the rain would seem like a dream. Leaf-cutters were streaming across the path, *Atta cephalotes*. A foraging raid, six deep, but separating into several thinner lines that fanned out in radial arms away to my left, like a great river flowing backwards, unnatural, in urgent search of its every source.

'The fungus-growing ants are wise,' Quinn would say in his lectures, 'not because the Bible says so – "*Go to the ant, thou sluggard; consider her ways, and be wise*" – but because they are the only creatures on Earth properly to heed that great atheist Voltaire.' And then he would describe the manner in which they cultivated their mighty fungus gardens.

The Judge had the best of the guest huts, the last on the right. Ahead, the path to the generator went on into the jungle – improbable, ill-kempt. I turned aside.

She was motionless in the hammock and so I only noticed her belatedly – the same woman who had arrived that afternoon on the jetty. I nodded. She was wrapped in a sheet, which was drawn up beneath her arms and tight across her chest like a strapless evening gown – stark white against her skin and the black tangle of her hair. She must have been watching me all the while. She was a *mestizo* and the capital's jealousies and calculations animated her appraisal.

'Is the Judge here?' I asked.

Her hazel eyes did not leave mine. 'Raúl?' She said his name without raising her voice much above a murmur and still without taking her eyes off me. I had never seen provocation and indifference blended so exactly.

'Raúl,' she called again, 'there is a man here.'

I heard a clattering and then a second sound that I did not recognize – a steady low-pitched roar. The door was pulled open awkwardly and the Judge appeared. He was stripped to his slim waist, grizzled hair on his chest and his face half-concealed by an Old Testament beard of shaving foam. In one hand he was carrying a blue-flamed gas burner and in the other an overfilled pan of water.

He stopped and regarded me as though astounded at his own patience with the world.

'Were it not for Rafaela's morning ministrations, then today I would be minded to cut my own throat,' he said. 'I do not sleep any more, Doctor. I do not sleep well and fully. All night, my mind teems. Imagined voices, imagined conversations.' He set down the little camp stove on the table. 'It is an unendurable agony. Sleep comes only briefly and as frugal as the rain. Do you suffer? The harrowed mind?' Foam slid slowly off his jaw like snowmelt – against the continued roar of the flame, it created the impression that his entire face was liquefying. 'How are the ants this morning? Do we have long to go before we can finally hand over? Or are they dragging the damn thing out like sadists?'

'I want to talk to you.'

He fixed his pale eyes on me as if reading something in my face that I did not concede. 'This is a great habit of yours, Dr Forle, if I may say so – saying that you *want* to talk to a person when in actuality you already *are* talking to a person. You are here. You are talking to me. Let us not dispute it further.'

'How long do you plan to use the Station as a registration post?'

He balanced the pan on the burner. The water slopped and brimmed its weight in chasing circles. The tiny stove would topple, I thought. The hut would surely burn, the trees, the forest.

'Do you have a difficulty with this policy?'

'No, I think it is a clever idea – thoroughly thought through and very well organized.'

He looked up sharply. 'You are not without a sense of humour, Doctor. This is good. Those without a sense of humour cannot be trusted with anything.' A precarious equilibrium had now been achieved and he straightened up to face me. 'Well, what shall we do, then – you and I? What do you propose? What next? Every morning, it's the same question – no?'

'The jetty has collapsed,' I said. 'It's unsafe. You can't do anything else here until it is repaired. You can use our computer if you wish to send a message.'

'To whom?' His thumb had found the woman's foot and begun a slow massage. She shifted her legs apart a fraction the better to accommodate his attention though her eyes remained on me. 'To whom shall I send this message?'

'I don't know – whoever you want – but I'm telling you that we are here for four months and that I will not let you use the Station as a registration post until you have mended the jetty.'

'I am enjoying this assertiveness, Dr Forle. Is it the woman or the drugs – or is something else inside you uncurling again?'

'When that is done,' I continued, 'if you want to carry on here, then we will need to organize a system so that there are not too many people registering at once. We will also have to cordon off our side of the clearing.' Our side. 'I don't want people wandering anywhere near the lab. The equipment in there is irreplaceable. We can't afford to have anything damaged or stolen. Not just for our sake, but because – presumably – your government is going to want to rent the place out to scientists in the future.'

'The savages are thieves and hooligans – is that it?'

'In the meantime, you will have to set up somewhere else.'

Foam fell from his face. 'I agree – I agree absolutely,' he said.

'Good.' I was taken aback but I spoke without showing it. 'Then that is decided: no registration here until the jetty is fixed.'

'As you wish.' He raised her foot to his lips.

'Thank you.'

'I will peddle my democracy elsewhere.' He kissed further up her calf and she smiled. 'Where it does not affect you.'

The water had started to boil. He let go of the foot and stepped smartly back to the table. I saw for the first time that he was carrying a cut-throat razor in the waistband of his pyjamas.

'That look in your eyes makes me feel better, Doctor. It reminds me of home. Of the men I have sentenced.'

I hesitated. 'Where is the Colonel?'

He took out the blade and sat as if to eat soup.

'I have no idea. But he will be doing as he sees necessary. He goes on despite, Doctor, *despite*. Much like your friend, the German, I notice. It is you and I who are to blame with our observational natures. The absurd sham of non-engagement.' He raised his jaw to scrape the blade up his throat and looked down his nose at me. 'Who knows where the Colonel is? The Colonel is out there.'

He flicked foam from the blade. The woman had still not taken her eyes off me.

'Ah, you may feign your disagreement and your disgust – especially in front of the women, Doctor – but you don't really believe in all the mud and the huts. Not in your heart. Nobody does. When they ethnically cleansed America for those angry and disaffected Europeans, they also brought industry and endeavour and fortitude and civilization and law and medicine and welfare and technology and, yes, science. And in your heart you believe – despite the genocide – in your heart, you believe that *it is better this way*. We all do. It began – as it always begins – in blood and slaughter; it became conquest and slavery; and by way of shame and in need of disguise, it pulled on the robes of religion and then the suit and tie of the market; until eventually it came to' – he laughed – 'conservationism.'

'I will see you both this evening, I hope,' I said.

Close beside the veranda, there was a maddened tree: the walking palm, *Socratea exorrhiza*. They lurch slowly through the forest on stilted roots in search of more light.

V

We gathered in the sanctuary of the lab. Lothar had made a flask of his treacle-thick morning coffee, which he poured into whiskey tumblers. We sat together at the bench amidst the welcome orderliness and calm.

I relayed the Judge's assurances.

Kim wondered who would tell the Indians and the *ribereños*.

I said that my guess was that the Judge had either already decided to leave or that he would set up somewhere else and that, hopefully, everybody would come to know of the change by mid-afternoon in the same way that everybody in the jungle always did: quickly and mysteriously.

Felipe, meanwhile, felt that it was his pressing duty to spend the day attempting to return the Station to a measure of normality and cleanliness. He was worried about Jorge, who had not been seen since the trip to Machaguar. But most of all, he wanted to know what we thought he, Felipe, should do about the jetty.

Jorge would most likely come back on the same boat as Sole, we reckoned, and he might as well forget about the jetty.

After that we got on to the work and Lothar argued

that it would be quicker for him to carry on cataloguing the results his marathon had generated rather than for Kim to take over and decode his jottings.

Kim agreed and expressed a great deal of appreciation for the hours he had put in.

I suggested that without Lothar or Felipe to act as guides, the best course was for Kim and me to go together to the cluster of easily accessed sites directly upriver that we both knew well. And that we should not waste any more time but start straight away.

VI

Stage Three

Not only did Darwin realize that the ants were his 'one special difficulty', but he was also the first person to think of a solution. This later came to be known as 'kin-selection'. And, for a long time, this theory (developed and expanded by others) gave science a way around the problem: a way of explaining the cooperative ants without running up against the laws of natural selection and what came eventually to be thought of as the selfish gene.

Kin-selection works because of the strange way ants inherit their sex: fertilized eggs become female and unfertilized become male. The consequences of this method of gender determination are profound: it means that each new female ant is born three-quarters related to her sisters. Why? Because each sister has inherited an identical half of her genes from her father (since the male father was in effect a clone) to go alongside the standard shared quarter set of genes inherited from her non-clone mother. In other words, ants are more closely related to their sisters than they are to their parents or would be to their offspring.

Thus, it makes more sense, in terms of the genes, for a worker ant not to produce young but to devote herself instead to caring for her close-kinned sisters. And, once it becomes more beneficial to favour sisters over children, a colony is formed. As long as the queen is able to have more offspring as a result of each of her daughters' communal attention to their sisters, then the shared genes will still be favoured and so disperse more quickly through the population.

In this way, for a while, biologists were able to preserve the gene's eye view of natural selection and explain the cooperation of the colony.

But the ants defy us at every turn. For now we know that they – our Myrmelachista *more so than most – mock even this explanation. How so? Because in the Devil's Gardens there are many queens. And the daughters of one queen behave cooperatively towards the daughters of another – behave cooperatively, that is, towards other ants to which they are* not *related. (In truth, we have long suspected that the lemon ants are cooperating between colonies. And this was the really significant work that Dr Quinn and I had in mind when we first began.)*

So, in the third and most important phase of our study, our aim is to demonstrate – to prove – that the Myrmelachista *are 'helping' one another when there is no good genetic reason to do so. Such a finding, we hope, will bring us directly into the crucible of the debate. For the only thing that ants cooperating across colonies have in common . . . is their species.*

The stakes could not be higher.

On the one hand, we have the selfish-gene merchants, who claim that traits can evolve only for the good of the individual and not for the good of the group. This has many implications for biology, but also for our society: most of all, it turns the individual into the king of the biological hierarchy. Most of science covertly or explicitly subscribes to this view.

On the other hand, we have those who say that evolution is multi-level: yes, individuals evolve traits, but groups also succeed against one another and these groups will beat other groups in the evolutionary game. Evolution works both within the group and between the group. Further, the most successful groups may well comprise many altruistic individuals. Again, the implications echo through every aspect of our existence.

VII

Sole was lying asleep sideways on my bed. She had been waiting for me. In five strides, I was across to her. Her eyes were smiling, drowsy, as she shifted onto her back, but now they widened as she saw my intention. She feigned a playful fright, raised herself and offered her lips. I slipped her belt and slid her jeans leg from leg.

Afterwards, we lay together listening to the evening calls of the forest. During our separation, something had changed between us: the acts of lovers no longer acts, our bodies become messengers of deeper things.

'So what was it?' I asked. 'What was wrong with Yolanda?'

Sole smiled. 'It was a boy.'

'What do you mean?'

'She had been with a boy from one of the villages . . . and she got hepatitis. B and D together, the doctor said.'

'How old is she?'

'Fourteen.'

'Christ.'

'She couldn't tell her father. Only her mother. She thought she was dying from bad magic.'

'She would have died?'

'The doctor said it happens – especially when you get

complications.' Sole rubbed her hand back and forth across my chest. 'But Yolanda was lucky: my doctor, who is not a doctor, saved her life.'

'I went to a party. You went to the hospital.'

'That's true.' She smiled. 'And I spent a lot of your money. You'll probably have to sell your house and get a big drainpipe in Laberinto.' She raised a finger – a bird was calling, three notes ascending in a minor key, sad and beautiful and hypnotic. A *seringueiro*. The light was beginning to fade.

After a while, she propped herself on her elbow and said, softly: 'Tell me?'

'What? Tell you what?'

'Whatever it is that has changed your eyes.'

I felt my shoulders tense.

'Please don't lie,' she said. 'Or this becomes like everything else.'

I was aware of the sound of my own breathing.

'I met a man at Machaguar,' I said. 'He introduced me to a soldier who went out to the plane that crashed . . . the plane that Quinn was in. The soldier told me what he had seen – the wreckage, the dead.'

She murmured.

'I stayed at the bar after he left. I was drinking. Then one of the girls came over and sat with me. I bought some cocaine from her. Maybe that was what she was supposed to do – sell me cocaine first and then sex. I don't know.'

'Did you go with her?'

'No. I took some of the cocaine. But it was strong – really strong. I left her the rest and went back to the river. I don't know how. I was drunk. I felt like death.'

Gentle fingers traced the bones of my face.

'Cocaine has always been here,' she said.

'I know that but after wh—'

'And part of you has been hoping all this time that Dr Quinn was alive.'

'Yes.' I looked up at her steady eyes. 'Yes, I have been hoping. And I have been lying to myself, too, about lots of things. But no more. What happens, happens. We just have to live.'

'We do.' She lay down beside me.

The room was almost dark. I wanted only the feeling of where our bodies met. The *seringueiro* called again – closer now.

'What did you get in the city?' I asked. 'What was it? Why did you want to go?'

'No. Not now, I will tell you later.' She was silent a moment and then she said: 'My mother was a cocaine girl like that once. That's how she met my father.'

I reached for her hand and side by side we fell asleep.

SEVEN

I

For a few days, Kim and I worked hard. Absorbed in the forest, it seemed as if we had never been away and I began to feel that the Devil's Garden was at the heart of things, that the affairs of the ants were the real business of the world and everything else fleeting and tertiary. I thought about Quinn and about his idealism – how he loved the Greeks and talked about them as if they were his friends. My mind stood up to its full height and I began to see the importance of our study again: the human effort to understand life – the only meaningful chance of salvation. Science had helped overthrow the beautiful deceits of religion but at what cost? A new age of uncontested materialism – so painfully antithetical to human well-being with its relentless appeal to insecurity, jealousy and accrual, ignoring need where found, creating need where none. We had to go deeper – into biology, chemistry and the laws of physics. We had to understand ourselves and our place in the universe – with dignity and without flinching.

Phase one – the poisoning – was merely a matter of the proof we were day by day collecting. Phase two – the limitation question – Kim would lead. And phase three – the cross-colony cooperation – this, we would work on together. My intention – if only we could proceed fast enough – was that this would become the denouement of my book. Thanks to Quinn, we had gene-sequencing equipment at the lab and at the storage hut. We could establish non-relatedness. We could provide evidence of cooperation. Was it beyond the bounds of possibility to start some early experiments straight away?

My idea was that we devise a way to measure whether one colony was lending workers to another for tasks – fighting off predation, for example – and then see if those same workers were returning to their original nest without any obvious recompense or benefit. Except it was not at all clear – to me, to Kim, to anyone – what exactly 'recompense or benefit' meant.

'It's a big problem,' Kim agreed, as we sat eating boiled potatoes on our field stools in the forest. 'Altruism is messing with the universe.'

'Maybe we just have to watch the helper-ants' bank accounts for the rest of their lives,' I said, 'to make sure that they never cash the evolutionary cheque.'

'Assuming this place lasts that long.' She raised her wrist and passed the sweatband across her brow. 'It feels like a very human trait, though – don't you think? I just can't imagine any other animal bothering with altruism toward strangers. Not for long, anyway. It's too close to self-delusion for any other species.'

I looked about the forest. 'Maybe that's what we have here, a self-deluding ant. Now how would you test for that?'

'Psychometrics,' she grinned.

I smiled. 'Anyway, I have a theory that self-delusion is the best indicator of intelligence.'

She swigged her water. 'You might be on to something there, Doc. Think of all the most successful and charismatic people – totally self-deluded.'

Opposite where we were working, I noticed a branch broken so that it formed a sharp and splintered elbow pointing up. It could have been snapped by any one of a dozen creatures, but I also remembered how Lothar had said that he came across evidence of the un-contacted peoples' warnings all the time.

II

Back at the Station that same evening, we found Tord waiting at the *comedor* with a bag full of gifts: baseball caps bearing the legend 'C.I.A. (Christians in Action)' and T-shirts which proclaimed in English: 'You don't know Jack if you don't know Jesus'. Felipe and Estrela, neither of whom spoke English, managed a display of gratitude on behalf of the rest of us.

Later on, and feeling more irreligious than usual, I went up to the Judge's hut to ask him if he wished to join us for dinner. Despite everything, I was still hoping for cordiality between us. His hut was dark though – and there was no answer when I rapped on the locked door. Nobody had seen him or Rafaela leave. And there was no way of knowing if he had simply been true to his word and set up his registration post somewhere else or whether he had vanished for good.

In the continuing absence of Jorge, Estrela made one of her guinea-pig casseroles, which we ate with uneasy conscientiousness. After dinner, Sole went to use the computer. And so we made a four for cards. We were almost as we were before the first arrival: Tord, Kim, Lothar and I sat at the dining table; Estrela lolling on the lounge chairs, muttering occasionally, one thickened leg propped up; and Felipe busy beside her, snipping fantasies from his lifestyle magazines with rusty scissors. Kim had crushed fruit to drink. I had added vodka. Unusually, she was bare-skinned in her shorts and T-shirt and she had been spraying herself with insect repellent all evening. The heat stuck the cards.

Was there a moment when we became aware of a commotion coming from the river? Perhaps it was gradual. But we seemed to stop our game and look up at one another in unison.

I pressed out my cigarette, slowly, as if this would somehow improve my hearing. A distorted bass, a thudding drum; a voice that did not sing but spat. Kim's chair faced inwards. She swivelled in her seat, her brown arm crooked over the high back. Tord's eyes followed her. Raised voices. Cries over the music; crisscross lights in the trees. Lothar put on his hat. I braced myself.

Darkened figures emerged from the river path – arms aloft, their faces obscured by the crazy dance of their torches. We waited in a rigid silence. Only when they entered the range of the *comedor*'s lights did we see them more clearly. Tribesmen. And the Judge.

He walked at the front like the conductor of a military band. His hair was slicked down and the more unsettling for that. Beside him was an older man with a tattered open shirt and a heavy scarf around his neck. Half a dozen boys danced around them; they were barefoot and wore only shorts with polished-bone necklaces over their bared chests. The raging music came from a massive machine, shouldered by the oldest. He was taller than the others and he wore red lines and some sort of white beading across his cheekbones.

'Drunk,' Tord mouthed at Kim as she turned back to face us.

'Tupki's son.' Lothar's hoarse voice was raised against the music.

Kanari – I hadn't recognized him with his face painted. And now I realized that the scarf around the older man's neck was not a scarf but a snake. I had seen this before; some of the villagers kept anacondas as pets to deter the rodents – they drugged them with some kind of root. But this one was big: head and tail, either side of the old man, it writhed slowly, sedated.

The Judge stopped and held up his palm. Kanari turned down the volume. The sudden silence was as shocking as the noise.

Kim stood.

The Judge spoke as though addressing the stage from the footlights. 'Hello there, my good Christian soldier.' This to Tord, who now also rose. 'I see you have come among us with your blessings. How about we all drink to your poor under-achieving God tonight? He's not done all that well, has he? Not so far.' He mounted the steps one at a time. 'We require more wine. And then more music.' He extended an arm back out into the night. 'For how do we charm the snakes if not with music and wine?'

Tord's voice was querulous. 'What are you doing, sir? What are you doing with these people?'

The Judge paused a moment – affecting to consider Tord anew. Then he started slowly towards our table, his palms before him as if for an aria. And before I could guess his intentions, he had dropped to his knees in front of Kim, clasping her bare legs to his face. The gesture was horribly intimate. She was caught, trapped, frozen by the joke, the seriousness, by a burning embarrassment and alarm. She tried to recoil but she was too strongly grasped to step away without greater force or a kick that she was unwilling yet to risk.

'Miss Van der Kisten, you are right, you are right: the world has not cared for these men. But see, we are all here debased – the black man, the red man, the white man. Will we ever forgive one another? How many generations does it take?'

'Sir, let her go!' Tord's shout rang out into the trees, his voice powerful, declamatory, a firebrand as he started towards the Judge. 'You justify yourself in the sight of men, but God knows your heart. For that which is exalted among men is an abomination in the sight of God.'

But the Judge – suddenly spry – was off his knees and on his feet in an instant.

'She is yours.' He threw his hands out violently then sent them vigorously through his hair so that it stood up in its customary fashion. 'Be wary of this ridiculous man,

Miss Van der Kisten, be wary. His intentions are worse than mine. I want a night. Less. He wants to steal your life and plant his resentful little seed up and down your womb.'

Laughing, the Judge stepped backwards and bowed, ushering Tord and Kim together.

'I'm fine.' Kim pulled away from Tord's arm, fury and embarrassment and repugnance fighting in her face. 'Let go of me.'

The Judge wheeled his arms. 'Why is the music quiet?' He looked about. 'And get these men a *drink*. We are desperate. We are all desperate.'

This last was thrown in Felipe's direction. But he was frozen where he sat, his scissors half-raised as though trying to cut invisible cords in front of his chest.

I stood. 'You can't have any more,' I said. 'Not here. These are our supplies. And you should take these men back. They've had enough. I think we sh—'

'You.' The Judge pointed at Felipe. 'Come with me. I have two cases. Help me fetch them. It's a matter of honour. We don't break our promises, Dr Forle.'

'Felipe,' I said.

But Felipe had risen. 'I will stay up here, Doctor, and ensure that there is no damage. Please. It's no problem. There's no problem. It's better if I stay awake here. I will be back in two minutes.'

He did not allow himself to look at me as he stepped down after the Judge.

I turned to where Kim was standing apart from Tord. 'Are you OK?' I asked.

Her face was defiant but beneath I could tell that she was frightened.

'I am going to bed.' There was accusation in her voice. 'We have work to do tomorrow. We can talk about this later.'

She stepped down. Tord made a move to follow but changed his mind or his priorities. Instead, he began to speak to the younger boys at the base of the steps. They stiffened, shocked perhaps at his facility with their language. He gestured and pointed at the old man and the Judge, enunciating his words with a supple-jawed determination that I could not help but admire.

On hearing Tord speak, the Judge had turned and was standing in the half-shadows with Felipe hovering in agonized attendance. His voice seemed to wheel and hiss about the dark walls of the clearing. 'Press your vile God upon them with bread. Press your God. The old ways are the best ways. Work on the children. The younger the better.' Then to Felipe: 'Come on. Let's fetch the cases.' He set off, calling over his shoulder, 'Work on the boys. Work on the boys.'

Tord endured all of this with a clenched and practised

Christian fortitude while staying about his task. But the animated conversation had clearly become an argument and he was holding up his hand in an effort to exclude Kanari, who was attempting either to exhort or to mock the younger boys, I could not tell. A minute more and whatever point he had been making seemed to carry. For now he mounted the stairs and collected his pack from where he had neatly placed it out of the way on his arrival.

'I am taking three boys back to their house,' he said. 'They are worried about returning to their father without the beer. Actually, the Judge promised them a case each. I will go with them and try to prevent their being beaten. The others will not come.'

He took out his big yellow torch, checked the light and shouldered his pack. There were many things I did not like about Tord but I saw then that he was a brave man; he travelled alone and he travelled at night.

The others appeared as indifferent to his going as they were to losing some of their number. The old man sat down on the stairs. The two remaining boys followed suit. But Kanari continued to watch me with an animal menace from where he stood – tall and painted and mute.

'The Matsigenka do not like the river stations.' Lothar spoke as if reading my mind, his voice calm and all the more unnerving for that. 'There was slavery here – the mountain empires, then the old world, the rubber barons.' There was a weariness in his face that I had not seen before as he stood. 'There is still slavery here – by other names,' he added, quietly. 'I'm going to bed. Kim is right. We need to talk again tomorrow. So. Let's meet first thing in the lab.'

'I'm going to stay here.'

He stopped. 'Don't do anything silly.' His eyes were steady but there was concern in the tilt of his head. 'This . . . this registration – or whatever it is – it's not your concern.'

'So I'm told. But I don't live in isolation any more than they do.' I relented. 'I have to stay with the bar, Lothar. Otherwise I don't think there will be a bar by tomorrow morning.'

He nodded – relieved at the triviality of my motives.

'We meet in the morning,' he said. 'This was not good news.'

I watched him go, feeling for the first time a pulse of anger towards him. Perhaps because he had done nothing for Kim, something in me was disappointed. I had thought that he held himself in reserve only so that we might count on him when the moment required.

I crossed to the lounge chairs by the bar. I poured myself what remained of the crushed fruit juice and added the vodka. Long-tailed bats were flying. The older man was sat facing away on the last step. The boys looked up but said nothing.

'Do you want some water?' I asked.

The man did not turn around. The boys stared at me: ragged, shuffling, limbs slack with the drinking. I guessed that they could not speak Spanish. I addressed Kanari who was crouching a little way off.

I asked again: 'Do you want some water?'

He spat and cursed to himself but so that I might hear.

And so we sat: me in the lounge chair, sipping my vodka and guarding my supplies in the lighted circle of the *comedor*; the four Indians in the semi-darkness on the bare ground beyond. I sought refuge in Felipe's magazines, which seemed to me then the most spurious things upon the Earth.

III

No more than ten minutes passed before I heard the Judge noisily returning. The Indians stood. Felipe was carrying two cases of beer, bottles clinking as he hurried along behind. I wondered how much of the Judge's authority was in his bearing and how much in his title. Would men heed him in other places, in other times? Why so?

He indicated that Felipe should set the cases down on the stairs and then clapped his hands.

'Music, music,' he called out. The blast was ferocious and instantaneous. Unperturbed, he beckoned up Kanari, who now mounted the steps like a communicant. He pulled out a bottle of beer, held it at arm's length for Felipe to prise off the cap, and passed it solemnly over. One by one the others followed Kanari, the old man coming last. But even then, the Judge remained at the top of the steps, encouraging them to dance with motions of his hand while Felipe stood stranded at his side.

When at length he turned, I could see that the Judge was speaking to me but I could not make out what he was saying; it was impossible to hear anything above the music. He took the bottle-opener from Felipe and bent down, prising the tops off all the remaining bottles indiscriminately. Then he smiled again in my direction, and offered me one.

I stood. For the first time, I wished for the authority of a weapon: a gun, or better, a knife. The music stormed between us. He offered the bottle a second time and gestured gracefully at the dancing. Then he bowed, placed the beer at the head of the stairs, stepped down and walked away towards his hut, one finger pointing high above his head, over and over, to the throb of the music.

I faltered. Felipe came up and took refuge behind the

bar. The dancing was grotesque. I could not tell how much pretence there was in their effort; the two younger boys moved from foot to foot, making pistols with their hands in a parody of gunshots; the older man slapped at his stomach, circling, clutching the neck of his bottle, first raising his head high with his eyes wide to the darkened canopy, then bowing down low to the earth and squeezing them shut. Kanari had put down the music and was pumping one fist then the other as though stabbing at a wall. I thought perhaps they were waiting for the Judge to disappear. I crossed to where he had been standing, indicated the beer and gestured for them to take it.

Already the younger boys were slackening. Only Kanari continued with any conviction – throwing himself into shapes, the sweat pouring across him. I realized with deepening unease that he was showing off. There was something more than adolescence in this display, something intended beyond itself, directed at me, something violent, or something erotic, perhaps, but in a language of movement that I did not understand. He closed his eyes and swayed his head. He seemed to hurl his weight through his body, first one way, then the other; he danced with so much energy that it was as if he had drawn out the souls of the others and that he was all four in one.

I did not see them coming.

I did not hear them.

The first blow was to Kanari's face – sudden, vicious, a sound like a muffled thud. His head jerked back and away, then forward, his neck flexing like untreated rubber. Blood surged from his nostrils. The bridge of his nose collapsed into a thickened gore and a dark stain burst across his cheeks and flooded his fluttering eyes. His hands covered his face. He went down. The follow-up kick was steel-toed and it cracked at his ribs but even as his boyish body recoiled and his head was thrown up a second time, he did not take the hands from his face.

The music caught, skipped, screamed, then died as one of the soldiers rained rifle-butt blows on the machine.

I was aware that the bottle of beer by my feet was rolling and spilling down the stairs. I was aware that the younger boys were running and the older man too, and that his speed was extraordinary. I was aware that they were all heading for the river path and that they swerved as they went; and I realized with a lurch of understanding that they were expecting gunfire. I was aware, too, that Tupki had arrived from somewhere and that he stood swaying in the silence, hands bound in front of him, half reaching out to his son, his face collapsing – slow and drunk and soundless – into an agonized grimace.

One of the men must have draped the fallen snake around his shoulders. And now Captain Lugo was moving decisively towards him. I assumed in terror that he was going to shoot the father in front of the son. He reached with his free hand for Tupki's wrists, raised the Indian's forearms and with them the snake, then he placed the muzzle soft against the sedated sway, paused, and fired into the reptile's head.

Tupki fell beneath the force of the thrashing body, trying to clutch his ear with his bound hands. Bone and brain and cold blood were spattered all over his face. I willed myself to move but I could not. Adrenalin was coursing through me. I was shuddering – my mouth dry, my eyes blinking, my chest sodden with sweat. There were more lights in the trees.

Lugo indicated father and son. The other men raised them up beneath their arms, dragged them to the foot of the steps and threw them down as if delivering rugs.

'Tie them,' Lugo said, then turned his eyes towards me. 'I need the key to your store.'

Cordero had appeared with more soldiers. The Boy was with him, the metal of his mouth gleaming in the torchlight.

The Colonel nodded curtly towards me. 'We have spies among us,' he said. He stood a moment beside Lugo looking down at Tupki and Kanari, his heavy face expressionless, using the beam of his torch though there was light enough to see.

Tupki had his eyes clear of the snake's entrails but he was visibly shaking, and still trying to reach for his ear. Blood was pooling around Kanari's head.

Cordero thinned his nose. 'This should be the end of it. But we will see – tomorrow.' He looked up at me with no emotion in his eyes. 'Doctor, can I charge you to make sure these men do not die tonight? Keep them conscious. Treat them at your own hut, please.' He used the muscles that in other men produced a smile. 'You' – this to Felipe still cowering behind me – 'make sure this mess is cleaned.'

I heard no more. I was pushing through the soldiers at a run.

In the store, I gathered disinfectants, bandages, scissors, painkillers.

Kanari wasn't moving when I returned. Tupki had shuffled over and was leaning by him saying his name. Cordero had gone. The Boy's associate, the rat-faced man, held out his hands for the medical equipment.

'Are you a doctor?' I asked.

'No.' He smiled.

I ignored him and fell to my knees. I had to wrench Tupki away. His son's breathing was clogged and wet and made a hideous sucking sound. His mouth was lined with blood and he was only getting the air in with great difficulty. His nose was broken. Teeth were missing;

others hanging by strands of gore. I did not know where to begin or what to do beyond the need to clean and swab and to keep his head back so that he might breathe.

'Thank you, Doctor,' Tupki whispered.

He began to mumble words I did not understand – prayers, I realized – the father wishing every moment of the son's agony were his own. In my own language, I cursed my uselessness over and over again. Our two voices mingled low, neither heard amidst the thousand calls of the jungle night. The heat crushed down.

IV

I do not know how long we were there clustered on the ground at the foot of the stairs. After Kanari, I cleaned Tupki's face as best as I could, listening to Felipe creak back and forth on the wooden floor of the *comedor* doing God knows what. I called him down three or four times but either he did not hear me or he was pretending not to. Eventually, I went up and ordered him to get me water from the kitchen. He came back quickly with one of Sole's big wooden buckets. But he would not stay and help.

'Why are you still here?' The Boy's associate returned and stood above us. 'Everyone is coming to eat here now. It's been a long day – with not much to get hard about.'

He kicked at Kanari. 'I would get him out of here if I was you, Doctor. Somebody might decide they want a face to stick their dick in after dinner. We like them better without teeth.'

I shouted for Felipe but still he did not come. Panicked, we rose – Tupki and I staggering on either side of Kanari and the three of us bound together like a single animal. I thought somehow to drag father and son to my hut and there gather Lothar and Kim.

Kanari stumbled and swayed, each breath a wet hiss and a low gurgle. I had no sense of Tupki's condition save for his stopping every few steps to reach for his ear. I had cut the binding from his hands. The remains of the snake were blasted against his neck where my wet rag had not reached and I could feel viscera caked on his forearm where we gripped one another round Kanari's back.

The voice came from behind us. 'Let me help. I heard the gun. I was watching.' Lothar stepped out from behind the kapok tree and slipped under Kanari's arm to take the weight from Tupki. 'Is Felipe here?'

'No.'

'Good.' He gripped my arm and we locked together. 'We can't trust him now.'

'What? Why?' I tried to see Lothar's face behind Kanari's head. 'I don't understand. What's happening? What is—'

'Let's walk. It's possible to get to the river through the jungle if we go past the washhouses. It's not far. We just have to cut through. We need to go now – *schnell* – are you OK?'

'Kanari won't get through. He can't walk. He'll bleed to death.'

'No choice,' Lothar said. 'They'll come for him tomorrow and beat him to death – even if he lasts the night. But if we get him to a boat, then maybe he has a chance. His brothers will take him down the river.'

'Lothar, what is happening?'

'Kanari double-crossed Cordero. He's been taking cocaine money as well. He's been telling some of the cocaine militias where the soldiers are. There was an ambush today on one of the rivers. Two soldiers have been injured. Believe me – Lugo will kill him as soon as Cordero says it is OK. And he won't do it nicely.' Lothar shifted Kanari's weight and I felt his head turn towards me. 'Lift him up more if you can.'

I re-gripped Lothar's arm; blood and sweat like glue between us.

'Where do we get a boat?'

'We go through the jungle then I walk along the river-bank and get one from the jetty.'

'In the dark?'

'Yes.'

'And if there's a guard?'

'Then I'll be careful and I'll be quiet.'

I did not think it possible that we would get Kanari out even had we daylight and ten more men. But I had moved beyond care. If we were caught, then so be it. Perhaps we would be arrested, I thought, but still, in my heart, I did not believe they would physically harm us. And this time there would be more than a report – photographs, witnesses, names, newspapers, everything.

Tupki was reeling along behind us. We were passing the first hut.

'Sole?' I asked. 'Kim?'

'Together,' Lothar said. 'Kim came out when they shot the gun and we stopped her going back to the *comedor*. Nothing more will happen tonight. Kanari is not important to them. Not really. And they are not going to think you are capable of cutting your way out to the river with him in this state.' He leant back and looked across at me behind Kanari's head and for the first time I saw the whites of his eyes in the darkness. 'It's over,' he said. 'I'm sorry. We leave tomorrow. We get Kim and Sole and Felipe – if he wants to come – and we get out of here.'

V

The insect trill was like some great tinnitus. Lothar's light swept the black. Fronds and leaves and twine lit up, white as fish bones in the darkness all around. Sometimes there was space, a deeper blackness; other times the forest closed in and we stood a moment – isolated, hemmed, claustrophobic. When we stopped to breathe, a dozen creatures gorged on our blood.

Lothar was ahead, his machete drawn, cutting a way through the undergrowth. We lurched and shuffled into a shallow dip. I felt Tupki's support weakening further and the weight of Kanari threatening to rip my shoulder from its root. He had given up tipping his head back and we were dragging him more and more. He groaned and sobbed. My face was smarting from a hundred scratches. I cursed. Tupki murmured. Lothar hacked at the jungle. On we went: another step, another step.

I began to believe that both of them would die. I saw José and Mubb – waiting, day after day, for their father to return, until, understanding before his brother and suddenly a five-year-old adult, José began the kitten game.

We stopped. I felt water thickening in my boots and I could smell wetness and rotting more intensely. Above, the fireflies vibrated back and forth in quick-shifting smears of light.

'The shortest route is up there.' Lothar came back towards us, his torch bright in my eyes a moment. 'The river is just on the other side. But obviously we cannot climb. So . . . So we must follow this stream down there a little way. It's not good to be in the water. But we have no choice.'

'How far?' I asked.

'Eighty metres.'

'That's not too bad.'

'We have only come sixty metres since we left the washhouse.'

Lothar spoke to Tupki in a language I did not understand. Then he took off his head torch and handed it to the old man.

'All kinds of *Scheiße* live in this swamp water,' he said.

'Caiman?'

'Yes.' We shouldered Kanari. 'But at least we can see their eyes shining with the torch. It's the other stuff that will kill us.'

The going was easier in the riverbed with Lothar on the other side; between us, we were almost able to lift Kanari off his feet. I became reckless with tiredness or shock or euphoria or fear and I tried to hurry. But the water suddenly deepened and I sank to my knees and pulled all three of us down sideways in the darkness and the mud – thrashing, sodden.

Lothar cursed. Kanari was howling, his face half submerged in the filthy water inches from my own. I tasted mud. His cries were terrible. Tupki had loped back and was begging him to be quiet. Lothar somehow covered his mouth in the darkness, muffling him. Something else was writhing in the water with us, churning against my legs. I struggled up. We bent to drag Kanari to his feet.

'Ready?' Lothar asked. There was no word of reproof. 'Let's keep going, then,' he said.

We came at last to a narrow tongue of mud that spat us out by the deeper darkness of the main river. There was a beach of sorts further along.

'It will take me half an hour to fetch a boat,' Lothar said.

'How are you going to get back along the river?'

'Carefully.'

It was impossible to see – and I could not guess his expression.

'Don't move from here.'

And with that he was gone.

We sat down. Tupki rested Kanari's head on his lap.

I wanted to wipe my eyes but no part of my clothing remained that was not soaked.

'I will look,' Tupki murmured.

He shone Lothar's beam around us in ever-wider circles. I did not understand at first. Then, across the bed of the shrunken stream down which we had come, where the far bank gave place to reeds, he stopped. No more than forty paces away: twin fiery diamonds were glowing in the light; eerie and empty, low to the ground, the eyes of the black caiman. At such a distance, it was impossible to tell if they belonged to some fifteen-foot leviathan or a mere hatchling.

We counted four. But even the near-futile precaution of placing them lasted no more than a few moments. For now came pouring out of the darkness, one by one, then dozen by dozen, a quivering swirl of giant moths. Heavy-winged as bats, they flitted about our faces, swarming out of the night, landing on us as fast as we could swipe them off, licking at our skin like a thousand tiny feathers. The light had attracted them and now they sought the salt of our sweat. Tupki extinguished his torch. I leapt up, swatting. I stumbled six paces in the darkness. They clung to me. I ran in what I thought was a tight circle, fearing to stray, fearing to fall.

When at last I felt them almost gone, I called out. Tupki flicked his torch on again a moment. He had not moved. He was sat fifteen paces away, holding Kanari in his arms, moths still fluttering all around his head so that it seemed grotesquely swollen and indeterminate. I walked back to wait beside them – the father and the son sat by the black water on the dark wet earth.

EIGHT

I

We hid the boat on the riverbank, the mists still curling over the water. Then we passed quickly through the milky light of the forest dawn and emerged like spies by the washhouse; the walk, this time, less than ten minutes.

'We need a story,' Lothar said, 'they will question us before we can leave.'

I glanced around. In fifteen minutes it would be fully light. I spoke quickly and softly. 'I'll say that I took Tupki back to my hut with Kanari. I cleaned them up as they asked. I left them both in there. When I went to find them this morning, they were gone. I'll tell them that I don't sleep in my own hut very often – the Judge knows about Sole. Whoever sees her first makes sure that she corroborates.'

'Good.' His sad grey eyes met mine a moment. 'We pack up the expensive stuff and we leave. See you in the lab.'

'One hour,' I nodded. 'Don't let Kim go to the *comedor* if you get to her before I do.'

He touched his hat. Then, carefully, he held aside a tangle of the undergrowth and ducked beneath. He was going to go back for the boat and take it round to what was left of the jetty so that it would not be counted as missing and cast unnecessary suspicion on us. He was confident that he would not be seen. If there was a guard, he would stop short and come back.

My plan was to walk back from the washhouse as though I had come down as normal to shower, as though I had taken no part in anything but love and sleep. I would steal a damp towel from the laundry and wrap myself in that to go back. The main thing was to hide the clothes I was wearing in case the soldiers were already looking for me; they would not believe that anybody would have spent the night in such a state – not unless they had been crawling through the jungle with a bleeding man.

We had arrived at Tupki's house, half relieved, half despairing. Two of the oldest brothers had been woken and they had left immediately with an unconscious Kanari in his father's boat. By torchlight and in whispers, his mother and his sisters had swept through the rooms gathering all that they could carry, loading it into their second boat with Lothar, hastening back and forth from the river in overburdened relays.

Meanwhile, in the grove of açai palms, we hung Tupki's biggest lamp. And there we dug the ground – another brother, Virima and I – mutely directed by Tupki, his haggard face streaked in the river's mud, the filth of the snake and his own son's blood. Close by, sat on a fallen log, José and Mubb kept silent watch – José pointing his flashlight on our spades while Mubb lay resting in his brother's thin little lap, looking out with wide infant eyes from his blanket.

When we pulled it out of the earth, the small metal box contained one hundred and ten American dollars, jewellery worth less than thirty, a man's watch and a necklace of jaguar's teeth. Tupki placed these items carefully in a small purse attached to a body belt and handed them to Virima, who raised her T-shirt and wrapped it around her waist.

As we approached the rise of the bank, we became aware that there was too much light and noise coming from the river. Fear slowed our steps and sped our hearts. Tupki and I went ahead – careful, silent, torch dark.

In a second, we understood everything. There were no soldiers but the brothers were back. I saw Tupki curl over beside me on the ridge, hands to his knees, tearless sobs rising from somewhere deep within him. Kanari was still lying in the boat. He was dead.

I came out of the wash room and looked for somewhere close to hide my clothes. There was half a parting in the forest wall at the very furthest reach, past the two big sinks that we used for laundry. Wearing my boots untied and wrapped only in two damp towels, I hurried that way.

I eased through the gap, conscious of the exposure of my skin. Three or four more paces and the shade gathered and deepened. Another half-dozen would do it – inside a hollow tree, perhaps. I stood on my laces, stumbled and looked down. The ground beneath my boots had been recently dug, the covering of the leaves was much thinner, the colour of the earth red. I kicked a little at a root. Then I stopped. A cold feeling ran up my spine and hunched my shoulders. I was standing on a shallow grave – barely that. The root was not a root but a dead man's arm thinly covered in soil – a rotting hand, insects, fingernails.

II

In my hut, I dressed quickly. I had thought for a second that it might be Jorge. But then I realized that this must have been the business of the Boy and his associate on the night that Sole and I had sat up listening to the squeaking of the cart. They had tortured the prisoner to death. And they had barely bothered to hide his body.

I hurried out into the clearing, glancing up the path towards the kapok tree, expecting to see soldiers at any moment. The door of Sole's hut was locked. I called her name. No answer. It was still less than an hour past dawn but already the heat was renewing itself. I considered going straight to the *comedor* but crossed instead to the lab as was our agreement.

Kim looked up sharply as I entered the dry room.

'Have you seen Lothar?' I asked.

'Yes. He just knocked on my door looking like he had been in some kind of mud bath.' She shook her head.

'What did he say?'

'He told me to get dressed and come here and to make a copy of everything onto the spare hard drive and then to wait for you.' She puffed out her cheeks. 'But the battery is as low as it has ever been. It's the photo catalogue that's taking the time.' She pushed back on the wheels of the chair. 'The generators didn't come on last night. We can't charge anything. The computer won't last more than another half an hour. The satellite isn't working either. What the hell is going on?'

'Let's sit.' I backed out of the plastic screen and she

followed me into the main area. 'Have you been up to the *comedor*?'

'No. I came straight here like Lothar said.' She swung her legs over the bench. 'What's happening? Someone fired a gun last night and Sole says you went out somewhere.'

'Where is Sole now?'

'I don't know. She disappeared with the mud monster.'

I drew a deeper breath. 'We're leaving, Kim – today. As soon as we can. After we've got the PCR and the field scopes from the storage hut.'

'No.' Anger tightened her brow. 'Why? No. I thought—'

'Kim – Kanari is dead.'

The shock stilled her.

'After you left, Lugo came back. They beat Kanari badly. I . . . I tried to clean him up. And I don't even know why or what he died from . . . But he died – on the boat. His brothers were taking him to a doctor.'

I began to tell her everything – about the violence, the trip to Tupki's house and all that had happened there. I told her, too, about the fire on that first night – the Boy, the white-hot rod. I told her that I believed the body of the prisoner was buried just beyond the washhouse. She listened in deepening silence, resting her head in her palms with her thumbs half covering her ears. When I had finished, she asked: 'Where will they go?'

'To one of the river cities – a favela, probably. Lothar says that's where they all end up.'

My eyes sought our formicarium, travelling over the plastic tanks and the test-tube trees where we kept our colonies and our specimens. When I looked back, though she had made no sound, there were tears on Kim's face.

I rose and went around to her but she motioned me away so I wandered over to look through the glass at my *Daceton*. When ants die, their sisters bear them from the nest. They recognize the pheromone. You can paint a live ant with the death chemical and its sisters will pick it up and carry it out. But you cannot paint a dead ant with anything that will make the others believe it is still alive and carry it back in again.

'I think we should stay,' she began. 'I think we should finish our work. I don't think it's dangerous for us.'

I did not speak. Her face fell. Instantly, she regretted what she had said – the 'we' and the 'them' – but still her eyes glittered.

'I think we should finish what Dr Quinn started,' she repeated.

'We will come back,' I said. 'We will finish this work, Kim. But now we need to go out to the storage hut and bring back everything that belongs to the department.

Then we pack up and we leave. I'm going to tell people what's happening here.'

'You don't *know* what is happening here.'

Another voice spoke. 'I do. I know.'

We looked around. Lothar must have stepped inside as we were speaking.

'I know what is happening here,' he said. 'We are in the middle of a small war. That is what is happening.' Though he had washed and dressed in clean clothes, the night seemed to cling to him and add a weight of weariness to his shoulders as he straddled the bench. 'The Colonel is cleaning up the area because there's an oil company coming in.'

'What?' I came over and sat down beside Kim. 'They're prospecting – right here?'

Lothar raised two fingers to his temples, pushed back the brim of his hat and nodded slowly. 'Welcome to Lot 13, *meine Freunde*,' he said. 'They have granted the rights to the subsoil. I thought we were too deep into the interior. But I was wrong. According to the reports, we can expect seismic testing and pipelines and a hundred and sixty-six heliports and more than a thousand unloading zones for the drilling equipment. And that's before they even find a single drop.'

'I don't get it. What do you mean, the Colonel is cleaning up?' Kim asked.

'I mean cleansing. Maybe that's a better word.'

'Cleansing what?' Kim persisted.

'Not what – who.' He spoke with a deep and heavy resignation that I had never heard from him before. 'To begin with – the drug-processors and the drug-traffickers. That's why there is a war. They're forcing them off the map. These rivers – they're important because they flow down from the coca-growing fields. It was quiet in the past because there was an agreement.' He shrugged. 'Last year, the army was *supporting* the drugs people – a different colonel, a different policy. Now, they have lowered the royalties on oil exploration, which has intensified interest from foreign companies. So there are many new concessions becoming active. But the oil companies, they will not pay the government all the money on the deals unless they have guarantees that the Indians and the traffickers will not attack them.'

'What about the Judge?' Kim's voice had lost all vitality. 'What about the registration?'

Lothar shook his head slowly. 'Because of previous actions from the pressure groups, the oil companies also ask for the cover of the vote. The registration is real but only so far: they want to collect all the new voters possible – so they can fix a referendum and make it look OK if they need to. But they will only start bribing the Indians once they have cleaned up the drugs people. What is happening right now is that the traffickers are fighting back – and they have some very good weapons and plenty of money.' He scoffed. 'And – oh yes – I am told that the oil people will be setting up health-care centres, too, right next door to Tord's schools.'

'What about the Matsigenka and the others?' I asked. 'What's happening to them?'

'It is the same as it is every time – the Indians are caught in the middle. Some of them are being paid by the traffickers to come out of the forest and kill the soldiers. Some of them are being paid by the soldiers to go back into the forest and kill the traffickers. Some of them – Sole's people – are furious because they are organized and they have already been made to buy their own land rights off a government that is nothing to do with them – only to find that this same government can still sell the subsoil out from under them. Others are happy for the oilmen to come and pay them for what they cannot use themselves – after all money is always money.' The mobility had gone from Lothar's face; it was as though his rubbery features had finally set hard. 'Half a village maybe wants the white man's bribes and half a village maybe wants the white men dead. There are disputes even between families – never mind the different tribes.' He took off his hat and laid it down slowly. 'It is a total mess. Everybody is fighting everybody. And of course, the traffickers and the soldiers cannot distinguish between one tribe and another. So people are being murdered for all the small wrong reasons as well as all the big wrong reasons.'

We were both silent.

Lothar looked at the roof that he had helped Quinn to build. 'Then there are still a few Indians – some Yora, the Mashco Piro – who never wanted to buy or sell anything. And they are disappearing deeper into the forest to get away – disappearing straight into the territories of other Indians . . . Which means more displacement and more fighting between groups . . . More of what we seem to be best at: *Scheiße* and death.'

Kim glanced sideways at me. 'How does this end, Lothar?' she asked quietly.

'It doesn't. It just goes on and on. When there is nothing left, there will be nothing more to fight for. We are not a moderate species. We are swarming across the world.'

I swung my legs back over the bench. 'Listen: we need to go out to the storage hut now and collect our stuff. We need to go together and we need to stay together. I will see if Felipe can help us. Then we must start packing things up here and—'

The door was thrown open and Cordero entered followed by three men.

The lab seemed to shrink – close and full with human

bodies. I felt the sudden, tight-keyed, animal concentration of the others.

Heavy booted, procedural, the soldiers took up station either side of their leader, their eyes incurious beneath their caps.

Cordero hooked his thumb through his belt as he assessed our workplace. His gaze halted a moment on the dry room beyond.

'You are well kitted out here,' he said. 'Impressive.'

Nobody spoke.

'You are powered by the main generator? Or you have your own?'

He already knew the answer.

'We use communal power,' I said.

'Oil.' He nodded slowly.

'What do you want, Colonel? This is a scientific laboratory. We're working.'

'So I see.' He thinned his nose. 'Very well, let me ask directly: are the prisoners dead?'

'We do not—'

'Dr Forle, if you don't mind. I would like to have a simple answer.'

Kim spoke. 'What prisoners?'

'Please, Miss Van der Kisten, I'm extremely busy. One of my men has been seriously injured. Now I'm told the prisoners have gone.'

'Miss Van der Kisten went to bed,' I said, 'last night – before your soldiers came in.'

Kim looked at me and then at Cordero. 'I went to bed before Tupki arrived, if that is who you are talking about.' She was careful to use his name – and placed a world of defiance in the emphasis with which she pronounced it. 'Your Judge was drunk again. He assaulted me. So I left. I don't know what happened afterwards.'

The Colonel inclined towards his aide, who stood, vaguely effete, and nodded assent – he must have been one of those who had arrived with Lugo.

'Good,' Cordero said. 'And you? What is your name?'

Lothar had replaced his hat. 'I am the same. I was at the *comedor*. I left a little later when the Judge went to collect some beer. I didn't come back.'

'I did not ask you if you came back.'

Lothar was silent. Beneath his brim, I could not tell where his eyes were. He had not given his name.

Again Cordero looked to the other. Again the nod.

'And so we are back to you once more, Dr Forle. What happened to you last night? Where are my prisoners?'

'I don't know.'

'You don't know?'

'I took them to my hut. I dressed their wounds. I took pictures of their injuries. And gave them what painkillers I had. Naturally, I did not sleep in there myself.'

'Where did you sleep?'

'That's not relevant. I didn't sleep with the prisoners – with Tupki and Kanari.'

For the first time, I saw the contours of anger in Cordero's features.

'Dr Forle, are my prisoners alive?'

'I would be very surprised after what your men did to them.'

'Let me explain something to you.' He passed his tongue from cheek to cheek. 'There are several lawless groups in this area – well supplied with arms and transportation. They seek to sabotage our efforts to ensure that the people here are registered and that some sort of order is created and maintained. But I am determined not to let that happen. This country *will* develop wherever and however it can. But my job is not made any easier by the fact that these terrorist groups are somehow being told of our positions and our plans ahead of time. My men were ambushed yesterday and again on tour this morning.' He took out a white handkerchief and dabbed at his crown. 'Now, I understand that you have chosen to take the side of these two drunks for some reason. I had thought them inconsequential. But this morning ... I am forced to reconsider. Another of my men has been shot and this time seriously wounded. The situation is deteriorating.' A second dab, of his neck. 'You see the problem:

we have an informant in our midst and had the prisoners still been here, we might have been able to eliminate them as suspects. Likewise if we knew them to be dead.' He put away the handkerchief, folding it down deep into his groin pocket. 'But now – because of my stupidity in allowing you to play the doctor – we are unable to draw that conclusion. You are helping nobody, Dr Forle. So, please, one more time: what did you do with the prisoners? Is that boy alive?'

One of the other men cleared catarrh from his throat and for a moment I thought he might spit.

'The boy is dead,' I said. 'And when he left my sight the father was in no fit state to give anyone any information about anything. I hold you personally responsible for what has happened.'

'When was this?'

'About two hours before dawn.'

'Good. Thank you. That is something.' Cordero hoisted up the muscles around his mouth before releasing them just as suddenly. 'We can be sure that this morning was nothing to do with those two at least.'

'Not unless the dead have learned to speak,' I murmured.

'Which means that we will have to look somewhere else for our spy. What is in there?'

'That is our dry room.'

'Who uses that computer?'

'Everybody within a radius of fifty miles who can type and quite a few that can't.' I shifted so that I was more squarely on to him. 'Colonel, we are leaving the Station today.'

'I'm afraid that I cannot let you leave.'

'All the same, we will be packing up and leaving today. Unless you intend to keep us here by force.'

'It is too dangerous for you to go anywhere at the moment. And there are now questions that we do not have the answers to.'

'Then you'd better ask them quickly, Colonel, because we will be gone as soon as we have collected and packed up our equipment. These people are my responsibility. Just as your men are yours.'

'Captain Lugo will be back in the hour. I will know more then.' He smiled his mechanical smile. 'I will see you at the *comedor* in two hours, please, with Miss Van der Kisten and the German.'

'We won't be here in two hours.' A monkey was running across the roof. 'As I said, we will be out collecting our equipment.'

'Then you will be accompanied there and we will speak after you return,' he said. 'To be clear: you do not leave the Station without my order. For your own security. The captain will detail some men to come with you on the river.'

'I doubt that whatever you are afraid of hunts scientists, Colonel.'

He stepped forward towards me and in that moment I saw the strange disunity between the heaviness of his frame and the delicacy of movement. And I saw how violence might breed in the cracks between.

'Is this the camera that you took your pictures of the prisoners on?' he asked.

'That is the camera that we use for our exp—'

I got no further. Carefully, so as to avoid an unnecessary splash, he placed the camera into the wooden pail of water Felipe had so recently filled.

III

On the far side of the kapok tree, we saw that the *comedor* had been all but overrun. There were people everywhere – milling, mustering. A temporary shelter had been erected in front. Beneath its blue tarpaulin, there was a wooden bench on which metal cooking trays, plates, mugs and pots had been placed; and behind this bench stood . . . Jorge. He was wearing uniform. He had pulled down his cap regulation-low on the brow, mirroring the men he served and preventing him seeing too much of what went on about him.

The soldiers slouched forward in a desultory line, their plates held like idle tambourines, until they reached the front and they offered them up, suddenly attentive. There must have been a dozen – all of them armed.

To our left, two smaller temporary shelters now flanked the mouth of the river path. More tarpaulins. Two desks; at one sat the Judge; and at the other, Felipe. Men, mostly tribesmen, grouped and drifted around, many of them holding incongruous pieces of paper, careful not to go near the soldiers or the *comedor*. Felipe appeared to be admitting them; one by one, they sat in the chair opposite him while he took their pictures. The Judge, meanwhile, looked like he was then discharging them – more or less immediately. A soldier was handing out parcels.

My eyes went back to the *comedor* and fixed themselves above Jorge's galley. Cordero was enthroned at the top of the steps. He had moved our dining table to the very edge and there he sat behind it, not facing outwards like the Judge but sideways on, as though the whole clearing were his office and the entire forest his barracks. He raised his head like a grazing bull disturbed.

Sole was serving him coffee. She was wearing one of Tord's baseball caps – also pulled down low. We had spoken. There was no question that she would be leaving with us as soon as we came back. She just had to get through the next four hours.

I stopped. The mud was cracking from the lack of rain. I knew that it would be foolish to draw attention to her in front of Cordero and his men. But, still, it cost me to turn away.

As we approached the river path, Felipe looked up and tried to smile but guilt and self-reproach were asphyxiating him and his grin looked more like some twisted choke. The Judge did not pause in his work.

IV

We took both of our boats. Three of Cordero's men followed us. They watched us beach the first and then they turned and sped off. I had agreed to a second meeting with Cordero. There was nothing to be gained from refusing and – now that he knew about Tupki and Kanari – there was nothing he could ask me that I could not answer directly. I wanted only to be able to secure our equipment and the lab and then leave. If he was going to arrest us, then I assumed he would arrest us regardless. If they escorted us out, then so be it.

Paradoxically, the river seemed friendlier than before – busier, certainly. Canoes passed. There were families, groups of three and four – many of them presumably travelling to the registration in the hope of whatever was being handed out. Some of them waved. Some of them did not. There were hand-paddled craft as well as *peque-peques*. But nobody paid us any special attention. And we were not unduly worried about being in the forest. As Lothar said, while the soldiers were based at the Station, then that was the most dangerous place to be; and everybody for dozens of miles around knew exactly who we were and what we were doing.

We had decided to work in relays for speed. Lothar carried from the storage hut and dropped off on our grey tarpaulin – roughly halfway along the path; I picked up from there and ferried almost as far as the river. Kim waited on a clay rise, standing on a second tarpaulin from where she could see the boats, then, as I dropped off, she took things down to stow. All the kit that we had taken out to the store haphazardly, one day at a time, now had to be brought back in a single trip. Besides the DNA amplifier, I wanted to collect the field scopes, the spare GPS, the camping gear, the emergency and first-aid bags. Everything that we used was owned by our department – under-resourced, under-funded – and I was determined to do my duty even if I was leaving my post. But after two relays – each a full fifteen minutes there and back – I was changing my mind. I wanted to be going.

I reached the tarpaulin where Lothar had left another load and stood a moment beneath a great *cumaru* tree. Ants were streaming up and down and around the trunk in thin diagonals like shiny black necklaces strewn by passing spirits. *Odontomachus bauri*. Trap-jaw ants; 130 microseconds to spring shut their mandibles and no living creature in the world that moved quicker. I had never seen them in the field before.

I resolved to do this relay and then wait for Lothar on the next return. I slung the additional pack over my shoulder and picked up the box of field scopes and the GPS and set off back down the trail. The jungle was rinsing every last mineral from my body. At a fallen trunk, I put down the box to swig my water.

Something ripped my shirt over my head.

Or this – in the quarter second – was all that I could think had happened. There was darkness – intense heat – but even before the panic had detonated, I was pushed over by a forceful weight – a body – or arms – or shoulders – some kind of animal – something that had barrelled into me with great force. And so I went down in worsening confusion – blind – crashing into the trunk ahead – calling out – my wrist twisting against some branch I could not see. I struggled to move, to find my feet – and now my mind came racing into the moment, chasing my body, and hot fear flooded my veins. What animal so big? Pain bloomed. I felt myself being yanked up and my head jerked back so that I thought my neck was about to be broken. I began to fight and flail and still I could not properly stand. Voices. And then horrified, understanding . . . that this was a hood and that I was a prisoner. The sweat on my back ran cold and I stood at last, dead still, sucking hotter and hotter air closer and closer about my face while a strange reason – or wild irrational shock – numbed the pain and shut the panic. And already I was assessing, bargaining, pleading – as my tongue found a rough mouth hole and my ears strained and I felt a rope being bound over my wrists.

V

Cracks of light. I was standing in a rough storage hut – similar to our own. The floor was dirt and little else. The roof sloped: as I faced the door, it reached up to my right no more than a foot higher than myself; to my left it came down as low as my knees into the deeper darkness. I paced carefully as my eyes adjusted: three and a half strides long, two and a half wide – though I must bend and then crouch to guess the width. Further into the gloom, where the roof was lowest, there were piled plastic sacks of the kind used for chemicals or fertilizer.

Moving spider-fingered down the wall, I put my eye to each light. If I was anywhere near another building, I could not see it. My guess was that I was in a clearing – though not a large one; nothing more than where two paths met, perhaps.

Panic swept through me like a storm again. I yelled and gripped the cross beam with my hand and shook and juddered at the door. But nothing gave. I threw my shoulder at it. Nothing. I kicked – again and again and then with my heel. The door moved a quarter of an inch each time – no more. My foot began to throb with the pain and I stopped, resting my hands on my knees, sweat dripping off me, breathing hard.

I forced myself to consider. I forced myself to be rational.

They had removed the hood so that I could walk. I had stumbled barely thirty paces and yet already my eyes recognized nothing of where I was – the same path, some other? With my hands roughly bound, I had followed the bare, brown, sweat-covered back of the anonymous man in front. He had never once turned. I had not been able to tell what kind of man he was or how old. He had not stopped, but somehow, though forever ten steps ahead, he had measured his pace to slow a little as I slowed and speed up whenever I did the same.

I could not be sure how long we walked. They took my watch along with my pack. My only gauge was that it had not grown dark. Twice I attempted to look around to see the faces of the men behind me, but each time I was met with a blow to my shoulder blade that sent me stumbling forward, crying out with pain.

When, at last, the figure stopped, I automatically did the same – as if mesmerized into mirroring his every action. But before I could shake off this spell the hood was back on my head. Then they cut the cord that bound my wrists and led me blindly by the hand – something momentarily tender and out of place in the gesture – before they kicked me inside the hut.

Bellowing, I tugged at the hood but it caught on my neck, the cord cutting hard into my flesh and the underside of the jawbone where it would not slip past my chin. I wrenched and twisted until I thought I would garrotte myself. Hot angry tears rose. I clawed at the mouth hole to make it wider; it ripped – easily – stupidly. I tore the more until the hood fell around me like a bandanna and I found myself in wider darkness.

I squatted now with my back to the hut door, listening to the forest squawk and trill. Fear came in pulses, threatening to take hold like the onset of sea-sickness. But each time it came, I pressed my back harder against the wood.

I could not have walked more than two hours. Eight

miles at the outside, then. Much less in all likelihood. But I had no idea who had put me in here or why. Cordero's men, the soldiers, the traffickers, other guerrillas, affiliated tribesmen, unaffiliated tribesmen? Was I to be used in some way? Was I to be ransomed? I knew it was not un-contacted Indians: my captors had spoken only two words to me, 'walk' and 'now', and though the accent was thick, the language was Spanish. Neither did the uncontacted have keys and storage huts. Who though? They had not spoken among themselves. I had guessed there were three but there could have been more. My mind circled lower and lower. If the intention was to kill me, then why bring me here at all? There would be water then, and there would be food. They would surely keep me alive. They would return. In any case, I told myself, these conjectures did not matter because there were only two possibilities: that either I found a way out myself or my captors let me out.

I stood up. I must check every board, every plank and every section of the roof. I must be systematic. I would escape.

I began at the door. I pushed at the bottom – then I pressed and kicked and tapped all the way up as far as I could reach. Next, the roof above the door. I reached up and thumped as best as I could. I would work my way clockwise around the hut.

*

Voices.

A language I did not recognize. Tribesmen?

Human voices. But sing-song, then chattering, then soft – 'ock-olock-olock'.

I moved from crack to crack hoping for a sightline. But I could see nothing. A shadow? The human shape? I could not be sure. The gloaming was thickening the forest from trunk to trunk. Now there was murmuring, calling; strange ethereal sounds that I could not understand. Two, three different voices – it was impossible to tell. Where were they? I chased along the walls.

I called out. Waited. Called out a second time. Listened.

A moment's stillness – silence almost.

I thumped on the door. I kicked. I shouted with all that my lungs could summon. I stopped. Listened again. Nothing. Nothing. The jungle noises were rushing in once more to fill the empty air – the toothcomb and the croaks and evening calls of the birds and no sound that was human. I pounded at the door. I was nothing but my physical self, howling inside my cage.

It was bitter to return to my task. More bitter still that the cracks were becoming merely smears and I was working with my hands rather than with my eyes. The wood was rough and splintered. I was reckless and despairing. And in the gathering darkness, my discomfort fed on itself and was soon grown to misery. Nothing was loose. Nothing moved. The cuticles of my toes were hurting in my boots from the kicking. I was stung and bitten and raging with the itchy compulsion to tear off my skin. My nails were cut, and my shirt clung to my back. I had tried to urinate through one of the gaps, using my fingers as a barrier to protect myself against the wood, but I had succeeded only in fouling my hands. And now I could no longer continue with my task because the only sections left were the low walls where the roof sloped down above the plastic sacks and I didn't want to lie in the dirt and probe blindly in the darkness. All this in less than six hours. I had no appetite, I was not thirsty, but I wanted to wash. I wanted to be clean. I was afraid of losing my spirit. And this fear merged into all my other fears until fear was my all.

The night began. The blackness was soon so deep that I could only see my hands when I raised them before my eyes. Whatever crawled on the floor, I could not crouch on my heels any longer. I allowed myself to sit in the dirt and it eased the pain.

Unsleeping, awake, asleep, awake again, I found I was slapping at my skin. The near-darkness whined with sound. With my head in my knees, I sought other places for my mind to go. But I could think only of the immensity of the forest, the river networks, the paths, the billion trees, this clearing, the hut and my body locked inside, isolated.

Against this loneliness, I spoke to myself. Are you injured? No – no, I'm all right, I'm OK. Good. You're lucky. They didn't really hurt you. You need to keep yourself injury free. You need to look after yourself the best you can. What about water? Shut up. You can last three days, even here. Longer. You wouldn't give it a second thought if you were heading to the station. You don't drink water for days at home. So put it out of your mind. And food will not be serious for a long time either. So you're not going to starve. Now, right now, you have your strength and you're not depleted. So think. Be systematic. This is just a shack. You can get out of here tomorrow. Stop wasting your energy, man.

There was surprising comfort in this. I knew well that it was absurd, but somehow the sound of my own voice stabilized me, held back the surge and press of other thoughts. And after a while, I no longer thought of it as my own voice. Time and space became as one – both dark, all around and neither passing.

In the blackness something moved and into my mind came the image of a snake. No longer a species I had memorized but a living creature of the night, worming beneath the walls, between the fissures, alive as I was, no more than a foot long, routinely fanged with a venom that would kill me – agonizingly, without significance or purpose.

I leapt up.

I would carry on. Anything would be better than this. Unseeing, I heaved out bags until I could wave my invisible arm in the empty space. Then I lay down on the bare earth and edged backwards, my hands held above my head, groping for the far wooden walls in the darkness.

Beading.

The telltale tunnels of the termites.

VI

Dawn. I had a gap six inches tall by eighteen inches wide, beyond which, if I twisted, I could just about see the tangle of plants. I dug in my heels and thrust myself deeper until I was close against the far wall, no more than a foot high. The air smelt of the heady sweetness of rot and ferment. My fingers probed back and forth. Towards the corner, the wood was completely beaded and less dense – the pieces came away in my hand more easily like icing from a cake.

The light was strengthening. I reached both my arms above my head in order to grip the cross-spur. I expected more resistance but a single wrench and it dropped to one side. I prised away the verticals above where it had collapsed – one, two, three, four came away easily. I twisted again. The job was almost done: I had a hole through which I could crawl.

I rolled onto my stomach. I wriggled and kicked myself forward. Soil packed beneath my fingernails. I pressed myself into the earth. My shoulders caught. I spat. The wood splintered. And suddenly I was through and looking at the outside wall of the hut in the blue light of the waking forest.

VII

The Termites

Termites are easy prey so they build their little tube-like tunnels across whichever surfaces they must travel – covered walkways inside which they can move protected. Some Indian tribes eat them. The workers have guts stuffed with soil and wood though, and the soldiers' heads harbour glands full of a noxious, sticky liquid that they use in their wars. So the alates, the reproductives, are the ones to seek out. Their dense little bodies are full of proteins and fats.

Raw, they taste of uncooked prawns, but with a nutty or woody flavour. They are easy to find. They wait near the surface of the mound for the rain to come so that they can begin their mating flights. Before they reproduce and burrow out their homes, they need the world to soften.

The termites are the enemies of the ants.

Their kings do not die moments after sex. They live in state with the queens. All the eggs are fertilized – male and female. There are no drone-clones. And yet their progeny cooperate without any need for the sophistry of kin-selection defence. In this way, the termites mock the myrme-cologists. They say, the reason you do not study us is because we live beneath mud and faeces and cannot be easily watched in the lab; they say, the reason you do not study us is that the ants are related to wasps, but we are related to cockroaches; they say the reason you do not study us is to do with human psychology; they say, Homo sapiens, *you fools, do you not see your own reflection staring back at you in the lens of your microscopes and your telescopes, obscuring every object on which you cast your gaze; they say, our soci-ety is more complex than you can imagine; they say, we are born altruists for we cooperate regardless; they say, our sol-diers are made to defend against our enemies the ants, which is why their heads are so big – so that they can block our tunnels against these intruders; they say, our soldiers stand behind one another – and when one falls, the next takes its place; they say, when the intrusion is bigger than a soldier's head, our soldiers range themselves like Roman infantry in tight formations and blindly bite and squirt their toxins through their horns; they say that these sticky sprays kill or immobilize the stinging ants at a ratio of twenty ants lost to only one termite soldier; they say that while their soldiers fight, the workers repair the breached tunnels behind them, leaving all the soldiers stranded beyond the repair with no retreat and so to die; they say blessed are the meek for they might inherit the Earth after all.*

VIII

I found the mound easily. *Nasutitermes costalis.* I scraped and sifted. Workers teemed about the damage. I watched the soldiers scramble. Then I scooped out handfuls of alates – white, winged, plump as beans – and filled my pockets. Three times, I stripped wings and swallowed. I would not be consumed by hunger at least. I would ward off that madness for as long as I could. I smeared the dirt from their mound on my skin against the mosquitoes.

I turned to face the little clearing.

A grey-necked wood rail was singing what remained

of the dawn – its call like hysterical laughter. There were no other buildings. The hut looked feeble from the outside – small, contingent. I circled the clearing seeking where the path came in and where it must surely leave. I breathed in the cool and filled my lungs as if it were some life-giving draught of resilience and resolve.

I found two tracks, diverging, and was pleased that there were no more. I remembered that while they had been leading me by the hand, the ground had sloped down a little. On this remembrance and nothing more, I chose the upward gradient and hurried away, smeared in filth, bruised and bitten and hobbling where I had damaged my toes.

But I had taken no more than two dozen steps before I faltered. Already, the hut looked like a place of great security. I stopped and the sounds of the forest seemed likewise to pause as though to say: you have half an hour's amnesty – be wise. Indecision held me. I considered the possibility of crouching in the forest, waiting for my captors to return. But what then – if ever they did? Attack them? Besides, the march here had not been that long. No, my hope was surely that this path on which I had started remained distinct and clear and soon intersected with that on which we had been carrying our equipment. If I was lucky, I would hit the river. If not, I could always come back to the clearing and walk out of the other side. I set off again.

The light was no longer changing but had settled into its uniform green-brown and time soon became impossible to judge. The heat was itchy and close – and it felt like the jungle was slowly being simmered, warmer and warmer, on the instruction of some malign spirit whose kingdom bustled beneath the thin topsoil. Whether I was following an old rubber trail or one of the Indian paths, I had no idea. Perversely, the places where the jungle thinned were the most treacherous – since the way was clearer where it had been hacked through dense undergrowth.

I became lost only when I turned around and saw that behind me the path forked and I did not know which of the two I had just emerged from. Instantly, the anxiety surged and I felt my fragile composure drowning in the onrushing tide. I retraced my steps. I was still holding to the idea that I might return to the hut if I did not come upon the river this way.

At a low thorn-spiked loop I did not recognize, I turned back on myself again – in the original direction of my flight as I thought – but now the path forked *ahead* of me. I ran on. Ten paces, twenty.

Here, inexplicably, the forest had almost no understorey; the ferocious impenetrability of vine and thorn and frond and bush had mysteriously disappeared. I had the sense of being in a cathedral. There were mighty trees all around me, their trunks soaring like columns towards the distant canopy. I swayed. Creation was singing all about my ears.

Tricks, I thought. Tricks of light and space and time. Everything looked the same. Everything looked different. I felt dizzy. My tongue felt alien in my mouth. I imagined that my sweat was thickening. Fear swamped me again. I dug in my pocket. My hands were cut and smarting and caked in every shade of dirt. I held up the termites in my palms, licking them up, swallowing them alive, greedily, without stripping their wings.

There was wildness in admitting that I was lost – exhilaration in the despair, in the abandonment of even the possibility of caution. Instead, I could now plunge on, fast, wherever the path led, without the anxiety of becoming lost, sure instead that the only new eventuality was that I would *find* my way again.

At every fork in the path, I chose the left and then the right, the left and then the right. My only rule was to alternate. Many times, I reached a wall of tangle and turned around. Panic raced in, overwhelmed me, abated a little, left me alone. My clothes were as a second rancid skin. But I knew that as long as the sweat continued my dehydration was not acute. There was water in the vines but I had no knife, nor could I trust myself to know which was fresh and which poisoned. No senseless running, Lothar had said. No panic. Time does not matter in the forest, only staying alive. Already, I had only the most primitive plan: to find the water and to follow it.

I fell into a trance. My forward stumble was broken only by a new sound or a gap where a tree had fallen and the sun could be glimpsed. Then I would come to my senses and rally. Anger permeated my limbs and I made faster progress and I called it progress. I told myself that I had been deprived for less than forty hours . . . that it was as nothing; a faddish diet; a minor illness; a busy day.

A bird was singing a song that sounded like a sparrow's. I saw my city and my former life and a spirit of great clarity overtook me. And I understood that the old relationship had been reversed; that I had been growing more sane with every step; that I was insane before I came here; that the jungle had not made me mad but that it had returned me to my right senses; that I would survive and come to know and see the world as it truly was; that I would no longer be uncertain, guilty, agitated, distracted, enraged, maddened, preyed upon against my will, isolated, isolating. Then my mind flew up and I saw my own human existence as a flashing moment in the endless expansion of the universe. And I saw, too, that it must always be our compulsion to fashion meaning – from soul to the stars and back again. What else could we do? We must throng the empty heavens with our imaginations. And our imaginations must forever outshine our reason – for how else could we redeem our solitude?

I saw that we are indeed the authors of our own story and that it is ours to write.

And laughing, I walked on.

I ate termites. I invented rituals. I counted steps. At forks, I broke branches and twisted them so that I would know if I came to the same place. I saw a snake and marked the place as evil with a cleft stick. And when I came on them again, I found that these signs made to myself had swollen into a great significance. The news that they conveyed – of intelligence, of concern – this news seemed transcendent to me; though I knew well, with another part of my mind, that the intelligence was only mine and the concern but a genus of my own desperation. And all the while the animal was there – thirstier and thirstier, sickening.

I stopped and stood by a tree bearing berried fruit. Everything was nourishment. Everything was poisonous. I

squeezed a berry and the juice ran. I dared not eat. I had
not seen even a stream.

The gloom was deepening when I heard a faint buzzing.
I was shocked out of my shambling stupor. I stood still.
Then I walked on. The noise rose a little. I walked faster.
I thought that it might be a chainsaw somewhere. I
thought that there must be people ahead – loggers, happy
loggers. I tore on through the undergrowth of the van-
ishing path in the direction of the noise, my hopes
surging uncontrollably. But the buzz had become a whine
and I grew more and more confused and could not tell
where the sound was coming from. I stopped and tried to
listen.

Ahead, I thought.

I stepped forward and caught my foot and the noise
disappeared and there was a great swishing sound and
something dropped from above and swung and slapped
heavy and wet and soft on the side of my face.

I fell and twisted around in the leaf litter. A glinting
black mass of flies swarmed above my head – seething,
shining, oily. Broken-necked and swinging from the vine-
rope, in the midst of their fury, was a dead monkey – its
mouth forced open into a silent scream by an upright
stake through the tongue. Beneath, hanging from its slit
belly by the congealed rope of an umbilical cord, dangled

a blood-stained foetus, curled up, pink and lipless, empty-eyed.

IX

I did not believe in the light until it revealed my legs to me: lifeless, rigid, twin cylinders of mud. I was the first man on Earth. I was numb. I raised my head from my forearm pillow and looked up, following the trunk of my tree far into the indefinite light of the canopy. My mouth was an open sore. I rocked slowly from side to side. My blood was surely thickening; I hauled my arms around my shoulders and so began a shooting agony as it pushed its sticky way into forgotten limbs. For a long time, I dared not climb down.

I lumbered and breathed in the grey-blue brume. I would choose a vine and split it open with my bare hands and I would drink whatever ran there. All my rules were broken.

I could smell the earth caked about my nostrils. Clay. Small pieces of grit had entered my mouth. I could taste the soil.

I could not see. There was a snowstorm in my eyes. My

bowels were squirting and I dared not stand but must crouch, holding myself against a tree. My head grew lighter. The stench of my own faeces caused me to retch.

There was a buzzing all about my ears again. The Meliponinae, stingless bees. Necrophagous, filth-gatherers, collectors of carrion and excrement, consumers of liquid salt; dead flesh not pollen their protein. They crawled across the skin of my legs seeking the sweat of my groin as I tried to run.

A terrible lethargy overcame me. My mind fell silent. I swayed as I walked. I was a dying animal.

When I came into the Devil's Garden, I fell to my knees amidst the wizened plants. One by one, greedily, I ate my ants. They tasted of lemon.

NINE

I

I do not know how long I knelt. But slowly I began to realize that I had all along been contriving a certain kind of madness so as not to allow the real thing; that I had been pretending the end of my endurance so as to garner covert comfort in knowing that it was not yet quite reached. Everything was my own creation: the signs I had made, the ceremonies of my path-taking. The sudden understandings were of no consequence and all that I had told myself to be true I had known in my heart to be false. The self that scrutinized was as unreliable as the self that hid. Everything was delusion except for my body and the forest itself. And my body, which did not lie or imagine or contrive a story where there was none, wanted only to convulse. I tasted acid and bile. Yet there was neither dignity nor cowardice in my dry weeping, only physical relief. The jungle had showed to me the meaning of my humanity: that I must eat and drink and void myself, that

I must sweat and sleep; that I lived only as an organism,
a body, a creature of the earth. I was at site fourteen – the
largest of the Devil's Gardens. The walk to the river was
no more than seven minutes. I would not lose my way.

II

I heard the drone and registered its constancy before my
conscious mind understood its meaning; but in another
moment I was calling out and crashing recklessly forward. This was not the whine of flies, nor the buzz of the
Meliponinae, but the deeper *peque-peque* of a boat.

My tongue was a monstrous clapper in my mouth. My
words were all cries without consonants. The engine had
slowed. I shouted. The ground rose and fell. I struggled
on. I yelled.

The engine had gone. I could not hear anything.

I hurled myself off the path, which had been parallel-
ing the river as if to torture me, and I plunged sideways –
directly towards the water. The undergrowth was dense
and thick and darker here and I had not the strength to
climb. I went on my belly beneath a tangle of thorns
thrown up across my way. I called out once more. I
squirmed the last of the rise until the ground fell away
and – through the trees below me – I could see the river.
I heard my name.

III

'Stay out of the water. *Zum Teufel nochmal.* Stay out of the water. *Komm nicht weiter ins Wasser rein.*'

I hesitated on the bank.

'Stay out of the water.'

I wanted to wash the filth away.

'Stay out of the water.'

Knee deep, beneath the overhanging forest, I stopped, swaying, faint, my heart like a humming bird, the river running cool in my boots. He was driving the boat towards me, drifting in across the glimmering river towards my shore – the cigarette and the hat and the glint of his earring.

I croaked.

He took a hold of the bow rope and leapt out. The sun shot through the splashes. And in a moment he had his shoulder under my arm, his arm around my back.

'Your hands are bleeding, my friend, and we don't want the piranha to know about your injuries, do we?'

He pulled the boat towards us and helped me collapse over the side.

Somewhere in the deeper shade of a long bend, he cut the engine and tied us up. He busied himself with his rucksack, his tobacco fingers working nimbly on the zips and straps.

'First, rehydration tablets.'

He climbed over the seat to where I lay, handed me a plastic bottle, examined my hands and then dropped two pills into the liquid.

'This. Slowly.' He watched me trying to drink. '*Du bist ein warer Glückspilz.*'

The fluid tasted like flat lemonade.

'Slowly,' he repeated.

I was choking and could not swallow.

'Little sips,' he said, pinching together finger and thumb.

'Sole?' I asked.

'OK,' he said. 'They have not bothered her. They're afraid of Cordero. But in a minute. Drink.'

'Where is Kim?'

'She wouldn't leave without you. Believe me, I tried. And now I think they are suspicious of her.'

'For what?'

'One thing at a time. Little sips.'

I drank as he instructed.

'Are you injured?'

I shook my head.

'Are you sick?'

'Diarrhoea.'

He opened another pocket in his pack. The river was strangely still. There were no other boats. I saw macaws flying overhead and thought that it must be the afternoon. I saw the sun through the branches.

'Chew this. Wash it down.' He held my head and placed a tablet into my mouth. 'What have you been eating?' he asked.

'*Myrmelachista schumanni.*'

He laughed his ugly rubber-faced laugh and I thought that he was some kindly forester from one of those old German folk tales after all – kings, kingdoms, princesses, wolves and woodcutters; a lesson in goodwill and self-reliance.

I drank again – with less discomfort. Already, restoration was seeping through me and I was becoming aware of the terrible itching of my skin, a tender pain radiating out across my shoulder blades, a crusted sore on my face, my splintered fingers, my savaged feet, my lips, my arms, a spasm curling in my gut. There was embarrassment, too.

'I didn't get lost,' I said after a while. 'I was kidnapped. Somebody locked me in a hut. I didn't get—'

'Easy, my friend. Easy. I know. I know you didn't get lost. Of course you didn't get lost.'

'You know? How do you—'

'Easy. Drink. Let me do the talking. You drink.' He

reached for his cigarettes. 'It was not Cordero – or Lugo.' He smiled sarcastically. 'They don't have to bother with kidnapping you. They can do whatever they want to you. Believe me.'

'So who?'

'What I know, I will tell you. Drink.' He turned his head to let go the first of his smoke but kept his eyes fixed straight on me. 'I waited for you at the fallen tree. You did not come. I waited longer. I decided not to make another relay. I walked to the boat. Kim was there. You were not. So. Something has happened. I run *schnell* to look again – and, this time, I curse the fact that I am such a pig-mounter – because now that I think to look, I can see clearly on the ground that there has been a problem.'

'Who?'

'Could be a lot of people.' He shrugged. 'But it's not going to be the oil – so it is either drugs or a resurgence of the guerrillas, or it's tribesmen working for one or the other, or even for themselves. Somebody wants to make money out of you, my friend. Or somebody wants the newsmen here. The bigger the coverage, the higher the price.'

'Why did they leave me without water and food?'

'They would have been back,' he said. 'If they wanted to kill you, then there is no place better in the world for murder.' He gestured about himself. 'Anyway, in that moment, it did not matter who it was. I saw that you had been kidnapped. And I was so angry with myself, I could have cut off my own balls.' He pulled at his ear. 'I was sure it was not Cordero. I decided that Kim would be better off with him than standing in the forest so I ran back to the river. I sent her straight to the Station. Then I returned to the fallen tree. I walked up and down until it was dark and I could not see my own stupid feet. But I could not find anything. So. I come back to the river. I sleep in the other boat with my head full of snakes. All night I hear people moving about. I begin to wonder if you are already dead. I begin to wonder if I am already dead.'

He exhaled his smoke through his nose. 'I am awake before the squirrel monkeys have brushed their teeth. But now who should come paddling along nice and quiet in the half-darkness, scaring the *Scheiße* out of me . . . it's Tord. He is searching for me, he says. He has intelligence. He tells me there are more soldiers at the Station and that the place is like a swine farm. He tells me that they are looking for you. He tells me Kim is OK. So. We agree we have to find you by the afternoon or we have to go back and alert every news organization in the world just in case Cordero decides not to do anything about you being disappeared.'

'How were you planning to find me?'

'Let me finish. Tord and me – we go back on the trail together. It is proven that four eyes are better than two – or maybe there are miracles after all – because this time we find the second path. We follow it together and we come to your little place in the jungle. We see the hut. We see the lock. We see the broken wood. I see the termites. I laugh.'

'It wasn't a good joke at the time.'

'But it improves – no? So, now, at the hut Tord says we have a bigger problem. And the little soldier of Jesus is correct. If you had stayed in the prison, we could have all been home by now, eating spider monkey and potatoes. But, no, you have broken out and you could be anywhere in the whole forest.'

Lothar fired a second cigarette. 'It was Tord's idea that we go back to our boats. There are too many paths here, from the rubber days and from everything else. The forest is not so dense either, which makes it easier to get lost. But we are also lucky because here we are between two rivers that meet not so far away and so the gap between is not so wide. Tord thinks that sooner or later you would hit the banks of one of the rivers – unless you managed to walk straight up, deeper into the interior, in which case maybe the Piro would find you and then eat your brain. So we decide to split up. I will go up and down one river and he will go up and down the other.

We meet at five and if nothing, we go back and . . . and then we raise whatever is left in hell that has not already been raised.'

I had finished the fluid. 'I think I saw the Mascho Piro. I heard their voices.'

He looked at me steadily. 'I'm sure they come down this way. People see their signs all the time.'

'Disembowelled monkeys?'

He shrugged and looked away – up the river. 'We are death to them. We make them ill. We rob them of their lands. We murder them. What else can they do? They can't speak to us. They do not *want* to speak to us. But all the signs they leave are as clear as one human being can be to another and they mean the same thing: "Go away. Leave us alone." They don't want democracy or Jesus or even science. We are the needy ones in the relationship. We want them to like us. We want them to agree with what we are doing to the world, we want them to participate. You should drink plain water now.' He handed me a bottle. 'And then try to eat something that doesn't crawl.'

'And then we go back. And we get Sole and Kim and whatever we can and we leave.'

'Exactly so.'

'Lothar – thank you. I owe you.'

'No.' He shook his head and smiled. 'There's no owing. We both know that.'

IV

They cruised up beside us like fighter planes appearing on either side of a passenger jet. One moment nothing – just the amber and gold of the evening river and the dull chug of our engine not quite echoing against the trees; the next – two boats gunning toward us from the shadows of the overhanging branches where they had been lying in wait. The uniformed men were sat in single file in their boats, just as they had been that first day on the jetty when I threw them the rope.

I twisted sharply around. I counted six guns. This time death was merely the momentary matter of a puerile finger on a perfunctory trigger.

Lothar raised his voice against their engines, his face somehow deeper within the circumference of his hat: 'They want us to pull into the bank.'

'How do we feel about that?'

'Right now, it seems like a great idea to us.'

I sank back. My body ached more than I had ever known it; but I was not as sick and the spasms in my stomach had ceased. Nor did I have any anxiety about what might happen to me any more. I could endure.

We stopped in the silt of the shoreline and raised our hands in the manner of all surrenders. But the two boats did not follow us in. Instead, they floated together thirty paces out, the guns still lazily trained. I recognized Captain Lugo. He seemed to be discussing something with a lieutenant who was sitting in the other stern.

With little more than a raising of his head, Lothar indicated where the water was darker beneath the overhanging foliage. No more than eight feet away, a black caiman lay absolutely still, all but submerged, the only motion its inner eyelid blinking – sideways – purposeful, patient, prehistoric.

He spoke softly from beneath his hat: 'They are looking for me.'

'I was beginning to suspect as much.'

'I hoped not to burden you. I was going to disappear after you had left the Station. But, well, now we may be in a bad situation.'

'Seems like life is just one bad situation after another,' I said.

He smiled and for a moment I saw the child in him again, the practical joker, but then it was gone and the lines in his face redrew themselves.

'I think they know. So you should know, too.' He winced as though his secret was leaving him physically. 'I take photographs and I report on what happens here – all the bad things. I am the spy they are looking for.'

Lugo seemed to be talking into a satellite phone. I

lowered my hands. They knew we were not going to go anywhere. If they wanted to shoot me, they could.

'What do you mean – spy? Who for Lothar?'

'I tell the Ashaninka where the oil people are. I tell the Matsigenka where the drugs people are. I tell the drugs people where the soldiers are. I even tell soldiers where the loggers are. And I tell the news organizations everything.'

'You write articles?'

'And other stuff. Some journalist usually re-writes it to make themselves look like they know. But it's me. Half the pictures in the newspapers are mine, too. Or they have come from cameras that I know about.' He paused. 'And I have been using your computer to send this information.'

'You mean you're an activist?'

'They say spy. You say activist. What does it matter what we call it? It's what I do that counts.'

'So who do you work for?'

'Nobody.'

Two of the men were climbing out of one boat and into the other. I looked across. 'You don't take money from anyone? You're not with anybody?'

'Not any more. Maybe you could say I work for everybody. I do what I think is in the interests of the long-term health of the forest and the remaining un-contacted tribes. I work for what is best.'

'I am glad you can work out what that is.'

The boats were separating.

'I have been here a long time, my friend,' he said. 'Once you free your mind of all the noise and the propagandas – you can think clearly.'

'Which is why you have been helping the drugs people – against the army?'

I heard a deep sadness in him now, the long-abiding spirit behind everything else. 'Against the army because – at this moment – the army is the government – which is – in reality – just the oil companies.'

'Which also means that you're helping arm the cocaine barons.'

'I don't arm them. But I do make choices. At the moment I prefer cocaine to the loggers – it's true – and I usually prefer cocaine to the oil concessions. Maybe this will change.' He raised his shoulders. 'I have to alter my position often. But the tribes have lived with coca for a long time. Oil threatens everything. Here. Now.'

The engines startled birds into flight.

'Why didn't you say?'

'I did. To Quinn.'

Lugo's boat sped off downriver.

'Is that why he hired you?'

'No. He hired me because I had a job in a zoo when I was a student and because –' he half smiled – 'I knew that the abdomen of an ant has seven sections.'

'Why are you telling me all this now? What do you want me to do?'

The other boat was coming towards us. 'I'm telling you because you should not act in ignorance. Because when they take us back to the Station, I want to be sure that you and Kim go – straight away – without any more trouble.'

'We leave together,' I said.

They pulled up alongside. There were only four men in it now – the Boy and his associate were at the front, the other two at the back with their guns still pointing at us.

'You should have stayed in the jungle,' the associate said, a sneer hovering over his bucked teeth. 'One of the Colonel's favourites has just been shot dead. And he's blaming you two. Now it's really starting.'

TEN

I

The sun had passed beyond the edge of the world, the sky was streaked in the colours of yolk and blood and the trees seemed almost sinister in the intensity of their stillness. If the rains did not come soon, I thought, the broken jetty would be all that told there ever was a river.

The Boy was to be our guard. Perhaps they did not take us seriously, or perhaps there was no one among them more suited to the job. We were ordered to go up the makeshift wooden walkway that they had laid across the mud. I closed my eyes at every pause and wished only to sleep. I imagined a cell in a holy place of redemption – a clean bed, bread, soup, bells that called out for prayers.

Some other soldiers must have radioed in Tord's position, because a third boat had evidently been despatched to arrest him. Halfway back to the Station, where two channels met, they had been waiting for us. Tord had waved across. And ever since, he had seemed almost pleased to have been taken – the chance to work among the servants of the enemy; courage was only ever madness anointed.

Now there were orders to climb the rope ladder up to the river path. I followed Lothar and Tord. We stood on what was left of the jetty, batting at the mosquitoes, waiting for the other men to come up while the Boy watched us – zealous, proud. I had not seen him close in daylight before. Behind his metal brace, his lower teeth were misshapen and twisted, sharp.

Tord began to speak softly: 'The Lord is nigh unto them that are of a broken heart.' His hands were clasped. 'And he saveth those who are of a contrite spirit. Let the wicked forsake his way, and the unrighteous man his thoughts: and let him return unto the Lord, and He will have mercy on him.'

I thought the Boy might strike him. I feared nothing save exertion and I doubted my strength even in getting out of the way. But the Boy seemed oblivious and simply continued to watch us – blank-faced but with an unnatural intensity in his eyes.

We were told to walk. Generators had been pushed into the undergrowth on either side of the path. They banged and throbbed, discharging heavy black fumes that were trapped in the understorey and that caused me to cough and smart as we passed. We emerged to sagging cables and lights above our heads; the deranged fizz of electricity. The makeshift registration desks had been extended – so that there was now a row of three or four structures built with corrugated iron and tarpaulin that flanked us as we walked in toward the *comedor*.

On our left, two soldiers guarded boxes of electrical goods, their rifles crisscrossed on the tables. On our right, another was selling beer to tribesmen who turned to watch us. More onlookers gathered as we passed. We were a freak show prodded forward by a juvenile circus master. My skin had become encrusted so that even to move the muscles of my jaw felt as though I were cracking my own face apart. Blood, sweat and the river had smeared themselves in dried rivulets on my arms where I had rolled my sleeves so that I seemed in part to be a striped creature. I was hobbling; half from the pain in my hips where I allowed my body almost to die in the tree; and half from the pain in my boots where I was sure that I had cracked my nails from kicking the doors. But I sipped from my bottle, amazed at the miracle of the water in my throat.

Ahead, where Jorge's canteen had been sited in front of the *comedor*, there was now a line of ramshackle stalls that curved from the stairs up towards their huts. Jorge himself was standing beside a fire in the middle, his uniform stained and his smooth head shiny with sweat. Half a dozen squirrel monkeys were hanging from rusted hooks that had been slipped over a portable clothes rail; they dangled – heads down, stretched and sagging in their skins, filmy-eyed. Above the fire, two or three had been skewered – anus to throat – so that they seemed to be crawling along the spit.

The Boy overtook us.

'Wait,' he said.

We stood – Tord praying quietly on one side, Lothar like a stone on the other. The older soldiers closed up from behind and bunched around us. They paid us no attention. Either they knew that any escape on our part was risible or they intended casually to shoot us if an attempt was made. Pleased to have returned to base, they talked among themselves, smoked and looked up at the women who were sat in frayed denim skirts on our lounge chairs at the lip of the *comedor*. In response, the women crossed their legs with studied casualness. Two or three of the soldiers pressed us forward so that they too might go closer. The women began smirking and giggling and turning away. A fat man with a chess clock on his knee sat beside them, drinking coffee through pursed lips. And I saw that the women were wearing their make-up to look older, not younger.

My side stung and ached where I had gashed it beneath my ribs. I was afraid I would faint. The smell of the cooking flesh was loathsome. I shifted my weight. I sensed Lothar stand in closer beside me. Jorge had stopped turning the monkeys on his spit and now stood staring – he must not have recognized me at first. He passed his hand across his head and flicked away the sweat. There was an acrid taste in my mouth. I swilled some water and spat.

The Boy reappeared, coming down the stairs eagerly. 'Captain Lugo is busy,' he said.

Several of the soldiers laughed. Others gave mock cheers and balled their fists. And only then did I realize that Cordero had left and that the Judge had been right after his fashion: that it was indeed the Colonel who had been sustaining what had passed for civilization.

We were under arrest for spying, the Boy explained, as if relaying news of a successful job application. We were to be held in one of the huts with the blonde bitch. There would be questions later. He had no idea how long for. He did not know where the Colonel was. We could not speak to the Judge. We were thanked for our excellent whiskey and the generous supply of cigarettes. He said this last in such a way that I could not tell whether he was being sarcastic or merely relaying sarcasm without understanding.

Tord spoke quietly: 'For the spirit of harlotry has led them astray. And they have played the harlot. And they have gone into the darkness.'

'Let's go.' The Boy raised his rifle like the bar of a gate that he must close to shepherd us into a pen. His associate set off ahead, looking over his shoulder every few paces.

The shadows between the trees were deepening. Frogs were barking. We rounded the kapok. A woman with a long frizz of straw-dyed blonde hair was sat on Kim's porch in red and yellow underwear. The Boy's associate called out. She blew him a kiss, which he made a show of catching and rubbing on his rump as he looked back over his shoulder at us again. Somewhere a radio was playing country music. My eyes went to Sole's hut. The door was open. I felt terror twitch inside me. Further down, towards the lab, vultures flapped the path like withered geese. My own hut was to be our prison.

Lothar went inside. I hesitated on the stairs. A pair of shear-tails fell and swooped and rose and darted through the clearing – so close that they must surely be lovers or deadly rivals.

'I need to wash,' I said.

'Later.' The Boy blinked.

Tord interposed. 'Actually, you would be doing the Lord's work if you accompanied him to the bathing hut.'

Still the Boy's face was impassive. 'Yes, later,' he repeated. 'Everybody will wash.'

He gestured for us to go inside.

A dog hovered below hoping for food or love or someone to throw a stick. The music had stopped. The radio announced the election of another president somewhere.

II

It was dark when I awoke. My body was stiff. And my mouth felt as though it were drying up like the forest. I rolled from the wall. My lamp burned on my desk. Kim was kneeling beside me, offering me water from a bottle. Her face was smeared and drawn and her clothes were stained with mud. Something had snagged her and she had a deep dark cut on the side of her neck.

'They say we can wash now,' she spoke gently. 'I'm going to have to borrow some of your clothes. They won't let us go anywhere.'

For the first time, I could smell myself. Shame rushed over me. I sat up, backing away.

Tord appeared and crouched down slowly, fingertips joined. 'Can you get up?' he asked.

I leaned against the wall. My skin was so itchy that I felt an overwhelming desire to tear it off and lay it down flat and work at it with a stiff-bristled brush.

'Where's Lothar?' I began.

'They took him.' Kim was unable to disguise the anxiety in her voice. 'They said to ask questions.'

Tord affected calm by way of contrast. 'He said he would answer them only if they would allow us all to wash. We should move now though – if you feel you can – before they change their mind.'

Someone had rigged up electric lights in the other porches. The cable snaked away onto the path. I could hear the sound of bamboo rats – cor, cor, cor. Opposite, the hulk of the lab seemed to loom in the darkness, dense and square. I had assumed we were going to the bathing huts, but the Boy's associate stopped at the bottom of my stairs and turned with a leer. There were three wooden pails.

'What are these for?' Kim asked. 'Why can't we go to the washhouse?'

'This is an army camp – the showers are for soldiers and for whores only,' the associate said with his twitching grin. 'Maybe we should go together.'

The Boy spoke as though relaying facts. 'We are not permitted to allow you into the forest after what happened with the prisoners. You are to wash here.'

His associate gestured at the pails with mock invitation: 'And the Captain doesn't like to work on prisoners who he can't stand to smell.'

Tord addressed us all: 'Who is a God like unto thee that passeth over transgression?' At the jetty, I had thought that either he was about some devious psychological ploy, or that he was proclaiming his piety with renewed vigour out of a desire to match every raise the Devil might make. But now I saw that he was afraid. As others might rehearse the law, or become terse, or underhand, these citations were how he met the strain of iniquity; and I saw, too, that he had thus far found their power equal to anything he had encountered in the world. Now he turned to us and said: 'I will wait. Your need is greater than mine, Doctor. Use my bucket.'

'Good. So you go back in now, Jesus.' The associate levelled his gun at Tord. 'We didn't want to see your shrivelled little dick anyway.'

Tord did not move. Without warning or changing his expression, the Boy, who was beside him on the porch, jabbed the butt of his rifle sideways, hard into Tord's stomach. The shock of the pain contorted the missionary's habitually tight features and he doubled, groaning, breathless. He struggled for a moment, almost on his knees, incoherent and gasping; then, with a great exercise of his will, he straightened up and mastered his expression. The Boy did not look down or even move his head.

'My friend, before we strike one another, let us talk among ourselves and find what brotherhood there is between us. You are a young man. You have the luxury of years. Your life may yet be worth a great deal to yourself, sir, and to our God. Because Jesus saves.'

'Go in,' said the Boy, his voice again without emotion.

Tord hesitated.

Abruptly, I peeled my shirt from my skin. I bent to untie my laces. I took off my boots and my socks.

Tord stepped inside the door and the Boy shut it behind him.

Kim hung the towel and the clean clothes over the rail of the porch.

I became aware of three people sat on Sole's stairs opposite. Others were on the path. The radio was playing a marching song. I unbuckled my belt and tried to remove my underwear at the same time as my grime-coated trousers so that I could discard them both without Kim seeing the filth and the mess. My feet were eerily white save for the dark u-shape of dried blood around my toenail.

'We need soap,' Kim said.

The Boy shrugged.

'We need soap,' she repeated.

'There is soap in my hut,' I said. Naked, I turned and walked up my stairs. My face and arms were black, my legs smeared where my trousers had been stained, my stomach scarred with bites and stings. I did not allow the Boy to look away. But neither did he attempt to do so.

Tord was kneeling inside – whether in pain or in prayer I could not tell.

In a hushed voice, I asked: 'Can you walk out of here?'

He looked at me a moment, then fixed his eyes somewhere above my head.

'No.' He shook his head, his voice hoarse. 'No, it is impossible. There is only the river – at least for three miles. After that, there is a path and you can go inland through the Matsigenka territories . . . but it would take days to walk anywhere – if you did not get lost.'

'What about upriver?'

'No. It's too dangerous. The Yora have left their villages and the killing is indiscriminate. Even the Matsigenka are fighting now. The loggers are armed. There are rumours of more soldiers in the borderlands. And nobody really knows the interior. Only Lothar . . . Only Lothar could go upstream.'

'Can you pilot one of the tribesmen's canoes in the dark without an engine?'

'Yes, I can.'

'As soon as there is a chance, I want you to take Kim and get her out. Go down the river – do whatever you think is the safest. Avoid Laberinto. Pick up a passenger boat somewhere further down.'

'Nobody steals canoes. It is the only law here.'

'There are no laws, Tord.'

'There are commandments.'

'Bring it back if you feel guilty.'

He looked at me. And for an instant, something in his eyes admitted the possibility that he doubted what he preached and I saw fear there; but then it was gone – replaced by the warm pity that one man might have for his vanquished rival.

'I will pray for you,' he said.

'Please do – there's a lot that needs praying for.' I took the soap from my wash bag and went back outside, six dozen devil flies following me as I went.

I held the Boy's eye again as I passed. His associate was smoking and staring at Kim. I stood by the pails and stooped.

'Let me help you,' Kim said, gently.

'It's OK.'

'I know it is OK but it will be easier if I help you. You can't pour and use your soap at the same time. It's too heavy.' She raised the pail in both her hands. 'Bend your head down a bit.'

The water streamed cold but only for a second before it became an intense bliss. I could feel mud running on my skin. I lathered myself – hair to toes until I was all but dry. Then Kim poured the water and I began again. My emerging hands were strangers to me – scratched and torn, arcs of dirt beneath every nail, pale aliens.

'Put your arms up.' She rinsed where I had washed. We had emptied the first bucket and started on the second. 'After this, we are going to the store room,' she breathed. 'We need to stop ourselves getting infected. Do you still have a key?'

'Yes.' A third time I lathered, filling my lungs with the smell of the soap. Again, she poured.

I used the small towel to dry myself. Then I began to put on my fresh clothes. The clean was beyond anything I had dreamt of – a sacrament, a new life.

'What happened to you, Kim?' I asked.

'Nothing. I went looking for you.'

'What happened to your neck?'

'I tried to go jogging in the jungle.'

'Away from the soldiers?'

'Well, not towards them.'

'Did they hurt you?'

'No. But they restrained me with their hands – a lot.'

Kim stood uncertain, seemingly far more in need of bathing now that I was washed myself. There were lines on her brow where smears of the forest had clung. I looked around at the gathering rag-tag of spectators.

'You are not washing here,' I said. 'We'll do it round the back of the hut. I'll screen you.' I picked up the full bucket and poured some of it into one of the others so that they were evenly filled.

The Boy stiffened.

'He won't shoot us,' I breathed.

'Where are you going?' The Boy's tone was neither sharp nor angry and yet all the more menacing for that.

'We're going around the back of the hut. My friend doesn't wish to wash in front of those animals.' I gestured to the figures sat watching.

'You are not going anywhere.' This from his associate.

I indicated to Kim that she should pick up her fresh clothes and walk in front of me and then I raised the two pails and, slowly, turned my back. I felt like every cell in my skin was excruciatingly aware – braced and tremoring.

But there was no gunfire.

Instead, they fell in close behind. Perhaps they preferred the idea of a private show.

We arranged the pails on either side. The Boy lit a cigarette. The associate stood beside him, stroking his moustache.

I turned my back to them again and held the towel wide, glancing over my shoulder as I did so. The associate moved round, not bothering to disguise his purpose. But where several onlookers would have been too many, it was possible to shield Kim from him wherever he stood. She raised her eyes to the darkening sky but he did not move a third time. I looked over the other shoulder. The Boy's expression was hard to see beneath his cap. I knew neither his intention nor his capability.

'Thank you,' Kim said quietly.

'Your turn,' I replied.

Quickly, she crouched down and squirmed out of her shirt. The forest's breath was more intimate here, warmer; the sound of the thumbed combs much closer. I held my eyes on the wall of the hut above her head.

She rose up before me and stepped out of her combat trousers, folding them and leaning to place them out of the way. Then she picked up the half-full bucket, bent her head and poured water on herself.

'Tell me about you and Cameron,' I said.

Her voice was little above a whisper as she turned her back. 'I loved the work first – before I fell in love with him. I met him three years ago. It started before I came to the department.'

I stared ahead. 'I am sorry – for your loss, I mean. I know what you must have felt. What you feel.'

Because I could not pour the water, she was using her underwear as a flannel. She spoke over her shoulder. 'He talked of you often.'

'We were friends.'

'He said that he was always skidding across the surface but that you lived your life more deeply than any other man he had ever met.'

'It's not true – I never had his ambition. He wanted to change the way we think about ourselves – about life.'

She turned to face me. 'What about you?'

I let my eyes slip down the fraction to where hers were waiting. 'I don't trust myself,' I said.

'I am going to prove what you both believed.'

'He believed. I hoped.'

'You're right, though. It's not just about competition. Nothing in the world wants to live alone with only its own success for company.'

She crouched down again and emptied the pail above her head to rinse herself. The grasses felt wet between my toes where the water had run from her body and was pooling into the ground. Then she stood before me once more – vital, ready for anything. She was as close as a kiss. She poured the last of the water on her head and I watched it stream her curled hair flat.

'Wrap me in the towel,' she said. 'I can dress inside it.'

I enfolded her body. Then I stood back.

III

We drank bottles of water. We ate muesli bars. With inactivity came boredom and agitation. After a while, Kim rose and rattled at the door.

'What are you doing?' The Boy's voice startled her, sounding close, like his lips were pressed to the gap in the frame.

She crossed the creaking floor and lay back on the bed.

'You can't escape.' The Boy continued, the strange immediacy worse than if he had been in the room. 'Where would you go?'

I sat sideways on at my desk looking out at the lab. I wondered if the Boy's associate was watching this window. My wallet, my money and my passport had gone. All that was left were my notes, pages and pages of handwritten nothing.

'Were you locked in here last night?' I asked.

'No.' Kim replied from where she lay staring at the ceiling.

'Did you see Sole?'

'Yes. We were together.'

'Was she all right?'

'She was tired because she had been working at the

comedor. But she was OK. Besides the fact she was panicking about you.'

'Cordero was still here yesterday, wasn't he?' I asked.

'Yes.' Kim looked over. 'Cordero was still here.'

We had no plan, except to ask to go outside to relieve ourselves and then, tomorrow, to try and get out by whatever means possible. Several times, we thought we heard the Boy breathing as though he, too, were in the hut with us.

Later, there came the sound of plates and voices outside. I looked out. A soldier was eating on Sole's porch.

'Why haven't they locked Lothar in here with us?' I turned to face the room again. 'When did he go?'

Kim was still lying on the bed. 'About an hour before you woke up,' she said.

'Who took him?'

'The Boy came with a couple of the older soldiers. Lothar just got up and went with them. They came back and said that we could wash and I woke you up straight away.' Kim cursed impatiently. 'This is a joke. What are they *doing*? They can't just keep us in here forever.'

'Actually,' Tord said, 'I'm afraid Lugo does as it pleases him to do.'

We had thought him asleep. He had been sitting in my easy chair with his hands clasped and eyes closed. Now they flicked towards me – quick and green in the lamp-light. 'They say that he is given licence to do the Devil's work,' he said.

Kim sat forward on the edge of the bed. 'What the hell does that mean? *Who* says?'

Tord gave a shallow nod by way of absorbing her antagonism. But there was a reciprocal anger lurking in the composure of his response: 'They allow Lugo to racketeer. They allow him to torture and fornicate and to commit all manner of abomination. In return, he creates such terror that the forest empties.' He thumbed his fringe to one side. 'And if ever he were caught or exposed by anyone, they would disown him. He knows this and serves Satan all the more while he can.'

'Shut up about Satan,' Kim said.

'He works underneath Cordero,' I said, quietly. 'Cordero uses Lugo at his own discretion. So Lothar says. Sometimes they cleanse nice, sometimes they cleanse nasty.'

'How does Lothar know this?' Kim asked.

'You should ask him that yourself.'

From outside came the low repeated gurgling sound that I did not recognize for a moment.

'Machine guns.' Tord rose.

Kim came over so that we were all three looking out of the desk window together. The rancour between us evaporated. Outside, the night sky was glowing red as if Satan's armies were indeed surging forth from a crack in the Earth.

'They're using flares on the rivers,' Tord said.

'Kim, if there's a chance for you to get out with Tord, you must go.'

She turned to me. 'What about you?'

'They may keep me here.'

'We should go together.'

'No. You must go – if you can, you must. I have to get Lothar . . . and Sole. You still have the disk?' I attempted a smile. 'You should—'

'I have the disk. I'm not going to lose the damn disk.'

'Good. Because you're right – it's important – you should carry on – you should prove what Cameron believed.' I held her eyes but perhaps she had heard something hollow in my voice because she looked away out of the window again.

'What is happening out there?' she asked.

IV

Deep in sleep, I did not hear the key in the lock. Flash-lights woke me, excoriating my eyelids, shining around the walls of the hut. Kim jolted and then kicked beside me, bad dreams broken by a worse awakening. I sat up, blocking their lights from finding her for a moment.

'We are going to see the Captain,' Tord said. He was standing by the chair, head bowed, in an attitude of pre-forgiveness. For the first time I thought that perhaps he was losing his self-control – that some particular kind of hysteria had him in its grip. He lowered his voice: 'Where the Devil sits enthroned in darkness, there shall the soldiers of Jesus venture without fear and bring all men back to the light.'

'Shut up.' The Boy's associate threw down my boots. 'Don't speak. Put on your shoes.' His light had found Kim behind me. 'And you.'

I bent to put on my boots. They flashed their light on my laces a moment; then, deliberately, they played the beams over Kim as she sat up beside me.

I stood. 'Where are we going?' I asked.

Though I could not see his eyes for their lights, I could tell that the Boy was looking at me. Again, I felt the strange sensation – a wordless recognition of something and yet a feeling that I could not fathom him, that I could guess neither his motives nor his inclinations. I detected a slight sway in his posture as he fixed on me and it occurred to me then that he was experiencing the same and that this was the reason for his persistent gaze.

He licked his metal. 'The Captain is ready now,' he said.

His associate laughed then leaned in towards Kim. 'Lucky for you – he has drowned his thirst in whores.'

I thought at first that we were going towards the *comedor* but instead we were taken along the back of the huts. The wall of the jungle pressed in again – the sounds of the night somehow solicitous beneath the din of the tinny music and the raucousness of men charged with drink and lust. I hobbled but only because with a certain way of walking, there was no pain. My mind returned again and again to Sole. How long had she and Felipe continued working after they realized that Cordero was gone? She must know that I had been found. Would she have already left? I hoped so. I did not doubt her ability to go through the forest if necessary. After I had seen the Captain, I would know better what actions were required. The next hour would decide everything.

I walked closer to the tendrils and the leaves. I drank in the perfumes of the hidden flowers. I wished to silence every other noise, every other person, so that I could truly hear the forest. I listened to the insects. Had Tord and I been reversed in our labours, I was sure that he would have had more things by heart – class, genera, species.

A pistol shot was fired. The retort ricocheted through the trees, where it was deadened and smothered. The Boy paused. We were behind the *comedor* – at the place where the fire had been that first night. The clamour had stopped. The music played clearly a moment. Then gradually the voices began again, but more softly now, hushed.

The associate came forward. 'Give me a second,' he said to the Boy.

We stood in line, waiting, listening. The Boy watched me. I looked up. All kinds of stars were massed and smeared across the heavens – bright, twinkling, shadowy, nebulous, twinned, clustered – their number so great that the sky could not be called dark and only an ignorant fool could imagine himself of consequence.

The associate returned, cigarette stub burning in his lips. 'Just that fat cook,' he said.

'What about him?' the Boy asked.

'Carlos shot him in the ass.'

The Boy nodded, indifferent. 'Let's go,' he said.

We passed behind the first hut and circled around the second. The path beyond was quieter. Up towards the generator, there were lights. I realized with a start that the Judge was still here – or else someone was using his hut.

Tord's voice was sticky with unctuousness. 'Thank you for guiding us,' he said to the Boy.

Kim coughed.

The Boy said nothing but instead pointed with his gun for us to mount the stairs.

Inside, maps covered the walls, the rivers like blue capillaries. A dim flickering bulb hung bare from the ceiling. There was a small table against the wall on which were arranged a few smeared tumblers, a bottle of my whiskey and an absurd lava lamp. A large field desk stood athwart the entire width of the hut; beside it crouched a surreal life-sized black puma – mid-snarl, stuffed or fake I could not tell; and behind it sat Captain Lugo cutting up what remained of a steak with an ostentatious knife.

'Captain, where is the Colonel?' I spoke immediately. 'And where's my colleague? Why have you arrested us?'

He forked himself a piece, keeping watch on me as he chewed, his eyes empty but somehow avid – the eyes of an addict, I thought, about to begin his ritual.

I pressed him. 'Captain, where is the Colonel?'

He swigged from his bottle of beer. There were boxes stacked under and all around the bed behind him – the firearms and ammunition with which he slept.

'We are leaving tomorrow,' I said. 'All of us. Including my colleague.'

With slow deliberation, he continued to eat. Beneath his toreador machismo, he was enjoying the theatre of this performance before the others, subconsciously seeking to enlist me in the role of an adversary against whom he could further burnish his authority.

I turned away.

'I want this to be easy, Doctor.' He spoke up though his mouth was full of meat. 'I've got plenty of difficult.'

The Boy held his rifle crossways to block my path.

This time I did not speak.

'Tell me,' Lugo said, swallowing, 'where were you yesterday and the day before?'

I swung back round and stepped forward to face him. Either he had placed a pistol on the desk as a paper weight or I had not seen it before.

'Yesterday, I was dying. But you know that. Your men arranged it.'

'No. Not us. You'd be dead.' He ran his tongue around his teeth. 'You were with your friend – the German?'

'Tell me what you want, Captain. Otherwise I am going to walk out of here and you will have to shoot me to stop me.'

'I wouldn't shoot you, Doctor. I would amuse my men first – take their minds off our own losses.' He toyed with his steak using the tip of his knife. There was a little pile of gristle that he had spat out on his plate. I felt a wave of nausea. 'The Colonel wanted you to sign these statements.' He indicated the papers with his knife. 'And now

I want you to sign them. That's all. Then, tomorrow, you will be escorted to Laberinto.'

'I'm not signing anything. And we do not need an escort to Laberinto. Where is my colleague?'

'You do. You need an escort with big fat bullet-proof balls. For some reason the people we are fighting think we care about you. We keep telling them we don't but – who knows? – they might resort to kidnap. It happens.' He grinned. 'Plus the savages can't be trusted one way or the other.' He lifted his gun and pushed forward the pieces of paper. His shirt was open and sweat slicked the dark hairs on his chest. 'Really, it would be easier for you and for me for you just to sign. You can guess what they say.'

'Sign what?' Kim's voice came from behind me. 'Sign what? What is this about?'

He sat up, displaying the fake chivalry of a man who believes women to find him attractive. 'Hello. Welcome to my office – and my bedroom.'

Kim stepped forward beside me. 'What do you want us to sign?' she asked.

Lugo kept his eyes on her. 'A declaration that the German has been spying. And that he acted alone.' With his free hand he swigged his beer. 'It shouldn't be a problem for you – it's the truth. Which we all love. Sign.'

Kim was looking at me.

He put down his bottle. 'Once we have your signatures, we'll let you go.'

'We do not know anything about this,' I said.

'I believe you. But I don't have to. All the evidence we need is on your computer and I'm told by my government that you're responsible for your equipment.'

'We're leaving.' I dragged his eyes back to mine with the aggression in my tone. 'We're leaving – all together – first thing tomorrow – and you will not stop us unless you plan to shoot us. For the last time, where is my colleague?'

He returned to carving his meat.

'You don't think any of this matters,' I said. 'But it will.'

I began to turn again.

The jab in my back was vicious. I stumbled forward, crying out. The pain was as shocking as the precision – an expert's strike targeted at a particular vertebra. I twisted my arm behind me, clutching at my spine, breathing through my teeth.

Lugo drew his gun towards himself, away from where I was holding on to the edge of his desk. His eyes were alight. The ritual had begun. I must end it now or there would be no chance of diverting him before blood was shed. I bowed my head and cursed and let the pain register so that the room would be absorbed by my hurt and the Boy would not strike again. I was certain it was he.

I straightened, pressing my fingers into my back, clenching my jaw as I spoke. 'If you let me read these pages overnight, then tomorrow I will sign whatever is true among the accusations.'

Lugo leaned forward, his thin nose the more delicate for the rest of his muscled frame. 'I can make you sign it in five minutes if I want.' He spoke softly but so that the whole room could hear. 'Or if I like it better, I can take my time. I can cut off your balls and leave you needle and thread to sew up the bleeding yourself. Five days later, I can make you eat them because you are so hungry you'll swallow anything I put in front of you.' He sat back again, picked up the gristle on the point of his knife. 'So: you do it. You sign this. We are happy. You go.' He became matter of fact and, as he did so, flicked the gristle so that it hit my face and I felt it wet on the corner of my mouth. 'Or you don't sign it. And you stay. And maybe you die here or maybe you don't. Or maybe I'll cut off your dick and feed it slice by slice to the dolphins myself. We like to enjoy ourselves in our work. Plenty of people don't get that chance.' He pushed the papers towards me for what I knew would be the last time.

But suddenly Tord was between us, slamming down on Lugo's desk with his right hand, half shouting, half incanting.

'The Lord strikes down those who strike against him and in his wrath there is great vengeance,' he said. 'Do you believe in the saviour Jesus Christ who comes and takes away the sins of the world?'

Again, he slammed. 'Do you believe in Jesus Christ? For I tell you outside are dogs, and sorcerers, and whore-mongers, and murderers, and idolaters, and those who loveth and maketh lies.' Spittle flew and his voice became high-pitched and raging as he leaned in past me. 'Oh yes and I tell you this. The fearful, and unbelieving, and the abominable, and murderers, and whoremongers, and sorcerers, and idolaters, and all the liars, shall have their part in the lake which burneth with fire and brimstone. Which is a second death.'

But Lugo had now recovered from the shock. He seemed to look past us and wink at the Boy as he stood up. Then he thrust forward with such force that the entire desk began to tip over. The plate slid and the bottle clattered, spraying beer in a dying arc. Somehow Tord managed to stand to one side, shouting all the while – 'which is a second death, which is a second death' – but I took the full weight of the desk as it fell. Struggling backward, trapped, I saw the puma's teeth snarling and then, vivid as in a vision, I saw the calm in the Boy's brown eyes as he rose up in slow-motion certainty behind a still-bellowing Tord. And in his right hand I saw a strange half-moon shape that shone beneath the length of his extended thumb. And I saw him seize Tord's nose in his left hand with great violence, dragging the slighter man backwards, head up, shirt buttoned, straw hair neatly fringed, still incanting loudly, 'Which is the second death, which is the second death.' And I saw Tord's face turn puce as he struggled to breathe and wrestle the Devil that had at last been made manifest, clinging to his back as his Bible had always said that Satan would. And I saw the Boy thrust finger and thumb of his right hand, deft and swift, into Tord's mouth and with a strong and sudden upward twist I saw him cut out the missionary's tongue and in one movement hold it up still twitching to the light. And behind his metal I saw the childlike smile of one who has added to his count.

V

Chaos came. Tord howled and gurgled and cried out thickly for his God through the blood that gushed from his mouth and down his chin like some dark liquid goatee, spattering right and left as they dragged him outside and threw him in the cart.

They made us walk ahead. Twice I tried to turn. Twice I received a blow to my shoulder that made me stumble forward. Beside me, Kim cursed and then begged and then threatened and then pleaded until she too was hit and fell silent. All we could do was listen to the squeaking of the wheels and the terrifying unnatural sounds that Tord made and the screaming of the howler monkeys that should have been asleep in the forest above us and the music that beat out from the *comedor* ahead boasting of murder and tribe and wealth and bitches.

Where before we had sat, now soldiers stood and drank and shouted, gathered in a horseshoe while a woman on her knees struggled against the hand that gripped the back of her head and the penis that was being thrust into her mouth. The associate raised his rifle and cheered. And his greeting was met with answering salvos. All around, underneath the tarpaulins, human figures stirred in the darkness – eyes, teeth, silhouettes. I looked for any sign of Sole, terror in my heart. But the point of the Boy's rifle prodded at my spine whenever I slowed. Tord choked and spat and bayed like an animal. Ants streamed the path. No god came.

VI

At the door to my hut, they told us to stop and began to speak among themselves. We dared not turn but listened, our heads bowed, silent, facing away.

They had forgotten the papers.

Lugo, in the exhilaration of his fury, had dealt out only violence and had not given any instruction. The Boy believed that they had been charged with having the statements signed. His associate did not disagree but disliked the delay. The Boy contended that it would be shrewd to have the accusations here, with them, since if we did not sign, then there was more . . . *razón*.

Like some grotesque parody of inseparable childhood friends, they were obliged to go back with one another. But first the associate came in close behind and placed one hand through Kim's ripped shirt, his fingers groping, while with the other he opened the door. He tried to turn her to face him. She swung her elbows. He shoved her inside.

'Ten minutes,' he said, in a coarse whisper. 'Then I'm yours.'

I turned and watched as they hoisted Tord up, his body sagging, his head swinging loose, blood and spittle stringing from his mouth. They mounted the steps with him, stopped, and without saying anything simply pushed him forwards onto me where I stood.

We rolled Tord over on the bed and took off his shirt. Already he was pale and clammy. His body bucked aggressively, the strain of his breathing showing beneath his ribs as he tried to suck in air. Our hands were sticky. There was so much blood.

Kim stood back. She turned to my rack, took off her own ragged blouse and selected a clean shirt. Quick and tight-fingered, she buttoned it up. She threw me a second. I tore it. She took a strip and wiped her hands. I did the same. Then she stepped forward again and wound a fresh band around her wrist and wiped at Tord's body with small hard movements of her thumbs.

Tord began to writhe. I held him down and looked up at Kim, wild-eyed beneath her hair. The violence had stripped through the layers of her person, leaving nothing but fear and the functions of the body that time and space demanded. She had been reduced to some essence of herself, something she had always been, but that civilization had previously transfigured. And yet she had also found her cunning and her instinct.

Tord was passing in and out of consciousness; his pale hair was congealed; his face, where we cleaned him, was alabaster white; his eyes, when they opened, glassy;

his lips, when we found them, blue. Kim must have known that he would die, but she would not be deterred by this.

'What do you want me to do?' she looked up. 'Talk. What do you want me to do? You're the—'

The door rattled. She stiffened. It seemed too soon for the Boy to have come back. They had barely been gone. They must have changed their plans and returned directly. Perhaps something had happened at the *comedor*. Or perhaps there was some kind of a raid.

I started to speak, quickly, my voice low and steady. 'When they come in, I want you to hold their attention. Don't let them look at me and don't look at me yourself. Do whatever you have to. Keep their eyes on you. But don't even glance at me.' The door rattled again. I could not understand why they were having difficulty with the lock. 'The Boy will be the hardest to distract, but he will watch anything that is physical so you sh—'

'The Virgin sent me.' A hoarse whisper. 'Doctor? Are you inside?'

'Estrela?'

'The Virgin sent me.'

Though she addressed us through a crack, I had never heard her speak so clearly. But before we could step over to the door, she had it open and the jungle night was pouring through – a rising wave of insects and sound.

She stood short and squat on the porch – her dark face closed in on itself, chewing at her cheek, her old black clothes stained and her grey hair wiry and unkempt. The reflected light of our lamps flickered in both of her eyes.

'Soledad is with the Judge,' she said. Then she held up her heavy key in front of her forehead and blessed us both with its crucified skeleton. 'The Virgin sent me here.'

'Estrela,' Kim breathed.

'Here.' From somewhere in her clothes, she drew out her carcass knife and raised it up to me like a religious offering. 'Go quickly.'

I glanced out into the clearing then pulled her inside.

'Estrela, have you got a torch? There is a way to the river past the washhouse. Lothar cut through. Could you find it?'

She shook her head. 'We go on the main path. There are many people. But the soldiers are busy. She must wear this.' Estrela took off her shawl.

'Kim, go with her.'

'Tord?' Kim asked.

'I will do what I can. Don't look at me like that. When you get to the river, go downstream and hide by the mud banks. Wait for me there. If I don't come by the time it starts to get light, pay one of the Matsigenka families to ride in their boat to Laberinto. Take Estrela, if she wants to stay with you.'

Kim's eyes were still now but I could not read what was written there.

'You are insane,' she said. 'I see it now.'

'Go.'

She hesitated another second, looking back at Tord, and then she was out of the hut and on the steps and hurrying with Estrela across the clearing and towards the far wall of the jungle beyond.

I wrapped up my soap and my notebook in a shirt. I took the last bottle of water. Then I closed the door on Tord.

VII

I limped swiftly through the shadows behind the *comedor*. The noise of the music had not abated and still there were voices and cries but now several of the upstream huts were lit as well. A man was grunting; a woman urging him to finish.

Ahead, the Judge's lamps were lit and it was quieter as I moved further away from the *comedor*. I began to hear a different music – a thin-voiced aria that seemed surreal and outside of time. Close by, a tree had filled the night with the thick scent of its resin. The heat clung like a familiar.

I passed around the back of the Judge's hut and rose silently up onto the porch from the far side. The lights from the other huts cast stretched squares of illumination either side of the path where it ran back towards the *comedor*. I stood a moment listening to the music from within. Then I placed the master key in the lock, turned it quickly, stood to one side and threw open the door.

'Sole?'

My voice died in the stifling air. For there she was, just inside, startle-eyed from her sleep, sitting on the Judge's reclining chair.

'Sole,' I said again. 'What—'

But already she had leapt up and embraced me.

'Dr Forle, I hoped it would be you.' The Judge's voice rang out. I swung around. He was sat upright on the bed, fully dressed but wearing a blindfold. In his hand he had my best bottle of whiskey, which he was drinking through a straw.

'I hoped it would be you because I am certain that this would have been the last hour of my restraint. Half the night I can survive – but no longer, man, no longer. What is abstinence but death's more presentable cousin?'

He lifted what I now saw was some kind of sleeping mask from his head and threw it down.

'There's no need to look like that. I have not touched her. You have my word on that – my word as a hypocrite.' He sipped directly from my bottle. 'As you can see, I have not even allowed my eyes the pleasure. It has not been easy.' He winced against the whiskey's burn. 'After all, I am a man, she a woman and this a bed – and none of us would wish to deny our own nature for too long. That would be contemptible – wouldn't it, Doctor?'

He laughed and took another sip.

'I've been hiding here since the Colonel left,' Sole said. Her eyes searched mine.

'It was the only way to save her,' the Judge rejoined. 'She told me her news. But who would have believed her? And what difference would it have made to the animals out there?'

'What news?' I asked.

'In another hour, I doubt it would have made any difference to me,' he continued. 'Beauty drives men mad.'

There came the sound of voices raised and then the growl of machine-gun fire. Sole ducked down and pulled aside the edge of the shade so that she could see out.

'What's happening?' I kept my eyes on the Judge.

'There are men all around Lugo's hut,' Sole replied. 'The door is open. People are going in and out.'

Softer, the Judge said: 'You'll have to stay with me. We'll be quite secure here – from the soldiers at least.

There's nobody alive dares to enter this room unbidden. Except you, it would seem, Dr Forle. Can I at least interest you in a drink? The quality is surprising.'

'Don't move. Stay on the bed.'

'The more I see of you, Dr Forle, the more I like you.' Across his eyes and around the side of his head there was a ring of paler skin where the mask must have been tightly drawn. 'Shall I continue with the music?'

I glanced down to where Sole was crouching. I did not know what she had told the Judge, nor his allegiances. But her kisses had been real.

'We have to get to the river,' I said. 'We have to steal a boat.'

She let go of the shade and looked up. 'No – there's a boat coming.'

'For us?'

'Yes.'

'There's a boat coming!' the Judge cut in.

'How?' I ignored him. 'I don't understand.'

'When she saw the soldiers bring you back, my mother gave a boy my money to fetch a boatman – someone who knows the back channels here. We were going to wait until they went to sleep . . . But it's just been getting worse and worse. And nobody sleeps.'

'Your mother has gone with Kim,' I said. 'I told them to wait for us. We still have to get to the river somehow.'

She bent back to the window. 'There are too many soldiers. We won't get past.' Without looking back up, she added: 'They forced their way into my mother's store. They desecrated her shrine.'

Outside, the noise rose. Somehow the Judge had started his music playing again but quietly. I stood facing him, still uncertain. He raised an open hand so that I could see it and with a passing flourish to the music reached out a cigarette from his box by the bed. 'Shall I tell you the real problem?'

'Do you have a gun?' I asked.

'I do.'

'Where is it?'

'In my other hand.' He dipped his head to sip.

'Use it now if you are going to use it.'

'I will use it when and on whom I wish, Dr Forle. But don't worry: I have no immediate plans to shoot you. I am not on any side.' He smiled. 'I am impartial. But the struggle is real and very much alive here – and, as you see, it is as tangled as the forest itself.'

'Will you give me your gun?'

'No.' He lit his cigarette. 'I am also an anthropologist, Dr Forle. Amateur, maybe. But I know what kind of man you are beneath it all. Mendax. *Homo mendax*. Does she know you yet?'

I turned my back on him and bent to watch outside.

But it was impossible to work out what was happening from this distance. Fire torches flickered. They must have known that we were gone. Were they looking for us? Or was this something else happening? Behind, the Judge's voice assumed the deeper demagogic tone that I had last heard on the only day of rain.

'The *real* problem, Dr Forle, is that a man cannot really see anything clearly until the moment of his death when it is, of course, too late. Only in death does the deception of our little self-story-making end.' I heard the sound of whiskey being sucked through teeth. 'And suddenly the successes we have sworn by begin to wither on the boast, the love we gave we see in truth was never really love, the qualities we claimed for ourselves we realize were but disfigurements masquerading, and everything we accrued through all those look-at-me years – instantly worthless. Yes, finally, we see them for what they are: the lies – the endless lies we have told ourselves and lived by and told one another. But explain to me this, Doctor: to whom – to what – are we lying when we lie to ourselves? What creature is it that lives inside? Of what are we so afraid?'

The smell of his cigarette smoke mingled with the smell of camphor.

'Meanwhile, the stars do not hear us. Never have. Never will. So, here we are, Doctor: you and me and this woman and the rest of our species. We dare not know that which is within us and we cannot know that which is without. We are marooned in time and space searching in the darkness for we do not know what. My advice, Dr Forle: sleep with a woman whenever the opportunity arises and learn a musical instrument.'

There were fewer men around the huts now but the sound of automatic fire had become more frequent.

'I wish you would have a drink,' he urged. 'You can have the bed if you like. I would be content to observe from the chair. There are a few hours of the night still to go. And tomorrow promises to be exciting. I have wine if you prefer.'

I stood. 'I need your gun,' I said.

'I know you do.'

I started towards him but just then Sole gripped my arm. I turned and bent down beside her again. A lone figure was coming up the path.

'It's Felipe,' she said.

VIII

He stood in the dim light thrown through the doorway, a small man, I saw now – oddly still, stiff, straight – abandoned by his smile and without spirit. Instead, he looked at me with ghosted eyes that could no longer express feeling.

'I'm sorry,' he said. 'I'm so sorry. I came as quick as I could but—'

'What, Felipe? What is—'

'Dr Forle, they're burning the lab.'

His stillness seemed to colonize my own body. I could not properly understand the meaning in his words. I turned slowly back to face the room again. I saw the Judge wave as a king might wave and Sole's face suddenly the face of every human feeling.

'Go with Felipe, Sole. Find Kim. Wait by the river.'

I turned to run.

The Judge called after me: 'What can you save, Dr Forle? Not even yourself.'

IX

Pain rattled and stabbed at my back, ripped at the raw flesh in my boots. There were people everywhere – as if Machaguar had come to the Station not as the carnival of lights but unmasked at last as the carnival of death. I ducked down and away, off the path, and ran the dark wall.

On the far side of the *comedor*, beneath the music and

the chug of the generators and the human tumult, there was a new noise: an urgent liquid crackle that seemed to feed upon itself, swelling and rising, as I loped on.

By my hut, I bent over and held to my knees – gasping, blinking. My eyes swept the clearing but could not consent to what they saw. Everything was illuminated in the febrile light of a fire that had already grown tall in its greed. Soaring flames writhed and twined, yellow, orange and red, tulip-curled around each of the wooden sides. Above, thick smoke barely rose. The air was acrid. The blaze would surely leap the gap to the forest. Men stood watching from the path, idle, with their backs to me.

My cheeks were wet. My lips tasted of salt.

Sole was there beside me. She held my face, pulling me towards her even as I resisted and wheeled away. Again and again she reached for me and I saw that she was screaming above the noise. I could not hear. I thought her likewise mad and gone.

'Lothar,' she was screaming. 'Lothar is in the lab. That's where they were keeping him. They tied him to a chair. Lothar is in the lab. Lothar.'

Unheeding, through the onlookers, racing, I ducked lower and lower. But the heat sought to scorch my face whichever way I turned my head. I bent lower again, trying to advance beneath the smoke. I shut my eyes and lay on the earth and crawled forward. Embers rained down, smouldering through my shirt, searing my skin. Pressed against the soil, I squinted up and it was as if I were in a molten pit and the flames were burning towers all above me. White heat rushed up from the base of the inferno in fearsome draughts that bent the air and sucked down the sky with a terrible hiss; and from within, I could hear timber cracking, beams falling, glass shattering, a thud, a cry. I crawled forward again. My brow was singed where I held my hand against it, my lashes thick when I blinked. I pulled my shirt above my head. I ceased to believe the flame was hot, that instead I might stand up and walk the last few yards untouched, that I might reach out with bare hands and prise away the wood where it flamed and cut him from the chair with my knife and put him on my back and bear him to the river and bathe and cool him in the water. But I heard only the roar and spit of fire and death.

X

Inside Lugo's hut, the lava lamp cast a purplish light. Beneath my bare feet, there was sawdust – for the blood that had been already spilt. In the corner, the puma still snarled.

Lugo was asleep.

The distance from the door was five short strides. At the third, he stirred. At the fourth, he spun around and raised himself up. At the fifth he found his gun. But he should have shot me without hesitation. For now I was over the desk and falling on him from on high, driving the carcass knife into the softness of the right anterior quadrant, precise and exact, just beneath the base of the sternum.

For a moment he thrashed and beat and clawed at me. But I lay heavy upon him and hunched myself against these blows and worked only with the knife, seeking to move the blade upward to lacerate the liver and puncture the gall bladder so that his acid and his bile would mingle with the copious blood already loose and swilling inside of him. He could not know the agony of the death that was coming. The Judge was wrong. I am *Homo necans*. I am man the killer.

XI

Downriver, sudden shards of light and ethereal flames lit up the night and the water was amber and oily black. Smoke drifted the surface and hung in the trees of the banks. The air was heavy with the smell of greenery burning.

I sat on my haunches inside the jungle wall. There were boats taking to the water. Voices called. The sedges stirred and the clay glistened beneath me. I waited.

There came the quiet, rhythmic splash of a paddle – dipped and held and dipped again. Then I saw a black shape moving towards me, whispering through the reeds.

I rose up from the forest and went down to the river's edge. I stood a moment. Then I walked into the water.

'My mother has gone – with Kim and Felipe,' Sole said. 'They're with the Matsigenkas. They'll get out.'

Vinton, the boatman, awaited my instruction.

'Upstream,' I said.

I eased myself into the canoe and took the second paddle from Sole.

'What I said to the Judge is true,' she said, softly. Then she leant in and spoke her secret to my ear.

After a while, we found our rhythm and the noise behind us dropped away and I listened only to the sounds of the night. The river darkened.

I am to be a father.

Acknowledgements

My thanks go to my agent, Bill Hamilton, for his continuing comradeship. I am also deeply indebted to Kate Harvey, my editor, for her intelligence and perceptiveness – and for taking the time to know this novel so well. Also at Picador, I am grateful to Helen Guthrie for her enthusiasm and commitment; to Rebecca Ikin for her thoughtful reading and for helping the book on its way in the world; and to Nicholas Blake for his care and attention to detail.

In South America, I owe a great deal to my guides on the different trips, Juan and Abi; needless to say, I would not have lasted very long in the rainforest on my own and I'm beholden for everything taught, explained and demonstrated – especially how to spend the night 'sleeping' in a hammock. Back at the various base camps, my thanks to Christophe, Miguel, Jan and Manuela for your conversation and the benefit of your long experience of 'life in the basin'.

Likewise, I am grateful to my guides in science. In particular, to Dr Megan Frederickson at the University of Montreal, the myrmecologist who is doing the real-life field work on the lemon ants that I have here described and who kindly answered so many of my questions. Also to Dr Charlotte Sleigh at the University of Kent, to Dr Cath

Long, who explained why and how the politics really work, to Paul Eggleton at the Natural History Museum, to Tom Fayle at the Zoology Department in Cambridge and to Dr Charlotte Foley.

I must have read dozens of books in the course of writing this one – too many to list here – but I am indebted to the following in some very obvious ways: *Journey to the Ants* by B. Hölldobler and Edward O. Wilson; *Families of the Forest: The Matsigenka Indians of the Peruvian Amazon* by Allen Johnson; *The Spears of Twilight: Life and Death in the Amazon Jungle* by Philippe Descola; and *Indigenous People in Isolation in the Amazon* by Beatriz Huertas Castillo. I have also plundered many papers, articles and commentaries from the science journals.

Some special acknowledgements . . . To Perry and Ross for the sanctuary and the pies. To Bob and Elisabeth Boas for the editing space. To Beatrice at Santa Maddalena. And to the rag-tag assortment of fellows who continue unawares to help and to hinder me in my work: Richard, Adam, Jon, Luca, Tim, Will, Dan, TT, Ian and Johnny who was there when we first met the ant men.

Closer to home, thank you to Adelaide and Leo for reading a late draft. Most of all this time, thanks to Gus, who lent me his quick and companionable imagination in the early stages. And finally, my heartfelt thanks as ever to Emma – for her constancy, her surety and her love.